Daughter of China

Daughter of China

C. HOPE FLINCHBAUGH

BETHANYHOUSE

MINNEAPOLIS, MINNESOTA

Daughter of China
Copyright © 2002
C. Hope Flinchbaugh

Cover design by UDG DesignWorks
Cover photo of girl in field: Paul Greblinas/Stone

Although fictitious, events in this novel are based on the real-life experiences of the persecuted house churches and orphanages in China during the 1990s. All characters and some cities in the book are also fictitious.

Scripture quotations identified NIV are from the HOLY BIBLE, NEW INTERNATIONAL VERSION®. Copyright © 1973, 1978, 1984 by International Bible Society. Used by permission of Zondervan Publishing House. All rights reserved.

Scripture quotations identified NASB are taken from the NEW AMERICAN STANDARD BIBLE®, © Copyright The Lockman Foundation 1960, 1962, 1963, 1968, 1971, 1972, 1973, 1975, 1977, 1995. Used by permission. (www.Lockman.org)

Published by Bethany House Publishers
A Ministry of Bethany Fellowship International
11400 Hampshire Avenue South
Bloomington, Minnesota 55438
www.bethanyhouse.com

Printed in the United States of America by
Bethany Press International, Bloomington, Minnesota 55438

Library of Congress Cataloging-in-Publication Data

Flinchbaugh, C. Hope.
    Daughter of China / by C. Hope Flinchbaugh.
       p. cm.
Includes bibliographical references.
    ISBN 0-7642-2731-9
    1. Christians—China—Fiction. 2. Women—China—Fiction. 3. China—Fiction. I. Title.
    PS3606.L56 D38   2002
    813'.6—dc21
                                    2002003948

DEDICATION

I dedicate this book to my beloved country, the United States of America, which by birthright has endowed me with the privilege to speak freely for those who cannot speak for themselves, to worship God in the place and religion of my conscientious choosing, to publish my beliefs, and to birth both sons and daughters into a land where liberty and justice will serve each one of them.

HOPE FLINCHBAUGH is a wife, mother, and freelance writer from Pennsylvania, covering the international persecuted church, revivals, and family issues for adults, teens, and children for magazines such as *Christianity Today, Charisma, Focus on the Family, World Christian, Campus Life, Brio, Breakaway, Clubhouse,* and *Clubhouse Jr.* You may contact Hope through her Web site, *www.seehope.com,* or send correspondence to:

C. Hope Flinchbaugh
Bethany House Publishers
11400 Hampshire Avenue South
Minneapolis, MN 55438

CHAPTER

One

"Father, slow down a little," I whispered, tiptoeing within the shadows of the sugarcane. "We could be seen in this moonlight."

My back hurt from walking hunched over for the last half hour, but my heart soared with expectation. Although the walk was grueling, I looked forward to the weekly house-church meeting. I gripped the handle on our food basket and caught up to Father, who carried our notebooks and unlit lanterns.

"This moonlight will make it easier for us to find the forest path up ahead," he whispered back.

"It's practically daylight out here," I answered. "We could also be seen by the cadre."

"Don't worry, Mei Lin." He turned and we crept on in watchful silence.

The air was cool for September and I shivered, pulling my jacket tightly around me. Father and I edged our way around the first two cane fields. The crops were nearly ready for harvest, and the air was thick with the sweet smell of ripened sugarcane. Under the soft haze of moonlight we could see ahead the terraced fields of rice, climbing like steps on the distant hill.

I wondered who was bringing the Bible this time. It was always passed secretly. Then if any members were questioned, they could answer honestly that they didn't know where it was. I kept an eye on the forest that covered the hill on the right side— a perfect place for a cadre to be hiding. My shoes, wet from the dew, squeaked when I walked.

Something moved.

Father stopped abruptly, and I came up close behind him. I motioned to the bushes on the right.

There it was again. Fear tingled down my back.

Father pointed to the ground and quickly went down ahead of me.

I dropped flat, my heart pounding wildly. Scraping our stomachs in the mud, we crept sideways, drawing closer to the tall stalks of cane for cover.

We lay motionless for a few seconds. *What if we're caught?* I wondered. Would I squirm like a captured serpent under the jolts of the cadre's electric rods?

Moving nothing but my eyes, I scanned the edge of the hill where I first saw the movement. Then I recognized broad shoulders and a familiar wave.

"It's Liko," I whispered hoarsely. Getting back up but staying hunched over, I ran toward him.

"Chen Liko, what are you doing out here? I thought you were the cadre!"

Liko motioned me to be quiet. His eyes searched until he saw Father crawling toward us. The three of us knelt in a huddle in the bushes.

"My father is uneasy," said Liko. "He thinks he's been watched this week. He sent me out to scout the trail and the main road for signs of the PSB."

Just last week Liko's father, Pastor Chen, had warned our church that the Public Security Bureau was putting more pressure on the village cadres to enforce Communist law and eliminate house churches from the surrounding counties.

"The trail looks clear," I said. I tried to sound fearless in front of Liko, but within I shuddered at the thought of being caught. Liko and I were both eighteen, and young people were the most forbidden at house-church meetings. The government prided itself in the loyalty of the young to the Communist Party.

"Still, let's use caution," said Father. We set off again, threading our way along the edge of the forest.

Father was right; we had no trouble finding the path in the moonlight. Liko led the way into the darkness of the trees. The abandoned barn where our house church met was nestled in the next valley. It could be reached either from the old dirt road or this wooded path, but the path was safer.

Fifteen minutes later we approached the weathered barn. An abundance of weeds had long overtaken the old gray structure— a perfect hiding place for our services. Father cautiously opened the creaky door, then motioned for us to go in.

The golden glow from lanterns hanging on the walls and the crackling fire in the old black stove near the door warmed my heart. And the cheerful greetings from our Christian family helped me forget my fears on the cold path.

I laid our food basket in the empty feeding trough at the back of the barn and returned to the benches, my notebook in hand.

"Liko, you can sit with me across from Mei Lin if you'd like," said Father.

"And your family will share our food after the meeting?" I offered.

Liko's eyes twinkled as he smiled. "I'll tell Mother."

I watched him walk toward his mother. He was tall for a southerner, but every bit the well-mannered Chinese gentleman.

Our parents were friends before Liko and I were born, often socializing during evening tea gatherings.

As small children we often slipped away from the adults in our courtyard to play on the hill behind my house. We'd race to the top of the hill, then fall flat on our stomachs and roll back down to see who could reach the bottom first.

That was before Mother became sick, just a few months before I started first grade. After she died, our family teas were less frequent. Still, Liko and I had managed to remain friends through the years. Even though we were both in the same class of 1997, planning to graduate in just eight more months, our schedules were different this year and we rarely saw each other. I looked forward to our talks at the house-church meetings.

A few more people trickled in, the men sitting on the right and the women on the left, about sixty in all. Our little gathering was growing in number. I sat in the second row and tried to imagine what it would be like to worship God freely as some do in other countries—to sing to Him whenever my heart was bursting with praise, to pray openly, to own a Bible and set it up on the mantel where anyone could see it, but no one would care.

My thoughts turned to Shanghai University. Like some of my friends, I planned to escape the poor peasant life and Communist oppression through higher education.

Liko returned and sat on the bench directly across the narrow aisle from me. He leaned across so we could talk. "Have you been well?" he asked.

"I applied to the university this week," I told him with excitement. "You're still planning on WuMa Medical College, aren't you?"

"At least WuMa is close to our village," Liko answered, suddenly very serious. "Shanghai is so far from here." He leaned forward on his elbows, his dark eyes flashing. "What's in Shanghai that makes you dream so?"

"The way to know the new China is to know Shanghai," I answered. "I want to walk down Nanjing Road. My political class teacher said that the whole road is one long line of department stores jammed with people as far as you can see. Many of the stores are just like the ones in the United States! And I want to visit Old Town and see the way our ancestors lived years ago."

"You don't need to attend the university to see all that," Liko teased. "Just go visit."

I ignored his comment and continued. "I want to stand on the top floor of the highest building in Shanghai and see the electric lights at night. Besides, I hear everyone in Shanghai owns a colored television and a bicycle."

"Mei Lin, you know there is more to one's destiny than colored televisions and electric lights."

"And your own bicycle, don't forget." I couldn't help giggling.

"Your father will be lonely for you, with only your grandmother to talk to," Liko pressed.

"He'll get used to it." I turned away, hiding a smile. Perhaps it was not just my father's loneliness Liko was worried about. But a hint of Liko's affection for me was not enough to make me want to stay in Tanching Village. Almost every family in Tanching had lived and died there for generations, never moving out to seek higher goals.

Turning back to Liko, I lowered my voice so our parents couldn't hear me. "I do not plan to be a lifetime member of Tanching's farming community, furrowing fields of rice and sugarcane for the rest of my life."

Now Liko was smiling that warm smile again. "I don't blame you for wanting to leave," he said softly. "I dream about the day I'll be a doctor with enough money so that my mother and father won't have to work so hard in the fields and garden. And I hear there are plenty of Bibles in Shanghai."

"I know! What if God leads me to some Christians there who have extra Bibles? I could smuggle them from Shanghai back home to Jiangxi Province. I wonder what the house-church meetings are like in the city."

"Probably bigger!" Liko glanced at his watch. "It's twelve-thirty. They're getting ready to start."

The meetings in this musty old barn were the highlight of my week. Here I could be who I really was and say what I actually thought without being forced to mouth agreement to communist jargon. I felt secure among my Christian friends. I knew I was entrusting my life to those who worshiped with me, but I also knew they would keep my trust, as I would theirs.

After everyone was seated, the room settled into a quiet expectancy. Pastor Chen always led the meeting standing behind a small wooden desk, with a spray of lantern light over the Bible. "I'd like to start our meeting with prayer," he began. "Of course, you are all welcome to participate. Please stand and make your requests known." Then he sat down in front of Liko in the first row.

A man in the third row stood up. "I have big trouble with my wife, who was once a believer but left God since her mother passed away. She always yells at me when I want to pray or sing hymns. She once took papers I'd written Scripture on and tore them all to pieces."

Before he could finish, Mrs. Huang stood to her feet behind me. Her daughter, Yan, was in my political science class at school. "I am in great distress too. My husband wants to divorce me. He strongly opposes my being a Christian and won't let our daughter come to the meetings here. Sometimes when I get home late from a house meeting, he has locked the door and will not let me in. He leaves me outside all night, all alone. In an outburst of temper he too has taken my papers with Scripture written on them and torn them to pieces. Please pray for me."

After a moment a young man stood and said, "I have a word of encouragement as well as a prayer request from my cousin in Zhaoyi Village. He wrote to us that their cadre has chosen to turn his face and ignore the house-church meetings! My cousin believes that the cadre's heart is softened. He asked that we pray for their cadre, that he will come to know Jesus and have wisdom to handle the pressure from the Public Security Bureau."

Mrs. Chen, Liko's mother, stood up in front of me. "My brother is a pastor in Guandong Province. His family is always being visited secretly by the PSB. When he was not at home, some people pretending to be believers came to visit his family members and questioned them about his occupation and his overseas friends. Please pray for his family's protection."

No one else stood. Then there was a moment when everyone

seemed moved, all at once, to pray aloud. Simple prayers for our brothers and sisters shot up like arrows over the rafters and into the heavens. A few of us were kneeling, some were sitting, some standing, and others lay prostrate on the packed dirt floor.

I prayed first for Liko's uncle and then for poor Mrs. Huang, who gets locked out of her house. The presence of the Almighty drifted down upon us. I could feel Him. I felt like a princess in the palace halls instead of a simple peasant girl in a deserted barn. God lifted me into a place where all things are possible and all things are perfect.

After a while, just as spontaneously as we had started, we all stopped praying. No one spoke. The atmosphere was charged with the presence of God.

My father, still on his knees beside Liko, led our small gathering in his favorite hymn about the cross.

See from his head, his hands, his feet,
Sorrow and love flow mingled down.
Did e'er such love and sorrow meet?
Or thorns compose so rich a crown?

A woman behind me began another hymn, and so it went until Pastor Chen stood behind the wooden desk and opened our Bible.

" 'Therefore, I urge you brothers,' " he read from Romans, " 'in view of God's mercy, to offer your bodies as living sacrifices, holy and pleasing to God—which is your spiritual worship.' "

The lantern light made his eyes sparkle as he spoke, and the obvious similarities between Liko and his father made me smile. Pastor Chen was shorter than his son, but Liko definitely had his father's kind eyes, full lips, and strong jaw.

"My brothers and sisters," said Pastor Chen, "we must live

every day as though it were our last, willing to sacrifice everything for the freedom of knowing God."

Pastor Chen spoke with great conviction. Inwardly I struggled with his words. I dated my sermon notebook and wrote: *Romans 12:1 says we must offer ourselves as a living sacrifice. My heart is set on teaching after graduating from Shanghai University. What sacrifices could possibly be required of me?*

Pastor Chen leaned over the desk and said, "I should tell all of you that I have been watched by the PSB this week."

I shivered, remembering Liko's warning on the path.

"I realize that all of you brought your food baskets for our meal after the service. However, I feel it would be better this evening if we dismissed our gathering earlier than usual and ate our meals in the protection of our own homes."

The bench sitters stirred, looking at one another.

One man stood. He shuffled his feet, glanced around, and said, "Pastor Chen, the PSB asked me questions about you this week while we harvested the sugarcane."

"They talked to me too," said another.

"And me," a man at the back of the room put in.

Pastor Chen hung his head for a moment, then looked up, studying each face. Our eyes locked for just a moment, and I felt as though he stared right into my soul.

"Do not be afraid," he began. "We are not a poor village church. We are rich in the love of God. Jesus himself was betrayed by Judas—a man, a friend, who had worked with Him for three years. Even though the Lord knew His betrayer, He continued to love him just the same."

A murmur rose among the villagers, and as I looked at each

one, it seemed their thoughts were written across their foreheads: *Will one of us betray our pastor?*

Referring to another passage in Romans, Pastor Chen said, "I am convinced that no matter what happens, nothing and no one will be able to separate us from the love of God."

Although I'd heard about people in other parts of China who pretended to be Christians just to watch the meetings and report to the PSB, I never imagined it would happen to us. I felt a little scared.

"I have no reason to believe that it is one of our own who is reporting to the PSB," said Pastor Chen. "But who is reporting our activities isn't very important. What matters is whether or not we will all love as Jesus loved—unconditionally, with forgiveness for every person."

Several people nodded thoughtfully, and a few mumbled "yes" and "that's right." The room settled into silence.

I glanced over at Liko and wondered what he was thinking. His father was definitely in danger—but what could he do? I reached up and put my hand on Mrs. Chen's shoulder. She glanced back at me, and I could see that her eyes were brimming with tears. She placed her hand over mine and patted it gently.

For years Father had warned me that house-church meetings were illegal and that we could be beaten or imprisoned if we were caught. Yet today, for the first time, it seemed that the warnings might become reality. I wanted to block out the horrible danger as I always had, but this night the realities seemed to find me, and I felt shaken.

After some time Mrs. Huang stood and ended our meeting in song:

That the Lord would allow me to live, to only love
    my Lord,
To use all my heart, strength, and talents, to only love
    my Lord,
Regardless of what happens, to only love my Lord.
In all my actions and words, to only love my Lord.

CHAPTER

Two

I was glad to leave the dangerous world of house-church meetings and return to normal life in Tanching High School on Monday. After school my best friend, Ping, and I walked home together, our habit since first grade. We always took the main road that ran through the center of Tanching, passing Liko's house and the open market, then taking the shortcut onto the narrow paths that wound between the village houses. Because both of us could only dream of having siblings, we often pretended we were sisters in grade school, braiding one another's hair and dressing alike.

"When are you going to apply to Shanghai?" Ping asked.

"I already did," I answered. "Last week. What about you? Have you decided what you want to do after this year?"

"You mean, besides marrying an officer in the PSB?" Ping said in her teasing way. "I am a member of the Communist Party, you know."

"I know," I chided in return. Ping always liked to remind me

that she had registered herself to become a Party member, placing herself in high political standing.

"I'd like to marry a *northern* soldier," Ping continued. "The men up north are tall and strong. And most importantly, they are paid well."

I tried to picture Ping married to one of those cruel men who touted communism over the microphone during our town meetings and threatened to put Christians in prison. But I couldn't tell her about Pastor Chen being watched in the fields. She wouldn't understand.

Instead I said, "Soldiers have guns and are trained to kill people. What if you marry a soldier and he is quick to anger? He may treat you badly or even beat you."

"There are chances," answered Ping. "But we'd have our own colored television and a real refrigerator, and maybe two fans in the summertime. Besides, I'd always have food and a warm house. And the government pays its soldiers well. I could send money to Mother and Father."

"Ping, do you believe everything they tell us in political class?" I teased.

Ping looked a little hurt. "Not everything," she said.

"I'm sorry," I said, kicking a few loose stones on the dirt road. "I didn't mean to offend you." Ping grew quiet, and we both became lost in our own thoughts.

I looked over at her. She wore her hair shorter than mine, just above her collar. This year she didn't pin it back as much but simply tucked the front of each side behind her ears. It wasn't hard to picture my beautiful best friend in a wedding gown.

I said, "The truth is, you would make a beautiful bride!"

Ping turned to me and grabbed my wrist. "Do you mean it?"

"Of course I mean it! I can see you now, your hair dressed high on your head and a red lace veil covering your face—"

"Wait—not a veil! Mother said she would buy me a phoenix crown with beautiful red beads and tassels to cover my face!"

"Ping, that sounds beautiful!" I exclaimed.

"That's the way some girls wear their veils in the northern provinces," Ping explained. "And that's not all! Mother showed my birth certificate to a fortune-teller at the summer festival and paid him to tell us the luckiest day for me to be married! She won't tell me the date yet, though. She says it would be bad luck."

"I thought they used both the bride's and groom's birth certificates to predict wedding dates. Do you have a groom hiding somewhere that I don't know about?" I teased.

Ping laughed. "There's no groom in hiding, Mei Lin, but you will be the first to know when there is one!"

We turned onto the shortcut path just in time to see the little Min girl waving a broom high in the air, attempting to shoo the family chickens back into her courtyard.

"Shake the broom down on the ground," I called to her. "They can't see it way up in the air!"

The little girl didn't answer me, but she brought her broom to the ground, still yelling at the chickens as they flapped and squawked.

Ping shook her head. "You are always teaching somebody something, Mei Lin, even if it's only how to shoo chickens."

"I do love to teach," I said, taking her jest seriously. "But I hope I'll be able to teach children more than just farming. I want to introduce children to what life is like in all of China—the rural farms, Beijing, the new cities, the old. I want them—especially the girls—to understand that they don't have to grow up and farm rice and sugarcane in Tanching all of their lives. They can work in other places and—"

"And become rich and intelligent and powerful," said Ping, finishing my sentence.

"Now, that's your dream, not mine," I replied, smiling.

We had reached Ping's house.

"I'll see you in the morning," she said, pausing briefly at her courtyard gate.

"Don't forget to study for the oral English test," I reminded her as I headed down the lane.

"I won't—I have to work on that *l* sound," she called after me. Her *l* sounded much more like the English letter *r*.

"Me too!" I waved as she disappeared into her house.

It was another ten minutes until I reached my house, the last one on the main road leading out of Tanching.

I had lived in the same house all of my life. It was the first one in from the fields and the one farthest from the center of the village, where my school was located.

Besides our portion of the rice field, we raised chickens and ducks and cultivated a large herb-and-vegetable garden that climbed the hill behind our house. We even farmed a small fish-pond in our backyard.

Our gray mud-brick house was topped with an even grayer tile roof, with the back of the house facing the main road. Except for the small wall of bamboo between the side of our house and the fields, our little house looked exactly like all the houses before it. Our neighbors, the Langs, lived in a house only five yards from ours, with their neighbors only five yards from them, and so on down the line. They were lined up in single file like the ducklings that followed their mother to our little pond.

"Amah!" I called as I entered the yard. "I'm home, Amah!"

My tiny, frail grandmother appeared at the courtyard gate, a small water bucket in her hand. Her long silver hair was pulled back in a bun at the nape of her neck, and her threadbare tan shawl hung loosely around her stooped shoulders.

I was Amah's only granddaughter, and she had been a mother to me ever since I could remember. I had vague recollections of Mother laughing with Mrs. Chen during our family tea gatherings. Just before she died, when I was six, I remembered her lying on the bed by the brick stove in the central room where Father slept now. But pictures of Amah crowded out the ones of my own mother.

Like most Chinese women, Amah had wanted a grandson to carry on her husband's family name. My being born a girl had been a great disappointment in her life. Still, she worried constantly about me, and I loved her dearly.

"Do you have to study tonight, Granddaughter?" asked Amah, crinkling her eyes in the late afternoon sunlight.

"Only for an English test, Amah."

"I don't know how speaking English will help a wife work in the fields or tend to her family," she complained as usual. Amah could not read or write in any language, and though I'd offered to teach her to read Chinese, she always refused, declaring that a woman's place was to bear a son and work the fields with her husband.

"Amah, you will be proud one day when your granddaughter rises up early to bring knowledge to children, instead of bending over rice paddies in the hot sun."

"Ach! Your head is full of wild ideas. Just like your mother, you are."

I crossed the courtyard. After stopping to fill her bucket at the courtyard pump, Amah followed me into the house, clucking in her usual way about the traditional role of women in China.

It took some time for my eyes to adjust to the darkness inside. Two glass tiles in the low-hanging roof let in precious little light. A single light bulb hung over the wooden table, but it was used only when the electricity was turned on at dusk. Brightly colored posters, left over from last year's Chinese New Year celebration, covered barefaced brick walls. Four straight-back chairs surrounded the table, with a few stools and a bench scattered around the room for guests at evening tea.

What used to be the family altar, used for worshiping our ancestors, now served as a mantelpiece on the left wall. It held school papers and knickknacks. Father's bed was straight ahead, pushed against the wall beside the mud-brick stove.

Amah carried water to the kitchen sink and began washing and dicing cabbages from the garden. After the evening round of cooking, eating, and dishwashing, I walked to our sugarcane patch. Part of it was already harvested. I pulled dead leaves and uprooted dead stalks for fuel. Tying them onto my back, I headed home, stopping to scatter grain for the chickens.

After sundown I worked on homework at the table while Father visited friends for evening tea. Amah went to our back bedroom for a while. She came out with her shawl in hand, grabbed one of the lanterns, and headed for the door.

"Amah, where are you going?" I asked.

"The granddaughter asks the grandmother where she is going?" she snapped. "I'm going out."

"Amah—"

The door closed.

That night I lay in bed listening for Amah to return. She and I shared the only bedroom in the house. There was just enough room for one bed, our two wooden chests of drawers, and a nightstand.

I'd never given much thought to what Amah did all day when I was at school or the house church. I never really thought of her doing anything except caring for Father and me.

The front door clicked. Amah was finally back.

I slid further under the blankets and pretended to be asleep. Amah came in to check on me, then went into the kitchen, where I could hear her moving about the cupboards. I slipped out of bed, tiptoed over to the door, and peeked out.

Amah held long, thin sticks and what appeared to be a picture frame. She set the frame on the mantelpiece, took a match, and lit the stick, laying it in a holder beside the picture of my great-great-grandfather. A spicy fragrance wafted through the room.

Forgetting that I was supposed to be asleep, I burst into the room. "No, Amah. It is wrong to worship ancestors."

"What are you doing, spying on your own grandmother?"

"Amah, you can't do this," I said. "We are to worship only the Lord God." I moved to take the picture, but Amah stepped in front of me, her eyes flaming with anger.

"You could use the favor of your ancestors' spirits right now, young girl," she said, shaking her finger at me. Her lips tightened into a pencil-thin line. "You may have offended them by going to that barn in the woods. The whole village is talking about Chen Biao, how he is being watched by the PSB for holding illegal religious meetings. That's how your mother's trouble began, you know."

"My mother's trouble?"

Amah's face went red. "It's time you knew the truth!" she blurted out. "Your mother died because they tortured her in prison!"

I stiffened, feeling as though I had just been hit in the stomach. "But . . . but you and Father always said she died of an illness."

"She was ill, all right. Deaf in one ear from a beating in the *laogai* camp—her fingertips seared to the bone from the fiery clamps they burned her with. And why? Why?" Her face got even redder. "Because she was a Christian."

My body began to shake. "Amah—"

"She came home to us almost starved to death from Shanghai Prison, with bruises on her forehead and cheeks. They put her through all that torture just to get her to denounce Jesus." Amah's voice turned to a hissing whisper. "Not once did she give in. They only sent her home to us because they didn't want their records to show that she died in prison."

My feet seemed glued to the floor. When my legs would no longer hold me, I collapsed to my knees and buried my face in my hands. I choked a sob, barely holding back the tears.

Amah hesitated a moment, then sighed deeply. "I didn't mean to tell you this way, Mei Lin. Your father will not be pleased. I just don't want to see you suffer needlessly, as your mother did. What can it hurt to seek the favor of our ancestors at such a dangerous time?"

"Amah, your thinking is all wrong," I mumbled. "The Bible says we must worship no one but God. He is the true God."

I thought I saw her shiver, and then she drew back from me.

"The house church took your mother to her grave, leaving my son without a wife," she answered angrily. She turned back to her altar and incense. "Doesn't your religious book say to honor your elders?"

"Yes," I answered. I knew where she was going with this argument.

"Then go to bed. Leave me alone."

"I am not a child, Amah. Father also will not be pleased to know you are doing this." I stood and took the picture from the mantelpiece. "Where did you go tonight?"

I knew I'd crossed a line with that question.

Amah put out her bony hand to take back the picture. "You are the granddaughter, are you not?"

I just stared at her as she pulled the picture from my hands and put it back on the mantelpiece. I had never seen her so angry.

I turned and walked back to the bedroom before I could say something I'd later regret. The herbal fragrance now filled the house, and Amah began some strange prayer or incantation. I lay in bed, feeling sick, my thoughts consumed with my mother. I tried to imagine going through such torture, never once denying my faith. My Shanghai dream sounded like Mother's Shanghai nightmare. How could anyone do such wicked things to another human being?

I suddenly felt a powerful surge of love for my mother. Incredible, I decided. She must have been incredible.

I'll go to Shanghai, I thought. *But not like Mother. I'll go as a student and a teacher, a Christian teacher. Mother was tough. I'll be tough too. And I'll beat the Communists at their own game!*

Within twenty minutes Amah had finished her ritual, donned a nightshirt, and was under our covers.

I tried once more. "Amah, won't you tell me where you went tonight?"

"Never mind where I go. You just see to it that you are not caught when you go to your meeting on Saturday night."

I knew she meant well, but I rolled over and put my back to her.

"We'll be careful," I finally said. "Good night, Amah."

Now she pretended to be asleep.

My thoughts turned to Liko. I fell asleep thinking about our house-church meeting at the barn on Saturday.

CHAPTER

Three

By Saturday I was so jittery about the threats against Pastor Chen that I couldn't take my usual nap before the all-night meeting. The midnight hour found me yawning on my bench.

After the last song Liko leaned across the aisle and said, "Mei Lin, you're going to suck in a fly if you keep doing that."

I made a sour frown at him, and Mrs. Chen turned around and laughed. "Liko, is that any way to treat our guest? Mei Lin, we'd like you and your father to join us up front for our meal."

"We would be honored to join you," I answered, bowing slightly in a playful way.

"Shall I set up a bench or a bed for you?" Liko teased.

"A bench will do," I answered. Liko walked away with a bench over his shoulder, turning back once to wink at me.

All around the barn, benches scraped the floor as families shifted them in order to eat their meals and talk. I put our notebooks in the feeding trough at the back of the barn and got out our food basket, filling our tin cups with water from the barrel by the wall.

Mrs. Chen and I arranged our food on the benches in the front, close to the barn door, while Pastor Chen grabbed a lantern and walked outside to check the perimeters.

There were only five of us, so Mrs. Chen and I sat on one bench facing Father and Liko. Pastor Chen came in and threw a few more sticks into the wood stove.

"Why are you so tired, Mei Lin?" Liko asked, leaning over from his bench toward me. "Did you have a lot of studying this week?"

"No," I said, smiling. "I just kept thinking about the dangers of coming here tonight, and I wasn't able to nap before we came."

"Try to turn your worries to prayers, Mei Lin," said Liko with great compassion in his voice. "Worry will only bring you fear."

Pastor Chen pulled his bench closest to the front door to guard it as we ate. "It's cold for September," he said, turning to rub his hands over the wood stove.

Father led us in prayer before we ate. The Chens shared their food with us, and I offered them some of Amah's delicious vegetable-and-egg omelet and rice.

"Your sermon was given with great passion, Chen Biao," said Father as he gathered rice and egg with his chopsticks. "Very sobering."

Pastor Chen didn't seem to notice his food but turned his cup of water around and around in his hands, deep in thought. "I was hoping to bring strength to our little flock."

Mrs. Chen and I exchanged worried glances.

"The PSB came to the fields again this week," he continued. "I was told they were questioning the workers about me."

"You mean they questioned your so-called counter-revolutionary activities," said Liko. "Father thinks some of the field laborers are even being paid to watch him," he explained.

"Did they question you too?" Father asked Pastor Chen.

"Ah yes. They questioned me. And what can I tell them without lying?"

"Well, I know lying is a sin," said Father. "But even King David lied and pretended to be a madman to escape a foreign king who would have killed him."

Pastor Chen smiled. "So you think I should feign the life of a madman now, do you, Kwan So?"

"Ah, the stories we could tell at evening tea!" said Mrs. Chen, and we all laughed.

I leaned forward in my seat. "But, Pastor Chen, do we always have to tell the PSB the truth?"

"That's a question we must all face," he answered, setting his cup on the floor beside him. "I was reading the life of David last week, and it shocked me to see there was a time when God actually told Samuel to withhold some of the truth from the king!

"Samuel knew that King Saul would kill him if he found out about his anointing David as king, so he asked God what to say when he arrived in Bethlehem. God told Samuel to bring a heifer and tell everyone he was coming to make sacrifices. Samuel did indeed make sacrifices, but his real purpose was to anoint David."

"Then why are we so careful not to know who has our Bible?" I asked, daring to question him further. "If we are asked, couldn't we just say we don't know?"

Pastor Chen stretched his legs in front of him, crossing his arms in thought. "Jesus said render to Caesar the things that are Caesar's, and render to God the things that are God's."

"So we should do our very best to give to our government what it requires?" Liko asked.

"Yes, whenever possible. But when the laws of God tell us to meet and evangelize, and the laws of China say we cannot, then we must obey God."

"Someday, perhaps, we will be free to worship and talk about God as we please," I said, but there was a sinking feeling in the pit of my stomach.

Suddenly the barn door flew open, cracking loudly against the wall beside Pastor Chen.

I froze in terror, staring at the green-uniformed men with electric cattle prods. All at once PSB police were everywhere.

"Counterrevolutionaries!" yelled the cadre.

"Bad elements!" one of the PSB snarled.

The officer in charge grabbed Pastor Chen and hit him on the back.

"Biao!" screamed Mrs. Chen.

Instantly, Liko pulled his mother to the floor. Father, who was sitting across from me, lunged over our food basket and pulled me down too, covering me with his body.

I heard the thud of rods over human flesh. With fear gripping every muscle in my body, I forced myself to peek from under Father's covering to see what was happening. Officers were everywhere, swinging their rods and fists at defenseless village Christians.

I heard the whistle of a rod in the air followed by a *thwack!* Liko groaned.

"Liko!" I cried.

"Quiet, Mei Lin," said Father, tightening his hold over me. One of the rods found Father's back, and he was struck again and again. For the first time since my mother had died, I cried.

"Do not beat them—I am responsible!" Pastor Chen cried, gripping the bench to support himself while he tried to stand.

The officer hitting Father momentarily stopped. He whirled around and slammed his club into Pastor Chen's chest. My own chest heaved in painful sympathy. I watched my pastor stagger, then slump to the floor. Several of the PSB dragged him closer to the front desk and continued to strike him with their sinister steel rods.

My body began to shiver and my jaw locked tight. I wondered when it would be my turn.

"Name the other leaders," the cadre demanded.

"There is no one else." Pastor Chen heaved out his words, trying to catch his breath.

The rods stopped momentarily. The cadre squinted as he leaned over and lowered his voice to a growl. "Name your foreign contacts, you poisonous snake."

"I . . . I cannot," came the choked reply.

"Beat him!"

Again they lunged at Pastor Chen, striking him with all their might. I had never heard such pounding on human flesh before, and it sickened me. I trembled with fright, still under Father's protective covering.

Everyone was on the floor now. People all around me were crying.

"Please, have mercy!" my father cried out, his voice cracking. I wasn't sure if he was talking to God or the PSB.

Liko was beside Father and me, covering his mother. She struggled to get up to help her husband, but Liko's strength easily overcame her. "No, Mother!" His hands trembled as he dragged her back down. "They will only beat you as well, and then Father's pain will be greater. If you were hurt, it would be unbearable for him."

Liko spoke the truth, and his mother knew it. She relaxed under him and sobbed.

Pastor Chen's broken voice pierced through the horrifying sound of the beating.

"Don't resist, brothers and sisters. Forgive! Forgive!"

More pounding. The officers' steel rods smacked against his ribs and back and legs. Every nerve in my body stood on end as I imagined the hammering blows bludgeoning me.

Pastor Chen lay groaning on the floor. Then one policeman kicked him and jumped on him until he vomited blood. Another picked him up and held him while the others continued the beating. My heart was screaming—how long could they go on?

Spying the Bible that had fallen underneath the wooden table, the cadre flew into a rage.

"Contraband!" He snatched it up, then looked around the room, leering at the stricken faces. "Burn it!" he ordered.

A collective gasp went up all over the room.

The Bible hit the floor with a thud. One of the other officers grabbed our greatest treasure, and within seconds our precious Scriptures were thrown into the fire. My heart felt squeezed and crushed. *How will we survive without our Bible?*

"Search for more contraband!" came the order.

PSB officers stopped beating Pastor Chen to search the barn, looking for more Bibles, notebooks, or anything to do with our Christian faith.

I felt my father's arms tighten. I knew he was hoping the PSB would assume I was his wife. It would go harder for everyone if teenagers were spotted at the meeting. I turned my head carefully to watch them as they all moved to the back of the barn. They turned the troughs upside down, dumping our food baskets on the floor.

Liko quickly lunged toward the wood stove, pulled out the Bible with his bare hand, and smothered the flames with a jacket.

"Notebooks," one officer reported from the back with a stack of them in hand. "Burn them!"

I felt myself growing more and more numb, until finally it seemed I was far away from what was going on around me.

More notebooks were collected. There was a shuffling of heavy boots moving toward the door. The door slammed. The PSB left, dragging our pastor with them.

We could hear the distant thumping of rods . . . the crackling of fire.

"Forgive!" Pastor Chen called to us in the distance.

We heard the sound of a truck motor pulling away with our pastor inside . . . then Mrs. Chen's sobbing, coupled with weeping all around the room.

A bench scraped the floor. Father moved to let me up, and I noticed that sweat was pouring down his face. Someone jumped to put out the fire. I wondered if any of the notebooks could be salvaged.

The weeping grew fainter until it stopped altogether.

Silence spread through the room like the soft summer wind over watery rice terraces.

My father was trembling now.

I wanted to throw up, but fear had left a lump in my throat and I couldn't swallow.

Mrs. Huang slowly stood up. "We do not struggle against

flesh and blood," she quoted in a soft, shaky voice.

"When you do good and suffer for it and take it patiently, this finds favor with God," said another.

"Our Lord Jesus struggled, so why shouldn't we?"

"When Jesus was reviled, He didn't revile in return. He uttered no threats but kept entrusting His soul to God, who judges righteously."

"Love your enemies. Do good to them that hate you."

Liko stood up, tears streaming down his cheeks. "I will build my church," he choked out. "And the gates of hell will not prevail against it."

The door slammed open again. Adrenaline shot through my veins, and my heart raced. Liko boldly remained standing.

It was our cadre. "From now on, you will all be watched," he said in a nasal tone. His thin, fuzzy mustache twitched when he talked. "The Chen Biao family is a disgrace to Tanching Village. The rest of you, however, will not have to pay fines—this time. You will all be given a second chance. Those who resist the Communist Party will be punished."

We were familiar with the rhetoric of Party loyalty. We had heard it from our earliest school days to the village meetings held by the cadre and the PSB.

"Now go home, all of you."

Without a word we obeyed, gathering our baskets, lanterns, and scattered food. The cadre stood at the door, writing down our names as we filed by.

My father passed through the doorway ahead of me; then the cadre blocked the door so I could not pass. I gasped, startled by his abruptness. Although Cadre Fang was not as tall as Liko, his frame was as rock hard as his disposition.

"The Party frowns upon influencing such a pretty young woman with counterrevolutionary propaganda," he said. His steel gray eyes narrowed with suspicion.

I looked down to avoid his gaze.

"You know, I could recommend Shanghai University for the daughter of Kwan So."

My eyes shot back to meet his.

"Or I could recommend no university at all," he added with a twisted smile.

I tried to stare resolutely at him but dropped my head again. I did not want him to see how I hated the fact that he had discovered my Shanghai dream.

"Unless . . . perhaps . . . Kwan Mei Lin may be more interested in a job assignment in the political system. There are ways, say, through marriage, to enjoy the privileges of the position of cadre."

My face flushed hot with anger. One thing the government could not do was tell me whom to marry! How dare this small-minded, egotistical man offer me marriage based on government privileges and a few small *yuans*! Besides, he was too old for me. The government's marriage age for women was twenty-one. I was only eighteen. But I knew I could never convey these feelings of revulsion openly. Biting my tongue and trying to look calm, I looked up again and chose my words carefully.

"Although I consider the cadre to be a friend of the family, I would hope he could find someone more . . . suitable . . . for his age and experience," I answered.

"You are stubborn, like your mother. Do not be foolish, Mei Lin, and throw your life away as she did."

I had learned my lessons well under the People's Republic of

China. Pretend to agree, even if you don't. And don't give in to fear—Communism's way of controlling people.

"May I go?" I asked.

"For now."

The cadre stepped aside, and I passed by. My legs were trembling, but I walked as straight and tall as I could.

Liko and his mother were behind me and had heard the whole conversation. We could say nothing, however, for fear of being seen or heard, as we walked back to our village under the watchful eye of the cadre.

The sun was coming up, casting fiery reds and pinks across the mountains as we made the journey over the hill and back to Tanching. I heard someone coming up behind me. It was Liko. As he passed by he brushed my side and stuffed something deep into my jacket pocket.

Then he was gone.

CHAPTER
Four

Father and I walked back to the village that morning on the dusty main road. A steep bank with clusters of bamboo lined the right side, while on our left there were multiplied acres of terraced rice paddies and sugarcane fields.

When I saw we were well out of the cadre's hearing, I asked, "Father, are you all right?"

"I only took a few hits on my back, Mei Lin. It is Pastor Chen we must be concerned for now."

"What will happen to him?"

"They will take him to the county detention center, where they will most likely interrogate him."

"Interrogate? Does that mean more beatings?"

Father looked away, anxiously running his hands through his black hair.

"Father?"

"Oh, Mei Lin, it is such a heartless country we birthed you into. This is no place to raise a young daughter. And you have such high hopes for your future."

"I have strong faith in God, Father."

"Yes, faith and hope, just like your mother," he said.

Even Pastor Chen spoke fondly of my mother's strong faith and great love for God. I was secretly pleased that Father thought I was like her.

Father continued, "They may transfer him to a prison in another province, where he will be beaten and tortured. Or he may be sent to a laogai camp. There they will try to reform his Christian thoughts through hard labor."

"I keep thinking about us, Father. We could have been arrested today."

"Mei Lin, when your mother died, I determined in my heart to protect your childhood from such horror. We both wanted you to have the opportunity to be a child. We wanted you to laugh and play and dream. But look at you now," he said. "You're hardly a child anymore."

I smiled back at my father, again wishing he had remarried after my mother died. He was well over forty but still very handsome, with strong, rugged features. Large muscles showed under his white Sunday shirt, revealing his years of hard labor in the fields and paddies. His dark hair was swept back over his sun-browned forehead.

"We're home," he said.

Father and I veered off the road and took the narrow path up the small incline that led to our house.

"Let me explain to Amah what happened today," Father said. I nodded.

"Amah!" I called as we entered the yard. "We're home, Amah!"

Amah appeared at the door, her egg basket in hand. As usual she was up early to collect eggs.

"What happened, my son?" asked Amah, grasping his arm. "Did the PSB come?"

"Come inside, Amah," answered Father. He glanced over at the Langs' house as he gently took his mother's arm. "Our neighbors will know soon enough."

After we were inside he slowly laid the food baskets on the table and sat down.

Father told Amah about the PSB raid. Doing his best not to worry her, he carefully downplayed the awful beating taken by Pastor Chen.

As they talked I remembered that Liko had put something in my pocket on the way home. I pulled out the package, which was wrapped in a cloth from Mrs. Chen's food basket, and carefully opened it.

"Oh!" I exclaimed. Ashes crumpled out of the cloth onto the table. "Father! Our Bible!"

I carefully laid the charred pages of our house-church Bible on the table. "Chen Liko put it there."

Amah's face turned ashen.

"Amah, you look like you've seen a ghost!" I exclaimed.

"How long do we keep the Bible?" she asked, her voice stricken.

"Calm yourself, Amah. We will hide it well," said Father.

Amah said nothing but went to the stove and nervously began making a clamor with her pots and pans as though she were about to prepare a great feast.

"We'll keep it this week and pass it on to another church member whenever we can."

"This house hasn't seen a Bible for years," Amah said over her shoulder, apparently trying to recover her composure.

"Too many years," replied Father. "Looks like John, Acts, Romans, and First Corinthians, all intact. Some of the other pages are still readable halfway down. Praise God! Chen Liko must have burned himself getting this out of the fire. At least we still have a portion of the Bible to read."

As he turned the scorched pages a paper slipped out and fell to the floor.

I reached down to retrieve it. Father and I stared at the Chinese characters. The message was brief and unsigned, but I recognized Liko's beautiful calligraphy. *Meet me at the cow shed behind your house Friday night at seven o'clock.*

Father glanced over at Amah. "Don't say anything—it will only upset her."

I nodded. Since Amah couldn't read, the secret was safe unless one of us told her.

"The cow shed is the perfect place." Father spoke in low tones. "No one's used it for so long, most people probably don't remember it's up there."

"I guess that's why Liko suggested it," I replied.

"It's close enough for me to keep an eye on things. You must be careful, Mei Lin."

"I will," I promised. Despite the excitement of the whole night before, I yawned again. "Where shall we hide the Bible?"

Father smiled.

"What are you smiling about?" I asked. I couldn't help smiling back at his mischievous expression.

"Oh, there are still a few secrets you don't know about, Mei Lin."

"What?" I practically shouted, leaning over the table toward him. "What secret?"

Father slipped outside and checked the yard to be sure no one was coming. Then he came back in, shut the front door, went over to his bed, and scraped it across the floor. Leaning down, he moved the dusty boxes that had been under the bed and lifted a loose board with a dead stalk of sugarcane.

"Father! A secret hiding place!" I hurried over, curious to see what was under the board.

"It was your mother's idea," said Father. He smiled sadly, as though at some memory he hadn't shared with me. "She always said that if you could escape from the Communists or hide your Bibles from them, you should. Her notebooks are in here too, Mei Lin. She used to teach at house churches both here and in DuYan, just over the mountain. Besides her Bible, these notebooks were her most prized possession."

"She had her own Bible?" I asked in disbelief. "Her very own?"

Father just looked up at me and smiled.

The notebooks were inside old rice bags. He pulled them out, tenderly running his fingers along the edges of one, lost in thought.

Amah had stopped in her tracks at the cupboards. I had never seen her act so peculiar.

"May I see them?" I asked Father.

"Put them back in there," Amah demanded. "We don't need any more trouble."

Father glanced over at her. "It's time Mei Lin knew they were here, Amah," he said. "Maybe you should look at them later, Mei Lin."

I nodded. I brought the Bible over to Father to put in the hiding spot with the notebooks, then helped him move the boxes and bed back into place.

"How will they live without Chen Biao's income?" Amah asked, pouring hot tea into cups for us at the table. She seemed more relaxed now that the Bible was hidden.

"We'll take up an offering from the other members," answered Father, sitting at the table again. "Chen Liko and his mother may lose much of their harvest profits this year. They'll probably have quite a large fine to pay too."

"It's a bitter thing to lose your rice bowl," said Amah. "I had to feed five children without rice rations during the famine in 1960."

"What about Liko?" I asked, seating myself across from him. "Will he be able to graduate? We are in our last year!"

"I don't know," answered Father. "Liko may not want to go back when he finds out how difficult they will make things for him."

"Oh, Father. He wants to go to the WuMa Medical College. He must pass his exams."

"Much is at stake for you too," said Father. "Your education at Shanghai University may be overturned if our cadre gets his way."

"You heard the cadre this morning?" I asked.

"Yes, but I already knew. He's mentioned you to me in the fields. You chose your words wisely. To offend him would make your plans for the university difficult, if not impossible."

Amah looked straight at me. Her eyes seemed to assess my entire appearance in one piercing glance.

"The cadre has an eye for beauty," she said matter-of-factly.

"And what can we do to change that, Granddaughter?"

Trying to hide my embarrassment, I jumped up. "I know, Amah! I'll wrinkle up my clothes and put dirt on my face!" I rumpled my shirt and put soot from the stove on my cheeks, then I threw my shoulder-length hair forward over my face and stuffed Father's straw work hat on my head. "See if the old cadre wants me now!" I said, laughing.

"It'll take more than hair and a *cao mao* to hide that flat little Mongolian nose," said Father, teasing me.

"Father!" I answered in my best scolding voice. Even Amah laughed.

"A lotus blossom is a lotus blossom, even underneath an old cao mao," she said with a smile. "I told your mother when you were born that those long, curled eyelashes and full cherry-colored lips would draw many suitors."

"Oh, Amah." My tone was still scolding, but my heart warmed under such a rare compliment from Amah.

Father took the cao mao off my head, put it on his, and grabbed the water bucket by the door.

"I'm going to check our cabbages," he said.

I sensed he needed some time to be alone.

As soon as we cleaned up the breakfast dishes and teacups, Amah grabbed her shawl that hung behind the door.

"Amah, where are you going this time of morning?" I asked, forgetting this was the same question that had created an argument between us earlier in the week.

"Never mind where I go. You just mind that you keep the cadre on your side. You must be careful not to make an enemy of him, Mei Lin."

I didn't say a word. Amah was standing at the door.

"Mei Lin?" Amah was demanding an answer.

"I'll do my best, Amah. But I'm not going to marry him."

"See to it you don't tell him that," she replied in the same tone she once used to reprimand me as a child. The door clicked.

I was glad to be alone. Quickly, I moved Father's bed and retrieved one of Mother's notebooks, then put it all back in place again.

I touched the edges of the notebook the way I'd seen Father touch them just minutes before. I shut our bedroom door, then slipped under the blankets with Mother's notebook. I skimmed over pages of teachings she had written and songs she had copied. There were a few songs I hadn't heard before.

When my eyes would no longer stay open, I tucked the notebook under my side of the mattress. My thoughts turned to Liko, and I fell asleep thinking about our meeting at the cow shed next Friday.

CHAPTER
Five

Friday night was muggy and hot, and a thunderstorm was rumbling toward the village. Low clouds raced like so many chariots across the sky, allowing the moon to peek between them.

"Stay low, and be sure no one notices you," said Father. "Here's the offering." He stuffed a thick wad of money into my light rain jacket. "And here are some fish and vegetables Amah made for the Chens."

"Amah knows?" I asked, tucking the small burlap-wrapped meal into my jacket pocket.

"She's next door at the Langs for tea. She only knows that I promised to get the food to the Chens for her."

Father planned to join Amah at the Langs as soon as I was safely up the hill. He wanted to make sure they were distracted from watching the cow shed during evening tea.

I trudged up the muddy gardened hill behind our house, sloshing my way over the soft, broken earth. I glanced back and saw Father anxiously watching me from the dim light of the doorway.

The cow shed was just over the hill. It seemed senseless to try to hide myself. Who would want to come out on a rainy night like this to a cow shed?

I was there first. Stepping through the open doorway brought back memories from long ago. The only cow in the whole village was once kept here, and I had helped Amah take care of it. I could still smell the musty hay. Inside it was so dark I couldn't see my hand in front of my face. A mosquito hummed in my ear, and I swatted at it, wondering if Liko was going to bring a lantern.

The warm wind hissed around the corners of the old shed, whipping through the cracks of bamboo. The rain made a *shhhhhh* sound on the roof, as though it were trying to tell the wind to be quiet. I inched my way along the wall to the left to stay out of sight.

Someone appeared at the doorway. "Mei Lin."

I breathed a sigh of relief. "Over here," I answered. "At the wall on your left."

Liko moved in from the doorway, and I could hear his rain jacket brushing against the wall as he felt his way toward me.

"Have you heard from your father yet?" I asked. "Have they come to your house to collect the fine?"

"No word about Father," he answered. "And no one has come to collect the fine, but we are sure they will come soon."

"Did you bring a lantern?"

"Yes, but I'm hoping we won't need it."

I moved over to make room for him, and my foot sank into the ground slightly.

"Liko, my foot is sinking," I said.

Shuffling our feet around by the wall, we kicked away loose

clumps of dirt and touched what felt like bamboo sticks underneath a canvas covering.

"What is it?" I asked.

Liko felt his way to the doorway to see if anyone was coming. Satisfied there was no one around, he came back and lit his lantern. We pulled back the canvas and bamboo mat to discover a wooden box wedged into a hole in the ground.

"Let's open it," I said.

Our fingers quickly inched around the outer edge of the box. Once we found the seam of the lid we tugged on it. The lid lifted easily, and three sets of eyes stared up at us from the box.

"Oooh, what is it?"

"It's just some old Buddha gods," said Liko.

Six glass eyes glared out of the box at us. One of the statues was made out of pottery, the other two of wood.

"Whoever saw Buddhas with glass eyes? They're ugly," I decided. "And they have fat bellies, like the county cadre."

Liko laughed. "Who wants to worship a fat, ugly god made of clay and wood?"

We lifted the idols to discover something even more intriguing.

"Ancestor tablets," said Liko. He held the lantern closer, trying to read the Chinese characters listing the names of several generations of someone's family.

"Whose family?" I asked.

"Kwan." He turned to look at me. "They're from your family, Mei Lin."

"They can't be," I said. "Amah keeps her set in her dresser, since Father forbids the worship of them."

"They say *Kwan*. Look."

Liko was right. They were our family's ancestor tablets, passed down from eight generations of Kwans. Perhaps Amah's were just a copy. Like most Chinese, many generations of my family had laid food before the tablets once a year at the tombs of our grandfathers.

"Who do you think put them here?" asked Liko.

"Amah," I answered gloomily. "I caught her offering incense to a picture of one of our ancestors Sunday night."

Liko looked bewildered.

I shook my head. "I guess she couldn't part with her old Buddha idols. She probably put the ancestor tablets in with the Buddhas because she thought it would please our ancestors."

"I can't believe people pray to these ugly statues," said Liko. "I saw a lot of these in Old One Tooth's house."

"You've been there?" I asked, astonished. Old One Tooth was the fortune-teller, and Father had strictly forbidden me to go to his house.

Liko smiled. "My father says even Old One Tooth deserves to hear the Gospel. I went with Father once a few years ago to tell him about Jesus. He has Buddhas standing everywhere—on the floor, on shelves, in the middle of his table. You get this scary feeling when you're there for a while."

"Well, even old Buddha is not worshiped in the temple anymore. Not since they made the temple into the work-team hall years ago."

"There's no god welcome in China but the red dragon of Communism," said Liko. "Still, most of my friends have Buddhas sitting around their houses."

I nodded my agreement. Ping kept one in her house. She said it kept the demons away.

"Amah says that Old One Tooth tells people to keep them to ward off evil spirits," I said.

"But God says we are to have no other gods before Him," Liko countered. "Someone must help your honorable grandmother to understand this."

"I wish I knew how to help Amah understand. She has such trouble letting go of the old ways. I'm glad we didn't tell her I was coming here tonight."

"What should we do with them?" Liko asked. "Should we destroy them?"

"No, that is my grandmother's decision. One we cannot make for her."

Thunder rumbled in the distance. We carefully returned the tablets and Buddhas to the box, replaced the lid, and covered the secret container with the bamboo mat, canvas, and loose dirt. Liko turned the lantern knob, plunging us again into complete darkness. I shivered and felt the inside of my pocket.

"Oh, my father gave me this for you and your mother," I said. "It's from all the church members."

Liko accepted the envelope. "What is it?" he asked.

"An offering."

"No, Mei Lin, we can't—"

"Liko, you are to take it. It's barely enough for the long months ahead before spring. And this rice bag has food in it that Amah made for you and your mother."

Liko was quiet for a moment before he spoke. "I am grateful. Please, thank them for us. We'll have to hide the money in our garden." He stuffed the envelope in his pocket and squatted by the wall. I squatted beside him.

"Did you find out if someone in our church was secretly

reporting our meetings?" I asked.

"No. Father said it didn't matter. It's hard to believe anyone in our church would do that. We've all been together for years now. Even the newest Christians have been coming for more than two years. Maybe it was just the cadre spying on us."

"Maybe," I answered thoughtfully.

He continued, "My father left instructions with me for the church in the event he is arrested. He suggested we meet with another house church in DuYan. We can take the path to the barn. It divides at the slope and continues around the mountain. It will take about three hours to walk there after I clear brush from the path."

"When are you going to do that?" I asked. I wondered how he could find time for anything else besides his father's farm work and school.

"I've been working on it already. It'll probably take me another two weeks—if I'm not in school."

"Why wouldn't you be in school?"

"If Father is arrested, the Chen family may not be welcome in the market or the school. You've taken a great risk in coming here tonight, Mei Lin. It will go hard for you if the cadre sees you with me. He seems a little possessive of you."

"You know that I feel nothing but pity and contempt for the cadre," I said, irritated at the very thought of him. "As for school, I'm honored to be your friend, no matter what happens."

"Mei Lin, I . . ." His voice faltered in the darkness.

"What is it? Please tell me, Liko."

"All of my plans are gone. You know what they say. *Zhong-guo zhiye you san bao, siji, yisheng, zhuroulao.*"

I smiled at his quoting the little jingle, "There are three guaranteed occupations in China—driver, doctor, and butcher."

"Yes," I replied. "It is true. A butcher gets all the meat he can eat, a doctor gets free medical treatment, and a driver gets to travel all over."

"Perhaps I should have pursued a career as a driver. Then I could drive you to Shanghai," he said, trying to force a joke. "Mei Lin . . . I had hoped to make you proud."

"You do make me proud," I said too quickly, leaning over sideways to bump his shoulder. "Cheer up, Chen Liko. God has a plan."

He didn't move or speak. It was then that I realized how deeply he was hurting. Imagining his dejection and humiliation, I gathered my senses and prayed for just the right words. "It is true, I long to see the world. That's one reason why I want to become a teacher. But look at you. You have all honorable reasons to become a doctor. And there is always hope, Chen Liko. I believe what I said. God has plans for your future."

"Mother will need me at home now with Father gone. And there will be a fine. It may take years to sell enough from our garden to pay it."

"God has a plan," I said again. "What will you—"

"Shhhh!" said Liko suddenly, covering my mouth with his hand.

Footsteps.

* ★ *

CHAPTER

Lise

There was no time or place to hide. Quickly we ran to the back of the little cow shed and huddled in the corner. A short figure stumbled into the shed, breathing heavily and sobbing.

"Who's there?" asked Liko.

"No, please, don't hurt me," a woman's voice cried out in the darkness. The figure turned to leave again.

Liko rushed forward to catch her. "We won't hurt you. Who are you? Who are you running from?"

"The Women's Federation is after me. Who are you?" She peered out the doorway toward the village.

"I am Chen Liko, and this is Kwan Mei Lin."

"See the lanterns in the village below?" she asked, still puffing. Liko moved to the doorway.

"Why are they chasing you?" I asked in the darkness.

"I am pregnant with my second child. I've been running from DuYan Village since last night." Now she became hysterical. "They'll take me to the county hospital and force me to abort my baby. I'm in my sixth month. Please don't tell them I'm here, please! I want my baby! Please!"

"We will help you," I said as calmly as I could. "How many are there?"

"There are four militiamen armed with rifles and the head of the Women's Federation," she answered.

"They're heading this way," said Liko, still looking out the door into the valley below. "They're on the road behind your house, Mei Lin. We have to get out of here. But where? The roads are probably being patrolled."

"I know where," I said. "The paddies up on the hill behind the shed. The rice is long now. They'll never find us there."

Just then lightning lit the small shed, and we caught our first full glimpse of our new friend.

"Why, you're in your nightshirt," I said to the woman, embarrassed for her and for Liko.

"I fled quickly," she replied sheepishly, her voice shivering from cold and fright.

I quickly unzipped my rain jacket and handed it to her. "Here, put this on."

"Let's go," said Liko, grabbing his lantern and the sack of food Amah had prepared.

The three of us crouched down until we were behind the cow shed, then ran uphill toward the rice paddies for cover. The rain jetted down, stinging our faces. Once we reached the rice field, we carefully placed our steps on the narrow pathway that separated the individual paddies. The ridges were soft and slippery from the rain. Liko and I tried to steady the poor trembling woman between us as we walked single file.

"There's a good place," Liko said, directing us to a flat-looking rock jutting high above the tall rice.

"The rain is letting up," I noted. "And look, the lanterns are at the cow shed."

The three of us waded through shin-deep water, trying not to disturb the stalks of rice. We settled on the rock, watching the lanterns search the cow shed below.

The storm cast a gray fog into the darkness. The rain lessened to a fine mist, bringing out swarms of mosquitoes.

"Get out," I said, smacking my bare arms.

"I'm getting welts on my legs," said the woman.

"The only way to stop it is to get down in the water," said Liko. He was already edging himself into the cold water. "They won't bite you in the water, and it'll help the itching."

"Ugh," I said. "It's freezing in there, and muddy."

I held out, sitting on the rock while I watched Liko and the woman slowly lower themselves into the water.

The lanterns left the cow shed and moved across the hill toward the center of the village.

After about twenty minutes the bites became so maddening, I gladly sank into the muddy paddy for cover. Because the rice was close to maturity, the water underneath it was only shin-deep. I dug my hand down into the mud and smeared the thick paste over the exposed parts of my body, easing farther down into a squatting position.

The cool mud helped to relieve the itching, but when the mud dried, the mosquitoes came back and stung us again. So we kept applying mud and waiting for the Women's Federation to leave.

"Something's tickling my leg," said the woman.

"Mine too," I said.

"Leeches," Liko stated matter-of-factly.

"Leeches?" I had to stifle a scream. I immediately knelt in the water, curling my legs tightly against my body so I'd expose as little of myself as possible.

The three of us knelt, occupied with pulling off leeches, scratching mosquito bites, and packing fresh mud over our faces and arms. We tried to take our minds off our discomfort by talking.

"My name is Liu An," said the woman. "And this," she said, patting her round, protruding stomach, "this is Liu Manchu, my only son."

"You know it's a boy?" I asked.

She smiled, nodding her head. "Yes, I am a nurse. A friend did an ultrasound for me."

"Gongxi!" said Liko.

"Gongxi, Liu An," I chimed in, adding my congratulations.

"And you two—you are lovers?" asked An.

I could feel my face flush with embarrassment, and Liko's face went completely blank. Of course that's what this looked like. Two young lovers meeting secretly after dark in a cow shed. I tried not to sound as self-conscious as I felt.

"We, uh, we are Christians," I finally said, feeling more stupid than ever.

An giggled. "That's a new one," she said.

Liko finally found his voice. "It's true. My father was arrested last Sunday in a house-church meeting. We're making plans for church meetings in DuYan, your village."

"Liko, your food," I reminded him, glad to change the subject. "An is probably starving."

"Yes, here," he said, pulling the bag out of his coat jacket. "For you and Liu Manchu."

Liu An choked back a sob. "Oh, thank you. I haven't eaten since yesterday. I've been worried about the baby—if he'll be able to withstand. Thank you. Thank you so much."

An wiped her hands on the rice bag, tears cutting a white path down her muddy cheeks. She hungrily opened the bag and began to scoop the food into her mouth.

"Where will you go?" asked Liko.

"I don't know," An answered. "We had planned that I would go to a cave up in the mountain until I had my baby. My husband stocked it with clothes and bedding and food. But I hadn't counted on the speed with which the Women's Federation operates. No one knew I was pregnant until Monday, and by one in the morning on Thursday they were at my door. I fled in my shoes and nightshirt while my husband detained them. I lost my way in the dark. I didn't know where to go."

"You are not so lost," I said. "It's God's hand that has led you here and provided this food for you and your baby. And you may hide on my father's farm until we can find a way to get you to that mountain."

"But you don't even know me," said An.

"God knows you," I answered, "and He's the one creating baby Manchu. He cares about both of you. I'm sure my father and grandmother will welcome you as well. Will you come?"

"If you're sure it's all right," replied An.

"I am sure," I answered.

"Oh, thank you. What a night of good fortune this has turned out to be for me!"

We sat for the next few hours in the blackness, catching glimpses of the lanterns searching the village houses. A deep shade of purple colored the black horizon, announcing the dawn.

"It looks as though the posse is retreating," said Liko. "We should go now, while it's still dark."

"How will I know when the path is ready for the house-church meeting in DuYan?" I asked him.

"Check the cow shed on Fridays. I'll leave a note under the box to let you know."

Liko left first, scouting the way to the cow shed, and then turning toward his home in the village. Liu An's pursuers were out of sight now, probably at the other end of town.

My legs were stiff and rubbery from kneeling in mud all night. I thought about how An must feel, after two nights of hiding and running while six months pregnant.

"An, we must leave now, before there's any more light."

"Your father . . . he's a Christian too?" she asked, climbing to the rock.

"Yes. And Amah tries to love God. But she's old in her ways, if you know what I mean."

Hoping not to stir the village dogs, we made our way quietly down the hill to the chicken coop to draw water and wash ourselves.

"Here, use this bucket," I said.

"Aaaaaaaaahhhh!" I jumped backward. There stood Amah with her egg basket, trembling as though she'd seen a ghost. Dogs barked in the distance.

"Amah, what's the matter? It's me, Mei Lin," I said softly.

Amah didn't talk at first. She just stood and stared.

Then I looked over at Liu An.

"Well, no wonder," I said, bursting into laughter. "Look at us."

Soon all three of us were laughing. The Langs' dog barked next door.

"Shhhh," I said, suppressing a giggle.

"You look like a mud monster," whispered An.

"And you—you look like a Buddha mud monster with that big belly sticking out!" I exclaimed.

"Mei Lin, really—a Buddha mud monster?" Amah scolded. "Here, let me get fresh water and we'll clean you monsters up."

Amah hurried to the pump outside with the buckets. When she returned, I introduced her to An.

"Amah, this is Liu An from—"

"I know where she's from," Amah interrupted, handing each of us a bucket of clean water. "DuYan Village across the mountain. Members of the Women's Federation were here last night looking for you."

I started to speak, but Amah cut me off again. "Although how she found you, Mei Lin, I'd like to know." Amah gave me that old scowl that told me I was being reprimanded for my bad behavior of staying out all night. "Don't fret. Liu An can stay with us until she has that baby."

"Oh, Amah, thank you!" I had a strange urge to hug her.

Amah tossed me a towel. "I'm glad you are safe, mud and all." Then she went back to collecting eggs. "Whoever heard of such a thing?" she muttered. "Chasing down a pregnant woman like a chicken to kill her unborn child? Not in this home."

"Thank you, kind grandmother of Mei Lin," said An. She bowed formally to Amah, but Amah was too busy collecting eggs to notice.

* ✦ *

CHAPTER

Seven

Before leaving for the fields, Father emptied out our small storage room near the kitchen, moving the water barrels and dry goods into the kitchen and storage sheds. Then he squeezed a small mattress into the tiny room for An to sleep on. The storage room was usually cold, but Father promised to fix up a venting system later on.

School ended at noon on Saturdays so that the children could help with chores during the harvesting. I knew I had to go to school, welts and all, or someone might become suspicious about last night's search for An.

After a breakfast of rice porridge and tea, Amah pulled out one of her herbal concoctions. "Mei Lin, I'll put this salve on you before you go to school."

"Oh no, Amah. I'll be fine," I answered, gathering our muddy clothes to soak before leaving.

"It'll stop all the itching," she warned.

"I'd be a laughingstock with all that brown paste on me," I

retorted. "And I'd be the center of attention, with everyone asking me where I got all these bites."

Amah clucked on about my mosquito bites and used the awful stuff on An instead.

Father and Amah welcomed An as if she were a relative, and An in return practically stumbled over herself trying to be helpful.

"Let me keep the fire going," she said, all gooped up like a dressed duck. She walked to the corner where the sugarcane stalks and twigs were stacked. "If I can't go out to hang laundry, at least I can keep hot water going for the thermoses."

"You sit down and rest now," said Amah. "You'll need to sleep after Mei Lin goes to school. You must be exhausted."

"Thank you, kind grandmother of Mei Lin," said An. "I was a fortunate woman when I ran into that cow shed last night."

"Cow shed?" Amah said quizzically, looking back and forth at us. "How long were you in the cow shed?"

"Oh, not long, Amah," I said quickly. "An ran inside to get out of the rain. We hid in the rice paddies most of the night."

"So that's where you were," she muttered. I was saved from the long line of questions that filled her eyes, probably because An was in the room with us.

Amah pretended that the shed visit did not matter. She poured water into the stove pans and said to An, "You may call me Amah like everyone else."

I grabbed the carrying pole and two buckets and went out to the courtyard pump to get enough water to fill the wooden wash-tub. I dumped the cold water over a bar of hard soap, watching the frothing water slowly rise to the top. I dunked the muddy clothes into the suds to soak until I could return home at noon to wash them. Anxiously, I sat down at the table to review for a test in political class before walking to school.

Amah was sitting in her rattan rocker by the stove, showing An how to stitch the embroidery she was working on.

"Kwan Mei Lin, you had good fortune to be born into the Kwan family," said Amah.

I glanced up from my book and smiled at her. Amah was always saying things like that.

"There aren't many mothers like An. Most parents don't keep their baby girls. You know, your mother's sister's first baby was a girl, and your uncle Yiping would not hear of keeping it. It had to be a boy to help him on his farm." Amah leaned forward in her chair.

"I'll never forget the screams of that new mother begging the village doctor for mercy. I was there, you know, helping in the birthing. But that doctor turned a deaf ear to her crying. I was so horrified I couldn't move. He stuffed that baby into a glass jar and closed the lid. It was good for your aunt Te that she passed out. Sometimes in the quiet of the night I can still see that poor baby inside that jar, crying her last breath."

"Oh, how horrible," gasped An, her face going completely white.

"Amah, maybe you shouldn't—"

"Your aunt Te nearly lost her mind after they killed her baby," Amah went on, ignoring my warning. "I think the only thing that saved her was her second pregnancy. Luckily, she had a boy that time."

"Amah—"

"That could've been your story, Mei Lin. Your father could use a strong boy around this farm. All the other farmers kept only their male babies."

"*Almost* all the other farmers," I put in.

She knew I was referring to my best friend, Ping. Amah was right, though. Most Chinese kept their newborn sons because by tradition the boy takes care of the parents in their old age. Baby girls were mostly aborted, killed at birth, or abandoned.

"Both of you girls are lucky to be alive. You have your honorable fathers to thank for that. I suppose you can thank your God as well. Your mother used to."

"He's your God too, Amah," I said, but there was a question in my voice.

"Oh, an old woman is supposed to have a god. You are young, Granddaughter, one of three girls in all of the high school. You will be the first girl to graduate ever in the Kwan family. Why do you want to risk your future by going to these new church meetings in DuYan? An says the PSB and Women's Federation are very strict in DuYan."

"Shhh, Amah, someone will hear you," I said.

"Ah, no one ever listens to this old woman," she replied, slowly getting up to pour tea. "I had five children, you know." She looked at An. "Four daughters and a son. Five is the most fortunate number of children to have. All of my friends admired me. Of course, that was before the one-child law."

Amah talked relentlessly at times, but she was old, and I was careful to honor her age and position in the Kwan family.

"It's time to go," I said. "I'm glad you're here to give Amah company, An. She gets lonely here by herself every day."

I was relieved that no one seemed to notice my mosquito bites at school. And despite my exhaustion from the night before, I thought I did well on the political class test. Ping and I collected our books and walked out together in silence.

Ping interrupted my thoughts. "Mei Lin, you are so somber lately. Has Chen Liko sought after the affections of another?"

Her question startled me. "No. I mean—"

"Mei Lin, look!"

We both saw it at the same time. Gray smoke billowing up like a thin tornado.

"Whose house is it?" I demanded.

We ran down the dusty road, quickly passing several mud-brick houses until we came to a crowd of people gathered around a bonfire in the middle of the road—right in front of Chen Liko's house!

"This is a matter of state business," said a booming voice at the front of the crowd.

Leaving Ping in the back of the crowd, I quickly jostled my way among the people to get to the front.

Off to the side I saw our village cadre near the back of the PSB truck. The smirk on his face told me he was in full agreement with what was happening.

"Bad elements must be cleansed!" cried the PSB officer.

Flames were shooting up around what appeared to be books, baskets, and even a shirt. A chair flew out of the front door. Soldiers were throwing books and perishables into the fire. Other soldiers were loading all the valuables into the truck.

"The Chen family is counterrevolutionary," the commander yelled from just outside the doorway. "All valuables will be sold to assist payment of the fines owed by these vipers. Let this be an example to all of you. Our government has provided you with the

Three-Self Patriotic Church. All who wish to attend church must register with the government."

Yes, register and have the TSP Church confiscate our Bibles and tell us what to believe, I thought angrily.

Everyone around me seemed to be in a stupor. My eyes searched frantically for Chen Liko and his mother.

"Chen Biao has been arrested for disturbing the social order and normal religious life set up by our government," the PSB commander went on, yelling the charges. "Chen Biao is a bad element."

Suddenly I saw them at the corner of the house. Liko had his arm around his mother.

"Liko!" I started toward them, but Liko looked away when I called to him.

I hesitated. Why was he acting so strangely?

"Mei Lin, come away from here," Ping whispered as she took me by the arm and turned me in the opposite direction. "Don't you know that anyone caught associating with the Chens may also be arrested?" she asked. "You must go home now. Forget about Chen Liko, or you too will become an enemy of the state."

I looked back and saw the PSB officers taking beds and tables out of the Chens' house.

"Look," I said to Ping and pointed. The commander had begun to unbolt the door to the house. "They cannot even leave the door on their house!" I cried.

Ping pulled me out of earshot of the crowd, then spun me around and grabbed my shoulders. "You must think of yourself and your family," she said. "You will lose face if you sympathize with Chen Liko. Then you will have nothing."

"Chen Liko is a close friend, Ping," I said.

"Think of the university. Think of Shanghai. Your dreams will be ruined if you associate with him. He is a bad element."

"The Chens have done nothing," I said, anger rising up in my throat. "His father loves China, Ping. He's like your father and mine. Our meetings are not anti-Communist. We just want to worship the true God."

"You should listen to your friend."

I whirled around to see the cadre. Had he been listening to our whole conversation?

"Your friend's loyalty to the Party is commendable. You, Kwan Mei Lin, should follow her example."

"Sung Ping, this is Cadre Fang Yinchu," I said coolly.

Ping and Cadre Fang politely shook hands.

"You are right, Cadre. I would do well to follow Sung Ping's loyalty to the People's Republic of China. She often corrects me from indulging in poisonous Western thought."

I was careful to leave a good impression on the cadre about Ping. Saving face was very important to her, and she was my best friend.

"It is my pleasure, Cadre Fang Yinchu," said Ping with a bright smile. "Kwan Mei Lin will come to her senses when she sees the crimes committed by the Chens. Mei Lin is at the top in our political class."

"One of her many gifts," replied the cadre, smiling under his sparse mustache.

"I'm sorry I cannot stay longer," said Ping, "but I have to go. My mother will be worried."

"I'll walk with you, Ping," I said quickly, taking her arm and turning away.

"Wait!" said the cadre.

Ping and I turned back to face him.

"Mei Lin, what can Chen Liko give you that I cannot? He will probably be a doctor in another village. Then what will your poor father do?"

"My interest in Chen Liko is not as a future husband," I replied cautiously. I could feel my ears turning red.

"Then what?"

"I think of him as a friend. A brother. That is all."

He seemed pleased with that answer. "Then you're considering my offer of marriage?"

I looked over at Ping. I thought her eyes were going to pop out.

"I am pleased that you find me a worthy marriage prospect, Fang Yinchu. But I am too young to marry and—"

The cadre stepped so close to me I could feel his breath on my face. He took my hand and pressed it into his hands. "But I may be able to arrange something," he said, his mustache twitching again.

"Please, let me finish," I said, not withdrawing my hand but moving away from him. "My heart is very much set on becoming a teacher. I must finish my education before I can think of your generous offer." I nearly choked over those last words, but I knew I had to convince him of my sincerity in choosing a career over marriage—for Liko's safety as well as for my Shanghai dream.

"Then I will wait for you, Kwan Mei Lin. Until you are ready to become the wife of the cadre. I can arrange to have a teaching position ready for you upon your graduation."

"Your offer is most kind," I answered. He released my hand. "Ping's mother will be worried. We must go."

"Of course."

Ping and I were halfway home before either of us felt we were safe enough to talk.

"Mei Lin, you've had a marriage proposal at eighteen! Why didn't you tell me?"

"It's nothing."

"Nothing? Don't you understand that you would be one of the few peasants in Tanching to own a colored television? And he has *guanxi*—many connections. Friends in high places. You could ask for an expensive dowry from his parents."

"I won't marry him, Ping."

"What?" Her mouth gaped open.

"He's not a Christian. Besides, he's proud and egotistical, and I find him repulsive. And I don't love him."

"Love? Love?" she repeated. "Is there no end to your Western thinking? First you want to worship a Western religion, and now you talk of love. Will love put food in your belly and clothes on your back? You must let go of this religion you've found. It can only bring you unhappiness. Look at Chen Liko. What happiness has your religion brought to him?"

"He has inner happiness," I answered. "Inner strength and peace that all the bicycles and colored televisions of Shanghai cannot buy."

"But you told the cadre he was just a friend to you."

"I meant it. Liko is a friend. Next to you he's my best friend, but I'm not ready to be married. I want to see more of China, more of the world."

Poor Ping. She'd always innocently believed everything we'd ever been taught from grade school classes to town meetings. I felt sorry for her now.

"Maybe one day you'll understand, Ping," I said as we

71

walked. "I pray for you often that you too will become a Christian."

"You shouldn't. My ancestors will not be pleased if they hear of it."

I smiled at that. "Believe me, if you decide to receive Jesus, you'll have your ancestors smiling in their coffins."

Ping laughed. "You're hopeless!"

A boy came running up the road behind us, yelling. "There's a town meeting next Friday night at six o'clock. The PSB are coming!"

"Chen Liko's family," I said to Ping, watching the boy run on, repeating his message.

Ping nodded.

We both knew the meeting meant trouble for the Chens.

CHAPTER

Eight

News of the Public Security Bureau's struggle against the Chens spread quickly throughout our little village. School circulars went out, and a notice was tacked up at the cadre's office announcing the Friday night meeting. Such meetings were seldom held anymore, but when they were announced they were always mandatory. They were held at the outside basketball court in the center of town.

After the supper hour more than fifteen hundred adults shouldering wooden stools and benches crammed onto the court, the men seated on the right side and the women on the left. I sat with Amah.

The police chief, head of the local Security Defense Committee, took his place. With forms in hand, he began to read: "Comrades, under the direction of Jiangxi Provincial Communist Party Committee, the local Prefectural Party has determined we will hold a movement this winter throughout the towns and villages of our district. We will criticize all who do not conform to the

Communist Party. We will strike against class enemies—embezzlers, thieves, and black marketers.

"All loyal Party members will eagerly conform to the one-child-per-family law. All who organize church meetings secretly without registering with the Three-Self Patriotic Movement are illegal capitalist elements and will be punished as well. All must participate in this people's war to criticize, strike down, and rectify."

At this point the police chief changed his tone of voice and boomed into the microphone, "This is a serious warning to all criminal elements: Completely repent of your ways and confess your sins against the state. If you continue to resist, the state will mercilessly bring you under control."

Repent? Confess? It amused me that once again the Communists were using biblical words to intimidate us. "Mercilessly bring you under control" was a code phrase for execution. Such threats had been repeatedly spoken in these types of meetings for as long as I could remember, and the new agenda against the bad capitalist elements brought little more than a yawn from the bench sitters.

With hardly a pause in between, one of the lesser-known village cadres got up and began to read individual cases. "The title of the first case is, 'If You Refuse to Reform, You Must Be Reformed Through Labor.'"

This caused some murmuring throughout the peasantry, for we were all wondering what had happened to Chen Biao.

"Chen Biao, male, forty-eight years old, resident of Tanching Village, Jiangxi Province. Family class status: lower peasant. From the time Chen Biao was a small child, his parents nurtured him in a slothful and prideful character by smothering him with love. Before the Cultural Revolution, Chen Biao was a landlord, a bad parasite who owned the Teahouse Inn, which belongs now to the People's Liberation Army. At that time he refused to confess his crimes, forcing the Red Guard to punish him severely."

I looked around and saw Liko standing in back of the crowd. They were denouncing his father as a means of public humiliation for him and his mother. I tried to imagine his pain.

"After the revolution Chen Biao worked in Tanching's Production Team Number Fifteen, upgrading his class to peasant farmer. Two weeks ago, September 14, 1996, the Public Security Bureau police, aided by the Party's loyal village cadre, arrested Chen Biao at an abandoned barn. He was holding a subversive capitalist meeting organized illegally against the Party's communist structure."

I watched as many of the women around me gasped, putting their hands to their mouth. It occurred to me that our secret meetings were no longer a secret. The cadre continued.

"He compounded his offenses by having in his possession a Bible printed by foreigners. Chen Biao refused to repent, forcing the legal organization to punish him severely. He was sentenced to a fine of seventy-two hundred *renminbi* and five years in the laogai labor camps to reform his thoughts."

A sigh went up from the crowd at the harshness of the punishment. Seventy-two hundred renminbi was about two years' wages. No one had that kind of money.

"Chen Biao has been brought under criticism by the People's Republic of China. All must participate in this people's war to criticize and strike down the Chen family for the crimes committed."

I hung my head. Liko would never have enough money to

attend college now. His university training was gone!

All eyes turned to Chen Liko, but he had left. The cadre began reading another case title about a thief from another county. I wondered what we could do to help the Chens. We could share our food, but there was barely enough for each family to live on, even after selling at market.

Amah leaned over, nearly touching shoulders with me. "They are your friends, Mei Lin. Your loyalty will count the most now."

"Amah, you understand?" I whispered.

"Of course I do." She smiled knowingly. "I've seen you watch Chen Liko, flushing at the sight of him."

"Amah, you're imagining things."

"Am I?" she asked. "Or are you denying your heart?" She crossed her arms and paused. "Perhaps . . . in three years . . . when you are of the age to marry . . . all of this will have run its course."

"Marry?" All this talk of marriage exasperated me! Then I had a wonderful thought. Amah had seen the rise and fall of many political programs over the years. Her foresight that this whole thing might run its course in a few years could prove true.

"I don't know yet who I'm going to marry," I said finally. "And why doesn't anyone believe me that I want to go to Shanghai?"

"Is it not parents and friends who arrange premarital introductions?" asked Amah. She was smiling now, completely ignoring my reference to Shanghai. "I saw Chen Liko watching you as well, Mei Lin. It is not the Chinese way to marry for love, but the ones who find love after marriage are most fortunate."

I knew what she meant. In political class Mr. Jiang told us that Westerners view the Chinese approach to marriage as businesslike and unromantic. Marriages in China are arranged for procreation, parenthood, and financial security.

"How will they ever pay such an outrageous fine?" I asked softly.

"Time," answered Amah. "I am old, and I have seen that time can be a friend."

As soon as the meeting was over, Father joined us, collecting our benches. I knew he planned to walk home with us, but I desperately needed some time to myself.

"Father, would it be all right if I take a walk?" I asked.

Father nodded soberly. "Go ahead."

After leaving the village I strolled along the paddies before circling back to the cow shed. The warm September breeze brushed my hair off my face, and just breathing the sweet air seemed to clear my mind.

When I stepped into the shadowy cow shed, I smiled at the memory of my talk with Liko last week. The box was still in its hole; apparently it hadn't been spotted by the militiamen from the Women's Federation. I lifted it and was surprised to find a note. I read it in the arrows of light that shot through the bamboo: *The path is clear. Next Sunday, 4:00* A.M., *at the fork. Only twenty people allowed besides us. Pass the word. Bring Manchu with us to a new haven. God go with you.*

I ran back to my house and burst in the door. "An, come and see!" I shouted.

"Mei Lin, calm yourself," said Father, who was busy sharpening his knives and tools. Then he saw the note. "Oh, this is good news. Look at this, Amah!"

I read the note aloud.

"A new haven?" asked An. "What does he mean?"

"Liko's found a new place for you to hide until Manchu is born. Guess where?"

"Where?"

"In DuYan. In your village!"

"Oh, it is too wonderful," An said, laughing and crying all at once. "My little Manchu will be born in the village of his ancestors after all."

"God's hand is on your life and the life of your son," Father said to An. "He cares about both of you."

An looked down, suddenly serious. "That is what Mei Lin told me the night I came here from the rice paddies. I have thought much of your God. If He can bring my baby and me back safely to DuYan, perhaps I will believe in Him."

Father and I exchanged smiles.

"Kwan So, is it too late for tea?" came a call from the courtyard.

"Quickly, An, back into the storage room," Amah said, grabbing An's tea and embroidery. "It's Lang Zemin, our next-door neighbor. He probably wants to talk about the political meeting."

CHAPTER

Nine

Even the sound of the rain couldn't dampen my spirits as I bounded out of bed Sunday morning. Amah was up at two-thirty with the rest of us. She had cooked all day Saturday, packing food for An and the house-church journey.

"Amah, do you think An will be able to eat all of this food in a week's time?" I teased.

"It takes a lot of energy to build babies. You'll see one day."

"One day far in the future," I said.

"Here's something for the new baby," Amah said, handing An a package.

She unwrapped the brown paper.

"Oh, Amah," said An. "Thank you. I've never seen a baby blanket so beautiful! I will pass it down to my grandsons."

"I'd have done better if my hands weren't so stiff."

"I can't imagine anything more beautiful," An said. "You've been so good to me, Amah. You've treated me like a daughter. I will always think of you when I embroider the way you taught me." She hugged Amah good-bye, and I almost felt jealous. I couldn't remember ever hugging Amah. I wondered if things would have been different if I had been a boy.

"Please send us word after the baby is born," said Amah, wiping her eyes with the end of her shawl.

Is she crying? I wondered.

"There's something in my eye," my grandmother said, as though she had heard my thoughts.

I glanced over at Father, who gave me a knowing wink. Then he turned to Amah. "Good-bye, Amah. We'll be home again after sundown."

Father, An, and I put on rain jackets and ventured out under the dark downpour, following Father's careful footing. We were grateful for the dark, wet covering, which hid us securely from the watchful eye of Cadre Fang Yinchu, but it made it hard for us to see as well. An, now seven months pregnant, wasn't familiar with the path and had the most difficulty.

"Take my arm," I offered. "Even if it was daylight, I don't think you could see the path over that belly!"

We took the same route as before, but we stopped at the fork on the wooded path to light our lanterns and wait for the others.

"Mei Lin." I heard Liko's voice but could not see him.

"Liko?"

He came out of the bamboo thicket, his mother behind him.

"Mrs. Chen, are you well?" I asked.

"Yes, thank you, Mei Lin. I hear you have a visitor in your home."

I introduced Mrs. Chen to An. I didn't bring up the house burning or the political meeting. The whole experience was designed to humiliate his family, and I wanted Liko to know that what had happened didn't change my opinion of him at all. In fact, I admired him now more than ever.

"How did you get this path cleared so quickly?" I asked.

"Actually, I finished it just yesterday," said Liko, smiling at his close timing. "The brush and bamboo were thicker on the other side of the mountain. But it's cleared now. We'll have plenty of firewood to gather on the way home tonight."

When everyone had gathered, Liko and I took the lead, walking together over the lower mountainside. It was impossible to talk, with Liko's attention given to scouting the trail, but it felt good just to be together.

───────

Two hours later, when DuYan came into view, all twenty-three of us were drenched. It was still dark, but we covered our lanterns, snuffing out the light. Conversation stopped and we moved quietly, not just for our safety but for the protection of the DuYan house church as well.

Liko led us to the side door of a house, the back of which seemed to be built into the mountain. He tapped on the door, and it was opened immediately by an elderly woman who smiled graciously and stepped aside so we could enter. We took off our soggy shoes, and the woman placed them around the warm brick stove at the far right along the back wall.

There was a bed on the left side of the room and a table and a couple of wooden chairs in the middle. A stack of firewood was piled high against the stone wall at the back, to the left of the stove. Except for the stone wall, it was very much like the houses in Tanching. I wondered how we would all fit in here without being caught.

Sitting at the table was an older man, who stood and bowed slightly. We returned the formal gesture.

Noticing An's apprehension, I whispered to Liko, "What about that new haven for Liu Manchu?"

"It will be taken care of after the meeting," he answered.

The elderly couple served morning tea to each of us. The warm liquid quenched my thirst and took away the rainy chill.

Then the old man announced, "It is time."

He moved several pieces of firewood from the pile, and the whole stack of wood came sliding down. A gaping hole was carved in the stone wall! The man stepped back and motioned for us to enter. I looked at Liko, who was grinning in a smug sort of way.

"This is amazing," I said to him.

He nodded and motioned for me to lead the way. I stooped to make my way through the small black opening. There was a faint shaft of light ahead. The closer we moved to the light, the more I could smell and feel the presence of other people.

We entered a small windowless room carved into the mountainside, which I found out later was commonly used to store the vegetable harvest. In front of me sat a group of friendly, smiling faces. Several people in the back stood, extending their hands to welcome us. A man in the front row moved directly under the single light bulb and sat cross-legged on the floor with his Bible and hymnal in front of him. We sat down facing him on the floor in the same way, our knees touching the backs of the ones in front of us.

"We are ready to begin," he said. "We welcome the Tanching house church this morning. Let us thank Jesus for bringing us all together."

From six-thirty that morning until noon, fifty-two believers took notes and listened intently to teachings by Pastor Zhang. He spoke about being a disciple of Jesus, reading portions from the Gospels. I felt like a starved child in front of a banquet table.

As the hours passed, people took turns going behind a curtain in the back to relieve themselves. Everyone studiously avoided noticing the sound; therefore, to the Chinese mind, it really wasn't happening. As I made my way to the curtain, walking among the believers seated on the floor, I was surprised to see so many young people. Almost half of the people in the DuYan house church appeared to be under twenty-five. I hoped I would be able to speak to some of them at the noon meal.

At the end of the sermon I couldn't believe my ears when the people began singing,

Don't listen to sermons,
Don't listen to sermons,
We will not listen to sermons. . . .

After nearly six hours of listening to Pastor Zhang's sermon, they were singing "Don't listen to sermons"! But revelation came when they clenched their fists and sang the rest of the song:

We will live out the sermons,
We will live out the sermons!

"How is it that there are so many young people here?" I asked a girl named Fei as I opened my lunch sack.

"We keep bringing in new converts," she replied. "Our church holds a morning and evening meeting now just to fit everybody in."

"Really?" I'd never met another Christian teenager besides Liko, and Fei's answer astounded me.

"There's a meeting on Tuesdays just for the teenagers. We make plans to evangelize in our school and talk about any new political maneuvers."

"Political maneuvers?" I asked.

Fei pulled a magazine article out of her baggy gray trousers and pointed to the last paragraph: *The church played an important role in the change in Eastern Europe when Communism collapsed. . . . If China does not want such a scene to be repeated in its land, it must strangle the baby while it is still in the manger.*

"Strangle the baby in the manger?" I asked. "The state newspaper printed this?"

"Yes, in 1992. But they're still just as determined to strangle babies this year," replied Fei.

I looked over at An, who was sharing lunch with Mrs. Chen. "I know what you mean." Then I related An's narrow escape from the Women's Federation and her fight to save her baby.

"Satan hates babies, especially those in Christian families," remarked Fei. "Look at baby Moses and baby Jesus. The wicked kings of their day ordered all the babies killed. Many died. But a few survived. The ones who lived, lived for God."

"I never thought of it like that. I guess we have some wicked kings in China who hate babies too. So what do you do as a political maneuver?"

"Well, it's viewed as political by the Communist Party, but really it's just a spiritual maneuver. One week we decided to show this article to our Communist Party friends in school. Then we told them about the real Jesus, who did not die under the wicked king and still lives today."

I was skeptical. "Don't your school authorities reprimand such behavior?"

"We've taken much persecution in the past, but there are so many of us now that they can hardly expel us all. There would be only a few left to teach, and they would have no jobs."

"That's exciting," I said, feeling as if my heart were going to burst. So often I had wanted to tell my friends at school about Jesus, but I was afraid to risk my future at Shanghai University. Fei's story gave me hope.

"We made up some tracts," Fei said. "Would you like to have some of them?"

"Tracts?" I asked.

Fei handed me a small folded paper with pictures and writing. I was shocked.

"It's a cross!"

"Yes, to show a picture of how Jesus died."

"And the whole way of salvation is written inside?" I asked.

Fei laughed. "Of course. Would you like some?"

"Yes!" I felt like a little girl at Chinese New Year getting my red envelope full of money. An idea came to me. "Fei, red is China's luckiest color, right?"

"Right."

"So why not put some of these in a red envelope with the money gifts at Chinese New Year? We could color in red on the three points of the cross, to show that Jesus' blood was the most fortunate red color the earth has ever known."

"A wonderful idea!" exclaimed Fei.

So we spent the rest of our lunch making a plan to evangelize during next winter's Chinese New Year celebration.

After lunch break Pastor Zhang opened the meeting for testimonies. A twenty-five-year-old woman named Jiazhen was first.

"Ten years ago the political system struggled against me. I

was getting very depressed and asked myself why this was happening to me. I am a good Christian and have never done anything wrong. Why do they struggle against me and not against those who have really done bad things? 'Do you believe in Jesus?' they shouted. 'Yes, yes I do,' I answered.

"In time my depression left and I no longer felt sorry for myself. The men tied a board that was five feet high and twelve inches wide to my back. They plastered posters on the board detailing my alleged crimes. They put a dunce's cap on my head and gave me a gong to ring so that people would know I was approaching."

I sat stunned. I could hardly believe this woman was only fifteen when she'd endured such harsh treatment. She continued. "I felt like a leper crying out 'Unclean! Unclean!' Their mockery continued as they wrote four characters on my hat that read 'God blesses.' They meant it to shame me, but I wore it as a testimony that God indeed does bless. I walked up and down the streets, thanking God that I could spread the message that He blesses.

"After they let me go I returned home, and in the days that followed many people came to my home asking me about the God who blesses."

"Ahhh," came the cry from the group. "Praise the Lord!"

Pastor Zhang called on an old man. "Come, share your testimony with the Tanching house church, Gong Kai."

The old man carefully made his way to the front and sat down. "I was in a prison where we were very crowded, with ten prisoners to a tiny cubicle," he began. "We were not allowed to speak to each other or to doze off during the day. A guard periodically looked into the room through an opening in the door. Many fell ill, while others lost their minds.

"One day another prisoner whispered to me, 'We can see that your religious faith really gives you strength.' This was the beginning of my new ministry. Another day, a guard burst into the cell and shouted, 'Stop your smiling!' 'I'm not smiling,' I replied. 'Yes, you are!' shouted the guard. When he left, the other prisoners said, 'Your eyes are always smiling, and your face glows with joy!' Most of my fellow prisoners were not Christians, that is, not at that time.

"During one period of time, we were sent off to work seventeen hours a day in the rice paddies. We stood in water almost waist-high until our bodies were a mass of sores. For a person in his late fifties who was not used to such work, it was nearly unbearable."

I glanced across the room at Mrs. Chen. Her face was wet with tears.

"But even worse was having to listen continually to the foul language used by the other workers," the man continued. "When I complained to God about it, He said to me, 'Are you holier than I? I left the absolute purity of heaven to live in your sordid world.' There are times when it is difficult, but that is what it is like to be a Christian in China. It is a price we must be willing to pay."

Pastor Zhang got up. "These testimonies bring to mind Zechariah 13:9: 'I will refine them like silver is refined and will test them like gold. They will call on my name, and I will answer them. I will say, "They are my people," and they will say, "The Lord is our God." ' "

An abrupt sound of weeping broke the stillness in the room. It was An, on her knees crying. Mrs. Chen had her arm around her shoulders.

"Is there something you would like to share, Mrs. Chen?" asked Pastor Zhang.

Mrs. Chen whispered to An.

"No, but Liu An would like to say a word."

An stood up, still trembling and weeping.

"I would like very much to become a Christian . . . if God will permit me."

Tears sprang to my eyes. "Hallelujah!" I shouted. And hallelujahs echoed around the room. Mrs. Chen brought An to the front.

An knelt and softly prayed, "Jesus, I know you are the God of Kwan So, Kwan Mei Lin, and their friends. You found me and my baby when we were running and afraid, and now you have brought us to this safe haven. I like you because you are kind, and I want you to be the boss of my life. Please forgive me for the bad things I've done."

"In the name of Jesus," whispered Mrs. Chen.

"In the name of Jesus," An repeated.

I was so happy I wanted to stay in that little cave for the rest of the night.

Right after the meeting Fei came over to Liko and me. "My parents have offered to take An home with us," she said.

"What is the plan, Liko?" I asked, looking up at him.

He was beaming. "This is what Pastor Zhang and I prayed for. God has put the desire in the hearts of Fei's family to help An. I believe God made the decision for us."

Liko arranged the new hiding place with my father, An, and Fei's parents. I wrote down Fei's address, knowing Amah would be pleased to have it. We said our good-byes and left after sundown. The rain had stopped, and the Tanching believers were able to find their way back without Liko's help. I was glad that we finally had an opportunity to talk.

I told Liko about Fei's school evangelism and showed him under lantern light the tracts she had given me. "I had an idea about making tracts to tuck into the red money envelopes at Chinese New Year celebrations this year," I said. "Fei and I worked on some plans."

"The tracts would be received in a time of happiness and feelings of good fortune," said Liko. "I like your idea."

"Did you know that a state newspaper ran an article in 1992 that said our government plans to strangle the baby while it's still in the manger?"

"What a morbid thing to say," said Liko. "They don't know that the baby in the manger is alive today."

"Let's tell Tanching Village that Jesus isn't a baby anymore. He's alive, right inside our village!"

"Tell the whole village? How?" asked Liko.

"I don't know. Yes, I do! Let's make a big banner and put it up in a place where everybody will see it."

"Are you sure about this?" asked Liko. "You know, you could be risking your future at the university."

"Oh, I've never been so excited to tell people about Jesus. Fei and her friends are so bold. She said there were more persecutions at first, but now the authorities don't bother them much. Maybe it'll be that way for us too, Liko."

"How about the marketplace?"

"What about the marketplace?" I asked.

"To put up the banner. Even people passing by our village could read it."

"It's perfect!"

We were almost home.

"Let's meet at the cow shed again," I said. "Until then we can try to come up with more ideas on how to evangelize."

"Can you get a banner from somewhere?" asked Liko. "We could work on it Friday."

"Ping will help me find one. Her aunt is a teacher."

"Great. Then we'll meet Friday at the cow shed, after sundown?" asked Liko.

"Friday," I said, and we parted ways.

CHAPTER

Ten

We visited the DuYan house church every other Sunday, half of our group going one week, the other half the next. Our November and December walks were biting cold in the darkness, but it rained less frequently. An came every week with the Gongs, Fei's family. She looked as though she was going to deliver any minute. Still, she waddled in.

Liko and I met at the cow shed on Friday evenings. We sat shivering by the dim lanterns, warming our stiff hands over them while making the tracts and the banner, using every verse of Scripture we had memorized.

"When do you think we should begin passing out the tracts?" Liko asked one night early in December.

"Let's start on the twenty-fourth," I answered. "We can hang up the banner on Christmas Eve."

"Good plan. But why don't we prepare the way first? If we pass out tracts the week before, even the Buddhists will recognize the meaning of the banner."

"That's a great idea!" I said. "I can leave some tracts in desks and books at school. Where will you go?"

"I'll try the marketplace. And I thought about visiting Old One Tooth."

"Aren't you daring?" I smiled at his boldness. We sat side by side on the dirt floor, working on the artwork for our handmade tracts. "You know, if some young people respond and become Christians, we may have some help up here on Friday nights. Maybe we'll have meetings for young people, like Fei's church."

"And you'd be the group leader," said Liko.

"Me? What's the matter with you being the leader?"

"I'm not a talker like you," he said.

"Was that a compliment or a criticism?" I quipped.

Liko just grinned. "You know, I'm more the quiet type. I'll draw, you talk."

"You have this all worked out, don't you?"

Liko smiled and then grew serious. "Mei Lin, have you considered the effect this will have on you if Cadre Fang finds out?"

Just the mention of the cadre irritated me. "I think Cadre Fang is more concerned about a marriage license than he is about subversive behavior."

"Then he may become very jealous if he finds we are meeting together every week."

"He'll have to stay jealous. I'm not going to marry him," I said firmly, coloring in pictures on the new Christmas tracts. We worked in silence for a minute.

"Does he have . . . a reason to be jealous?" Liko asked slowly.

I could feel my face slowly turning red. Suddenly I noticed that Liko was sitting very close to me.

"I . . . I told him you were a friend, like a brother to me."

"Is that truly what I am to you? A brother?" he asked.

I looked at him, totally shocked, as he continued. "Ping told me what the cadre said. That he's willing to wait for you until after you graduate from the university. And that you let him hold your hand."

I jumped to my feet, sending tracts flying everywhere.

"She had no right to tell you that!"

Liko looked shocked, so I lowered my voice and tried to sound calm. "I told him you were only a friend and let him hold my hand only to protect you. It would go badly for you if he thought I had greater interest in you."

Liko stood up and faced me, putting his hands in his baggy pants pockets. "Ping said you were planning to marry him, and that you thanked him for his generosity in offering you a teaching position in Tanching."

"He made the offer just to get what he wants," I said hotly. "And of course I thanked him. I thanked him so he wouldn't stop my plans to go to the university. And to protect you."

"I'm sorry. I just didn't know what to think," he said, shoving his hands deeper into his pockets. He looked so sad it was hard to stay angry.

"I'm sorry too," I said. "Ping just doesn't want me to associate with you anymore because of your political status. She's always pressuring me to become a Communist Party member. She wants me to forget about you, and she wants you to believe I'm planning to marry the cadre."

I looked into his eyes, trying to figure out what he was thinking as he looked down at me.

"Is that the whole truth, Mei Lin? Why is Ping worried about your interest in me?"

Now I looked down at the floor. I had to tell him the truth, even if it hurt.

"She believes I have affection for you, that I'm Western in my thinking, wanting to marry for love instead of political and financial good fortune."

Liko lifted my chin and rested his other hand on my shoulder.

"I've been praying about us, Mei Lin," he said, staring deeply into my eyes.

"I don't know what to say," I said, fumbling for words and looking away. For the first time since I had known Liko, I felt awkward with him.

"Say nothing until you're sure you can be honest with yourself. And with me."

I could feel his gentle concern. His hand was still on my shoulder. Placing my hand over his, I looked up into his eyes.

"I care about you, Liko, but I'm not ready to think about marriage yet. I still want to go to Shanghai University. I will feel like a caged animal if I must stay in Tanching all of my life."

Liko nodded. "Thank you for being honest." A twinkle came into his eye and he added, "I guess there will be two of us waiting when you graduate."

I squeezed his hand and smiled, "Amah says that in a few years things may change with your political status. She says that new government programs arise and replace the old ones."

"I hope so," he replied.

"Cadre Fang will have a long wait," I said. We both giggled, breaking the tension between us.

Dropping to the ground, we continued our work, but something had changed inside me. I was certain I didn't want to marry Cadre Fang, but for the first time I felt I was honest enough with myself to admit that I really did care for Chen Liko. One thing I was sure of—I didn't want to lose my friendship with him. Liko was gentle and wise. And he was a strong Christian man.

"Liko, I'm not going to mention our conversation to Ping," I said. "It may be best if she thinks we're not associating anymore. She may report me if she thinks it will help me in the long run."

"I'm sure you'll see to it that she receives one of these tracts. Maybe she'll come around."

"Maybe. If she finds a Christian soldier who'll buy her two fans and a colored television!"

"That'll take some prayer," said Liko.

Liko always made every effort to protect me from danger during our secret meetings. So once our job was finished for the night, he left first, taking our materials home with him and hiding them safely. I waited and watched his tall figure disappear in the distance, then set out for home, my steps light. I knew that Chen Liko would keep praying about our relationship. I felt secure knowing that he was praying about us and not chasing me like Cadre Fang.

"Father," I called, once inside my house.

Father turned from the wood stove and smiled at me. "Yes, Daughter?" he answered.

"Father, I want to tell you something very exciting. Liko and I have a plan to pass out tracts Christmas week and put up a banner in the marketplace on Christmas Eve!"

Father hesitated and motioned me to sit with him at the table. "I don't know, Mei Lin," he said. "You are taking a great risk."

"Isn't that what it means to be a Christian in China?" I asked, quoting the old man from the DuYan house church. "I thought you would be happy."

"I am happy, Daughter," he said, squeezing my hand in his. "You remind me of your mother, so happy with your missionary work."

I thought now would be a good time to bring up my argument with Amah.

"Father, Amah told me about Mother's imprisonment."

"What?"

"She was cross with me because I tried to stop her from burning incense before our ancestor's picture. She said she was doing it to appease our ancestors because they were offended by our house-church meetings in the barn. She knew Pastor Chen was being watched, and she said that's how Mother's trouble started."

Tears filled Father's eyes. "Mei Lin, I wish you hadn't found out that way, but I'm glad you know. Your mother was the most wonderful Christian I ever knew. Now you can understand why I caution you about this new missionary work of yours. Although prison terms today are usually only three years instead of twenty, the labor camps are cruel. Many prisoners are tortured and even killed. You must understand the risk you are taking and be certain it is truly God who has called you to do this."

"I will pray some more about it. But please, tell me more about Mother."

Father leaned forward and clasped his hands together. He looked almost as if he were going to pray, and when he spoke, his voice was low and somber. "Your mother became a Christian soon after we were married. I was not a Christian, and I made her life extremely difficult. I would often stop her from going to house-church meetings. But I couldn't stop her love for God and people. Many times she passed out literature about Jesus, even talking about Him to the peasants she worked beside in the fields."

Father beamed now, his pride in my mother causing his face to shine. "She was very courageous. Even after you were born, she would travel over the mountain to DuYan Village to get Bibles and Christian literature."

"DuYan? You mean where we go to church now?" I asked.

"Yes, the same church. After the cleansing in 1980 all of our tapes and Bibles were taken. All foreigners were forbidden to come here. We were lucky to have the Bible your mother buried."

"You mean, the same one the PSB burned?" I asked.

Father nodded his head. "They released her in 1983." He looked away as tears slid down his sun-darkened cheeks.

A knot formed in my throat, and tears brimmed my eyes. I'd never seen my father cry before.

He continued, "When she came home, she begged us to forgive her persecutors. 'If you do not forgive them, you will become like them, full of hate,' she used to say. It was her forgiving heart that finally turned my hard heart to receive Jesus as my Savior." He released a deep sigh. "I'm so glad I did that before she died. It has been my one comfort all these years."

"And Amah?" I asked. "What did Amah think?"

"Oh, Amah tried to forgive, but it was difficult for her. She thought maybe your mother's torture was her fault because she threw away her Buddhas during the Cultural Revolution and no longer prayed to Buddha every day. To ask her to convert to Christianity after seeing her daughter-in-law suffer so because of it was too much for her."

"Father! That explains why Amah hid three old Buddha idols in the cow shed with our ancestor tablets underneath them."

"In the cow shed?" he asked.

"Yes, Liko and I found them in a box in a hole in the floor. Oooh, they are ugly."

Father rose from his chair and walked to the door to make certain Amah was not within hearing distance of our conversation. "That old woman is always up to something. That explains her odd behavior. Maybe now you can understand, Mei Lin, why I want you to be sure God is calling you to witness."

"I will pray more, Father," I promised, getting up and walking over to him. "Please, don't worry about me. It's my last year in high school. I'm sure God will protect us in our efforts to spread the Gospel."

"Sometimes He calls us to suffer in the cause of the Gospel," Father replied slowly, his hands on my shoulders.

I was taken aback. "Surely God wants more Christian teachers in China! Why would He want me to suffer when so many more can be won to Jesus through my teaching?"

"God's ways and thoughts are higher than ours, Mei Lin. Just be certain you are doing His missionary work and not your own."

I felt a little deflated and looked down at my feet, away from his penetrating gaze. "Yes, Father. I said I'd pray more, and I will."

"Meanwhile, I'm going to have a talk with Amah about her ancestor worship!" said Father, and he walked out the door.

CHAPTER

Eleven

The next two weeks went by quickly as Liko and I prepared all the materials for our Christmas missionary work. The preaching and testimonies at the DuYan house church challenged us and encouraged us to continue.

Finally the time arrived. Christmas Eve fell on a Friday night, which gave us the Monday through Thursday before to pass out tracts and boldly witness. We met at the cow shed Sunday evening. After organizing our materials and realizing all was ready, we dropped to our knees and prayed for the upcoming week.

"Father, we ask that you bring many people into your kingdom next week," I prayed. "Nudge us in our hearts so we will know who wants to hear your Gospel."

"Give us direction and help us to be wise," Liko prayed. "We don't want to be foolish when we boldly witness for you."

It felt as though Jesus and Liko and I were having a conversation. I guess we actually were.

"God, I ask for your power to be inside of us," I said.

"Yes," Liko agreed.

"Give us the words to talk to people. Help us to see their hearts as you see them. Give us assurance that we're on your mission and not our own."

"And keep your protection around us," Liko said to God. "Most of all, we want to honor Jesus on His birthday."

"In the name of Jesus we pray."

"Amen," we said in unison.

Quietly, we stood to our feet.

"Liko, let's—"

"Shhhh." Liko put his finger to his lips.

Then I heard it too. A sort of shuffling coming toward the cow shed. Liko turned out the lantern just moments before a form appeared in the doorway.

"Mei Lin, you must come home."

We sighed with relief.

"Amah, you scared us. What's the matter?"

"Cadre Fang Yinchu is at the house to see you. Your father is talking to him so I could come find you. I told him you took a walk."

"It must be a business matter," I said, trying to convince myself as well as Liko. "A man can't just come visiting a young girl unless—"

"Unless he's planning to court her," Liko finished for me.

"In which case he needs to be invited," I said. "It can't be that. I have to think for a minute. What will I say?"

"Liko, you should stay here for a while before leaving," cautioned Amah. "The cadre has *bong-yen bing*, the red-eyed disease of jealousy. If he sees you with Mei Lin, there will surely be trouble. Mei Lin, you must leave now before he comes looking for you."

Amah looked around the cow shed and folded her arms to keep warm. "It's freezing in here, Mei Lin. I can't believe you still meet up here in the winter."

But I didn't feel the icy wind as we walked down the hill toward our house. I felt numb. What would I say? What could the cadre possibly want?

"Give me the words I need, Lord," I prayed quietly.

"Don't offend the cadre, Mei Lin," Amah told me for the third time.

"A man can't just force me to be courted. And he cannot coerce me into marriage." I quickened my pace to get ahead of her.

"Father!" I called as I entered the house.

"Mei Lin," said Father. "Cadre Fang would like a word with you."

"Perhaps we could walk," said the cadre.

"You're just in time for evening tea," I countered, walking briskly toward the stove, anxious to have a moment to collect my thoughts. "Would you care to join us?"

Cadre Fang looked uneasy. "Yes, thank you."

Amah reached for some fruit to serve the cadre, but I shook my head at her. The cadre needed no further encouragement in his pursuit of a wife.

"What would you like to speak to me about?" I asked, pouring hot tea water into the cups.

The cadre looked at Father and Amah.

He smiled broadly, "I've come to tell you that your application to Shanghai University has been accepted."

"Already?" I was astonished.

"Pending the outcome of your final exams, of course," answered Cadre Fang. "From what your friend Ping said, they should pose no problem. Even so, Shanghai is a very difficult university to be accepted into. You would have never been accepted without guanxi."

Although I didn't allow myself to show it, I was infuriated by his insinuation that his connections had gained my acceptance.

"Forgive me for asking, Cadre, but how did you come to find out?" I asked.

Amah raised her eyebrows.

"The high-school administrator informed me," the cadre said. "He also speaks highly of your academic record."

"Mei Lin studies hard to make the grades she gets," Father said. "She's up many hours working on her papers."

"Sometimes I take walks to clear my mind before going to the next subject," I put in.

"And you must keep up with your work in the gardens," Amah added.

"I see," replied Cadre Fang Yinchu, looking suspiciously at each one of us. "Mei Lin is very busy her senior year."

"Ping is busy too," I said, trying to lighten the conversation. "She has more work to do than I because both of her parents work long days in the fields and on their farm. I have good fortune to have Amah at home and Father carrying so much of the load."

"Such spoiling will not last long," replied the cadre, straightening his back, his black mustache twitching nervously. "Labor is good. The great Chairman Mao said, 'The more students learn, the dumber they become.' "

Now I was boiling mad, and Amah recognized it.

"Labor is good," agreed Amah. "It is what our country has been built on. Through it our rice bowls are filled."

My anger was immediately diffused by my admiration for Amah. She knew how to quote communist propaganda and soothe political strife better than anyone I knew.

The cadre had half a grin on his face. I was sure he thought Amah was on his side. Although it wasn't very Christian, I just wanted to scratch his eyes out. But Amah had inspired me to play the communist chess game too.

"I hope I will be able to influence many children and youth during my years of teaching to conform to the efforts set forth by the great Chairman Mao," I said.

"Ah, you have a worthy aspiration in your pursuit of a teaching career," replied the cadre. "I am impressed at your daughter's loyalty to the Communist Party, Kwan So."

"Mei Lin has a mind of her own, Cadre, for better or worse," said Father, grinning at me.

"Father," I said, pretending to scold him. Everyone laughed.

I was relieved when the cadre got up to leave. "Thank you for the tea, Mei Lin," he said. "Perhaps I can join you on your walks sometime?"

"Well . . . midterms are coming up, and I'll only walk between studying. It may be difficult to—"

"It's all right. Perhaps after midterms, then."

"Thank you for informing us of my acceptance into Shanghai University. It is wonderful news," I said, steering the conversation away from prospective dates.

"You're welcome," he answered. "Good night, Kwan So, Amah."

"Good night, Cadre," answered Father.

"Please come again for evening tea," said Amah.

I pinched the back of her arm.

"I may take you up on your invitation, thank you," he replied. Then he was gone into the night.

"Our cadre is persistent," said Father.

"Persistent? He's a cunning old fox, that one," retorted Amah.

"And was I careful enough not to offend him, Amah?" I asked.

"You covered yourself nicely, Mei Lin," she said, busying herself with cleaning up the dishes.

Father waited until Amah was at the stove before he spoke. "Mei Lin, Cadre Fang may be watching you more closely from now on, looking for opportunities to speak with you. Handle yourself with discretion in your missionary work."

"He can't see me in school. Most of my missionary work will be done there."

"He's quite bold to make himself known to your school officials. He may have asked someone there to watch you."

"I'll be all right," I said, trying to convince myself as much as Father.

As I lay in bed that night I tried to put the cadre's visit out of my mind. I looked forward to our exciting week of passing out tracts and witnessing, and I was determined not to let thoughts of the cadre ruin my zeal.

Liko met me on the way to school the next morning. He shouldered a carrying pole loaded down with sacks of produce and two chickens to be sold at market.

"What happened with the cadre?" he asked.

"He came to tell me that I have been accepted at Shanghai University, pending my final exams, of course."

"Is that all he wanted?" asked Liko.

"He asked if he could take walks with me. I discouraged him, telling him I was too busy with schoolwork. Amah says he's a cunning old fox."

"Amah is wise. Perhaps we should move our tract ministry to another week."

"No. I'll need to be more discreet, that's all. And you too, Liko. Don't take any chances. We still don't know who reported your father."

"You didn't hear?"

"Hear what?" I asked.

"It was Huang Yan's father who reported my father to the authorities."

"But why—" Then it came to me. Mr. Huang was angry with Yan's mother for attending the meetings. She said he locked her out of the house sometimes. Reporting Pastor Chen to the authorities must have been his way of seeking revenge for his wife's conversion to Christianity.

"That's awful!" I exclaimed.

"Mrs. Huang is very upset. She wrote a letter to Mother yesterday and told her how terribly sorry she felt. It's really not her fault, but now you must be especially careful at school. We don't know if Huang Yan is spying on you there. Everyone knows that you and I are friends."

"I'll be careful, Liko. But I still think we need to carry on with our plans."

"Then I'll see you at the cow shed Friday night?"

"Yes! I can't wait to hang that banner. 'The Baby Born 2000

Years Ago Lives in Tanching Today.' Woooo."

"It will turn heads for certain," said Liko.

"And hearts too, I hope. We'd better meet after sundown, just in case the cadre finds another excuse to come for tea."

"I'll see you then, Mei Lin. God go with you."

"And with you, Chen Liko." I slowed down to allow him to walk ahead.

I stared after him, watching his long strides, his strong shoulders, and his short black hair shining in the morning sun.

"Thank you, God," I whispered. "You've granted me such a good, caring Christian friend."

"Who are you talking to?" asked Ping, jogging up behind me, her book bag flopping on her back.

"Who are *you* talking to?" I countered.

"That's Liko, isn't it?" she asked, looking far ahead as he disappeared around the bend in the road. "Life of a peasant farmer, that's what it'll be for his wife. No. Worse than that. He can't even supply a ration card. What a waste of a fine future doctor."

"Amah says time has a way of changing things. Maybe things won't look so bad for him a few years from now."

"You don't believe that, do you?" asked Ping. "Look, your good fortune falls right into your lap, and you toss it out like an old homework assignment."

"Who says I'm tossing anything out? I just want to be sure that Shanghai University and a teaching career are still ahead for me."

"I can't blame you," said Ping. "I want to venture out of Tanching Village myself. Hey, did you study for the physics exam yet?"

I nodded.

"It is so difficult! I got lost in the first chapter."

The conversation shifted to the immediate cares of the day. Silently I prayed for Ping, asking God to soften her heart toward Him.

"I'll meet you outside by the tree for lunch, okay?" she said as we approached the schoolyard.

"See you there," I answered.

By lunchtime I had passed out seven tracts. It was so easy! I left one on a classmate's chair, three in library books, two in the outhouse, and the last one on my English teacher's desk. I thought perhaps she would be more sympathetic to a Western religion than the other teachers.

"Mei Lin, you look like the cat that caught the bird," said Ping as we opened our lunch bags under the large poplar tree outside the school, pulling our coats about us in the chilly December wind. "You did well on your physics exam today?"

"I'm not sure. Sometimes I think I did well, and it turns out I didn't. We'll see."

I bowed my head and prayed over my food, a custom Ping had seen every day in recent months. I used to be afraid to pray before my meals, but seeing the boldness of the teenagers in DuYan Village made me more daring to do so, whether I ate in public or at home.

"So what's going on?" she asked when I looked up. "Your face is practically shining."

I gathered my courage, taking this question as the opportunity I'd prayed for to witness to Ping.

"My face shines because I have Jesus Christ in my heart. I

rarely mention Him to you, but a day never passes that I don't think of Him."

"Who is He?" she asked, biting into an apple.

"See the blue sky?" I said, leaning back on my elbows and pointing up through the bare branches of the poplar tree. "Jesus spoke the word, and it was created. See the strength of this old poplar tree? He created its ancestors as well."

"You believe that?" she asked with her mouth full.

"Yes, and I believe whatever is written in the Bible."

"So these ideas about creation are in the Bible?"

"Yes. And there's a lot more in there too," I said.

"Like what?"

Words came easily now, and I couldn't have been more delighted. For the first time Ping actually asked to know about my God who made the earth and the skies.

When I was finished she said, "Well, I don't think it's for me, but there must be something to it. You seem so happy most of the time."

"It's the inner happiness from Jesus that you see," I told her.

Ping's eyes looked past me, and I realized someone had come up behind me.

"Kwan Mei Lin, I'd like to talk to you. Alone." It was Professor Jiang, my political class teacher. I immediately stood to my feet and greeted him respectfully.

"I'm finished," said Ping, getting up and looking concerned. "See you tonight, Mei Lin." She cast a backward glance before she entered the school.

"Mei Lin, you've been an excellent student at Tanching High School," Professor Jiang began. "I'm sorry to question you now, in your senior year, but I've seen you bow your head before you eat your lunch. Would you tell me why you do that?"

Fear gripped me. My legs felt like rubber.

"I bow my head before every meal, Professor Jiang."

"Yes, I've seen that. But why do you do it?"

"I pray over my food." I suddenly felt limp.

"To God?"

"Uh, hmmm . . . yes."

"Mei Lin, this kind of act is treason against the Communist Party. The Public Security Bureau would deem it intolerable. Where are your loyalties to the Communist Party? Have you heard anything I've taught you in political class?"

"I am loyal to the Communist Party," I said. Why was I struggling for words?

"If you are loyal, then this Western religion must go. It will poison you and rob you of your future as a teacher in the People's Republic of China."

"I'm sorry, Professor Jiang. I didn't mean to disappoint you."

"Then give up this praying and this religion, and I will forget about this conversation. If you are found engaging in any other activity involving this religion, I will report you. I should report you now, but it would be such a waste of talent. You'll make a good teacher one day, Mei Lin."

"Thank you, Professor. You've been very kind."

After he left I felt like a traitor. What kind of a Christian was I? All my boldness left as soon as I was threatened.

I spent the rest of the afternoon under a cloud of guilt and shame. Fear tingled down my spine when the school principal pulled me aside outside the door of my last class.

"Kwan Mei Lin, Professor Jiang talked to you this afternoon, did he not?" The principal leaned his short, stocky frame close to me.

"Yes."

"Then what is this?" he asked, waving one of our Christmas tracts in the air.

"It is a paper telling the story of the first Christmas," I replied as honestly as possible. My knees were shaking, but I was glad I did not cower under the principal's questioning as I had earlier with Professor Jiang.

"Such behavior must be dealt with at once. You will cause Tanching High to lose face. We will be the laughingstock of Jiangxi Province. I am taking measures to ensure this will not happen again."

"I'm not sure I understand," I replied.

"Go home. You are expelled."

"What? But I—"

"You are expelled until you write a confession of your sins against the state and this school. You must promise to denounce this Western religion, this . . . this Jesus Christ."

Stunned, I turned and walked out of the school. Then, with fear thumping in my throat, I ran. Faster and faster, over the pebbled road to home. My mind was a jumble of emotions and worries. No more Shanghai. No more teaching career. No more dreams.

Father saw me from the garden and met me at the house. Amah followed us inside.

"Oh, Father, it's so awful," I cried, throwing myself into his arms. "You were right, they were watching me. Professor Jiang said they've seen me praying over my lunch. Then after school the principal had one of my tracts in his hands. Oh, Father, I'm expelled. I'll never see Shanghai."

I was devastated, but I would not allow tears to fall. Tears were a sign of weakness, and I intended to be strong.

"This is only the beginning," said Father soberly. Suddenly I noticed he was shaking, holding the back of the wooden chair for support.

"What do you mean?" I asked.

"He means that now the authorities will know, Granddaughter," said Amah. "Oh, I knew that Bible would bring trouble."

"Enough, Amah!" Father snapped. I'd never heard him speak to her so sternly. "We will not be ashamed of the Gospel in this home."

"Father, what will I do? I must tell Liko."

We heard the unusual sound of a motor running.

"Kwan So, Kwan Mei Lin," a deep voice called from the courtyard.

Father went to the door. "Stay back, Mei Lin," he said over his shoulder.

It was Cadre Fang Yinchu, accompanied by five PSB officers with rifles. "These Public Security Bureau officers would like to speak with you both."

Having no choice, Father let three of the officers into the small home, while two stood guard outside. He motioned me to stand behind him.

"Your principal tells us you've been expelled, Mei Lin," said the one in charge. "Would you like to tell us why?"

"I pray before my meals. And . . . he found a tract I'd written."

"A what?"

"A tract," I answered, feeling strength come into my soul. "It's a piece of paper—"

"I know what it is," he snapped, throwing his briefcase on our table. "Here is paper and pen. We will stay here until you have written a confession of your sins against the state."

"Sins?" I asked, feeling incredibly stupid.

"You must admit that this poisonous Christianity is false and declare your loyalty to the Party. You must denounce this Jesus Christ."

"Oh," Amah gasped, holding her hand to her mouth.

"Officer, I respect your duties—" Father began.

"Shut up," the officer interrupted, using a hand motion that signaled the other two officers to hold Father at gunpoint. They pushed him aside so that I was face-to-face with the officer in charge.

"Cadre!" the officer ordered.

"Mei Lin, these men will do you no harm," said Cadre Fang Yinchu, his voice smooth as butter. "Cooperate with them, and I will see to it that you can return to school."

"Jesus is my Lord," I said softly. "I cannot deny Him."

"Cadre!" The commanding officer was ordering Cadre Fang to carry out his command.

"Mei Lin, this is suicide," the cadre pleaded with me. "All you must do is promise not to pray or pass out seditious religious literature."

I stared at the cadre. For the first time I felt a love for him. God's love. "I cannot do that."

"Mei Lin, this is serious! What about Shanghai University? What about your dreams for your future? Are they nothing to you? If you refuse to submit, you will lose everything."

I looked at my father and grandmother. "I cannot deny Him who gave His life for me."

"You counterrevolutionary!" shouted the commanding officer. "Cadre!"

Cadre Fang stared wildly at me. "Please, Mei Lin."

My eyes told him my answer.

"Arrest her," he said weakly. He turned his back to me and walked out of the house.

The two officers who had been standing guard outside now entered. Using a baton, one of them struck my back. It shocked me, and before I could react, a second blow to my arm threw me to the ground. I winced in pain and tried not to cry out for the sake of my father and Amah. My silence only seemed to cause the officer to strike harder.

"Let her go!" my father shouted, struggling to free himself from the two soldiers who held him firmly. "I'm the one at fault. I told her to do these things."

They held him back and forced him to watch the beating. Father was heaving with sobs now, crying out, "No, no. It's my fault. Beat me. No, stop!" I knew the thing he had feared the most was happening right before his eyes.

The officers stopped beating me and shoved Amah into her rocker. "Have mercy, have mercy," she cried out over and over again.

As soon as I managed to stand up again, the officer in charge raised his hand high and struck me hard across the face. My head filled with lightning, and I fell against the back of the chair, grabbing it for support.

"If your Christ is bigger than the Communist Party, let Him save you," he sneered. His body had broken into a sweat, and foul breath spat out the next words. "Confess your sins against the state. Denounce Jesus Christ."

Warm blood ran from my lower lip. In my stupor I suddenly saw Jesus on the cross and felt the hatred of the people who hit Him until the blood ran down His face. It sounds strange, but I suddenly felt honored to experience what He suffered.

With great calm throughout my being, I declared, "Jesus is my Lord!"

Enraged at my answer, he sent another blow to my back. I staggered forward, then stumbled down into an engulfing blackness. Lights flashed again in my head as it hit the floor.

I clawed at the kitchen chair, struggling to my feet. The pain was dizzying. Nausea filled me, and the room began to reel.

The officer yanked my arms behind my back. Another blow to the back of my neck. The floor came up at me.

The last thing I remembered was Amah's scream.

CHAPTER
Twelve

I woke up in total darkness. Was I awake or dreaming? Everything was such a blur. I felt something warm running down my arm. I grabbed for it, then realized it was blood from the beating. I tried to be strong, but the tears wouldn't listen. They leaked out in spite of my determination to hold them back.

My tongue and lips were thick from dehydration. I was viciously thirsty, and for a time I could think of nothing else. I rubbed the tears off my face with my fingers and used them to wet my lips and tongue. The salt burned, but the wetness of it was somehow soothing.

The acrid smell of human excrement choked my throat. The floor was wet with human waste. I could tell I was underground somewhere. How long had I been unconscious?

A shadowy movement in front of me caused me to jump. My head pounded at the sudden jerk, and my entire body was on fire with pain. There was the movement again. A rat.

"Get out," I yelled. "Oh!" I covered my mouth. Some of my

teeth were loose and bleeding. It hurt to talk. Overwhelmed with nausea, I threw up bile, dry heaving when nothing else was left.

When it was all over, I felt cold. I moved close to the wall and squatted so that my body wasn't resting on the filthy wet floor. I could barely move my lips to pray.

"Jesus, thank you for giving me the strength not to deny you," I began. My teeth chattered from cold and shock.

"Oh, God, I feel so sick. Please help me. Please help me." All at once I felt consumed with dark loneliness and fear. "Please, God, give me answers." My teeth chattered uncontrollably now. I shut my eyes tightly, squeezing back tears.

"I thought you would protect me so that I could bring your message to students. What happened? Would I have been a bad teacher?"

My thoughts went wild, condemning me for my past, making me doubt my future. "Lord, do you want me to live the rest of my life in Tanching or in this filthy prison? Am I a bad element to the kingdom of heaven? I'm sure I'm prideful, Lord. Please forgive me."

I thought of my mother, suffering until her death. And Pastor Chen, imprisoned while his family's belongings were confiscated, knowing they had to survive without him. "God, is there any justice?" I asked, my faith dwindling as I cried in confusion.

Then I thought of my own family. Would our home be raided? Would Amah and Father lose their possessions and be forced to fend for themselves? I felt crazy thinking about it.

"What have I done?" I cried out. "Lord, please keep Father and Amah and Liko safe. Forgive me for all my sins. Don't make them suffer for it. Don't let them come here, please, God. Please, God."

I groped for a way out of the darkness, praying haphazardly until my teeth hurt too much to pray anymore. I was exhausted, all of my emotions and physical energies drained. Drawing my knees to my chest, I slipped again into the subconscious realm of sleep.

———————

I woke up to face black solitude. After a time, my eyes grew accustomed to the darkness. I'd heard of such cells from the *Lao Da*, the house-church elders who'd survived similar prison experiences. Some gave eyewitness accounts of Christians who did not survive. My mother was one of them.

I was only eighteen. I wondered which group I would fall under, the living or the dead. And I wondered where I was. There were thousands of prisons and labor camps in China. Was I still in Jiangxi Province?

I decided to explore my new surroundings. The underground cell was much colder than what I was used to at home. There was no bed, no window—just one door without a handle. Weak and wobbling, I walked toe to heel, measuring the little room at ten shoe lengths long and eight shoe lengths wide. I could touch the ceiling with my hand.

I was tempted to pound on the door to let them know I wanted out, but I thought better of it. Remembering Mother's imprisonment and the elders' stories of interrogations and beatings during their imprisonment, I chose to try to let my wounds heal and use my time in other ways.

My strength depleted by my measuring tour, I lay at the door and began to organize my vacant little room. I decided to sleep next to the door. I would use the corner on my left and farthest away from the door as my latrine. The doorway would have to be the head of my bed, or the rats could beat me to my meals—if there were meals. The corner to the right of the door would be my praise-and-worship spot. Of course, my dinner table was located where my bed was.

I felt better once my room was organized. I lay at the door and longed to escape the cold darkness and slip into the world of sleep, where I would walk through the sunlit rice fields with my father, or talk to Liko on our walks to the house church. Finally, I drifted off.

————

I awakened with a jolt. Dark thoughts of fear surrounded me. Amah was right. I shouldn't have made an enemy of Cadre Fang. And the house-church Bible. Didn't Amah say it would bring trouble? Was it true? Was that why my mother and I were beaten and imprisoned?

I felt the tips of my fingers. Would I return home with fingertips seared to the bone? I shuddered and tucked my hands under my arms.

The darkness engulfed not only my cell but my thoughts. Without daylight to measure the hours, I lost all concept of time. I could feel depression's cold breath on the back of my neck. I felt as if it were watching me, waiting to swoop down and consume me at the first sign of weakness.

Then I thought of Father's words: *"God's ways and thoughts are higher than ours, Mei Lin. Just be sure you're doing His missionary work, not your own."* His wisdom tormented me now. Had I been doing God's work or my own? Why had it all ended up in such a terrible mess?

I knew that depression was part of the PSB's plan to weaken me. It seemed impossible to think of anything positive, so I said verses of Scripture out loud.

" 'I am with you always, even to the end of the world,' " I began. " 'I am strong in the Lord and in the power of His might.' "

Keeping my mind occupied was one thing, but what about my stomach? Could Scriptures fill my empty insides? My body felt hollow and weak. I had no idea how long I'd been unconscious, but I guessed from my hunger that I'd probably been here at least three or four days, maybe a week.

"Lord, please, send me some food," I prayed. "I feel weak from the beating, and so thirsty and hungry." I rolled over, bumping into an object. A bowl! It felt like a wooden one. Empty.

The rats must have eaten whatever was in it. I searched the floor on my hands and knees, looking for any other object I might have missed. I knocked something over. It was a jug of water, with a closed lid! I knelt, trembling with anticipation, and drank the sweet liquid. I poured just a little on my hand and wiped my face with it. I could feel the water reviving my hollow body.

Suddenly I heard a shuffling of footsteps.

A small window opened at the bottom of the door, bringing a glimmer of precious light.

"Can you tell me where I am?" I yelled through the little window.

"Give me your empty bowl and water jug," a woman barked from the other side.

I quickly downed the last of the water and slipped the empty bowl and jug through the small window. Thankfully, a filled bowl and new water jug were slid back through the door toward me. I felt large, cold grains of rice between my fingers. The window flapped down, and I couldn't open it again.

"Where am I?" I asked again.

No answer. She was gone. I hated the darkness.

I sensed movement beside me.

"Oh!" I screamed, feeling a rat crawling over my hand that held the rice grains. Instinctively, I threw it off my arm.

Suddenly there were more rats scurrying around my rice bowl. Shocked and terrified, I curled my body into a tight ball to protect myself. My bowl of rice fell, scattering its contents. The rice was devoured in seconds. With the food gone, the rats found some hole in the cell and escaped.

Again I felt depression's cold breath luring me into a darkness more real than the darkness of my cell. Anger came up my throat, and I grabbed the dirty bowl and flung it across the room, hitting the wall.

"I hate you!" I yelled at the rats. "I'll show you next time."

It felt good to be mad.

"And I hate you, PSB! And you, Communist Party. I hate—" I stopped myself.

"No!" I screamed. "God, forgive me." I began to shake, trying to hold back the rage I felt inside. "Help me not to hate. Help me to forgive. God, I feel so angry inside. I want to hate the people who did this to me. I want to hate them for what they did to my mother. Oh, I've never wanted to hate so much. Please help me to forgive. I just don't know how."

My prayers of desperation finally mellowed into hopeful silence as I strained to hear the shuffling footsteps that delivered my precious meal. Survival became paramount, and I formed a plan to guard my rice bowl.

Before the next beautiful ray of light flooded my cell, I sat on the floor and positioned my legs to form a V-shaped wall around the little window. That way I could keep the window open and the rats away from my food at the same time.

The window finally opened and the rats came, maybe half a dozen of them. Having no weapon but my hands, I held the rice bowl to my chest with my left hand and batted the rats away with my right, sending some of them flying and others rolling across the floor. My foot slipped, and the window closed.

Pitch black. The rats were relentless, coming back for more.

"Jesus, help me!" I cried. I jumped to my feet and kicked them away as I felt them touch me. The rat war continued until I'd killed two of them by flinging them against the walls with my feet. I was debating about what to do with them when I sensed the dark shadows of the others sneak back in and drag the two dead ones away. I tried not to think about what they were going to do with them. I had to concentrate on my first meal in prison. The "rice" turned out to be *kaoliang*, a kind of coarse Chinese sorghum. It was cold and chewy. I wondered how long such a meager diet would sustain me.

After I finished eating, I found what was probably the shirt of a previous prisoner and soaked it with some of my water. I set to work mopping up the place. Human waste was everywhere, mostly dried and putrid. Cleaning gave me a sense of order and stability. It was something I could put my hand to and be in control of.

The rice bowl gave me my only sense of time. I decided to count my minutes. I leaned against the stone wall and counted out loud—one thousand one, one thousand two—until I reached one thousand sixty.

"There," I said to the empty darkness. "That's a minute."

Then I prayed for my father and Amah, that they would not have to come to such a place and that God would send word to them that I was alive. Other prayers were for Liko, that he would not forget me while I was in this dark, stinking hole . . . and that he would never have to come into such darkness. Deep inside, I knew he was praying for me.

I thought about Shanghai. It was a meaningless dream from where I sat now. Still, I needed to have a dream, something to look forward to that the Communists couldn't take away. Over and over I wondered if God had stopped my plans because I would have been a bad teacher.

My solitude and pain made me long for the old relationships I'd had. Sometimes I prayed to go home. But then the old fight returned, and I longed to share the Gospel as I had to Ping that day under the poplar tree. I remembered Father's words: *"We will not be ashamed of the Gospel in this home."*

"Lord Jesus, I ask that you give me wisdom and strength," I prayed. "And no matter where I am, give me the courage to continue to preach the Gospel."

At times wild thoughts of hopelessness and even suicide surrounded me. During these moments I quoted the Bible verses I had memorized. Perhaps it was good our church had only one Bible. I had put much more of it to memory than I had realized.

Often I found myself singing praises to God. I used to be in awe of Paul and Silas, who sang praises from a prison cell. Now I recognized that this sort of music was as much for the prisoner as for their Lord. It was this kind of singing that lifted me above the constant darkness and solitude into the sweet presence of Jesus, the place where all dreams are possible and everything is light, love, and peace.

Then the day came—or was it night?—that the prison guards came for me. I was startled by the sound of footsteps nearing my cell.

The dead bolt was unfastened.

Light!

I couldn't see. I was blinded by the light I had longed to see. Two heavy-handed guards jerked me to my feet, pulling me outside the cell.

They were the first human beings I'd seen or talked to in many days.

"Please, tell me where I am," I said. "Is this Jiangxi Province?"

One guard guffawed mockingly. "Hey, she wants to know if she's in Jiangxi Province," he said to the other. Now they both laughed, pushing me ahead of them. The first one spat on the floor.

I stumbled and fell several times, groping for a wall to steady myself. By the time my eyes adjusted we were in an office. After being thrown into a chair across from a desk, the guards left, locking the door behind them.

I quickly scanned the room and saw a clock. It was two-thirty. There were no windows to tell me if it was day or night, but it was probably afternoon. A calendar hung on the wall to my right. March.

I'd been in the cell for at least ten weeks. Next month I would be nineteen years old.

China's crimson flag loomed high on the wall behind the desk, with a map of China underneath. I relaxed a little. This did not look like a room where they tortured people. Too orderly and intact.

The door behind the desk opened, and the warden entered. His light skin and brown hair told me he must be from northern China. He was large in build, much larger than the men from Jiangxi Province. I bit my lower lip and silently prayed.

Looking down at a paper, he began to read. " 'Kwan Mei Lin, age eighteen, born in Jiangxi Province, daughter of Kwan So, mother dead. Lives with paternal grandmother. Graduated from village high school.' " He looked up at me. "Is this true?"

"I was to graduate in May of this year," I answered. "Sir, could you tell me where I am?"

"You're in Shanghai Prison." He rubbed his square chin, then shuffled through the papers in front of him.

I had to suppress a giggle. *I guess there's more than one road to Shanghai.*

The warden continued. " 'Mother incarcerated from 1980 to '83 for inciting and propagating counterrevolution and distributing seditious propaganda.' True?"

"So I was told. I was very young," I answered.

Without looking up, he read, " 'Kwan Mei Lin is charged with disturbing the social order and normal religious life of Tanching Village.' "

I couldn't believe my ears. Was he sentencing me right here without a trial?

" 'Kwan Mei Lin joined church meetings not registered with the Three-Self Patriotic Movement. Engaged openly in religious activities and rituals in school. Distributed seditious religious propaganda, inciting and propagating counterrevolution. Suspected of collaborating with hostile forces from abroad.' " He looked up at me and leaned forward over his desk. "Is this true?"

I froze. The accusations were dizzying.

"I . . . I don't know," I finally answered.

"Miss Kwan . . ." He spoke with a grandfatherly tone. "Confess your sins against the state." He shoved a pen and a stack of blank paper toward me. "You can go home to your father and grandmother and receive your work-unit assignment. Perhaps even the university will accept you if your brain is washed."

That was a lie. No university would register a counterrevolutionary with a prison record.

"Simply write a confession of your sins and that you no longer believe in Jesus Christ."

I just stared at him.

"*Fanxing, fanxing!* Reflect on your mistake," he ordered. "Surely, three months in solitary has washed your brain."

"I still believe in Jesus Christ," came the answer from deep inside me.

"Miss Kwan," said the warden, ignoring my confession, "you were young when your mother died, too young to be greatly influenced by her counterrevolutionary thoughts. The Communist government can be forgiving of such things. If you stop believing in Jesus Christ, I can release you right now. Today."

"I still believe in my Lord."

His chair flew back, and all at once he was in front of me, the grandfatherly tone completely gone. "Your mind is incorrigible. You are hopeless. A bad element. The Kwan So family is a bad element. You shame your country and your father's name. Your brain needs to be washed even more. Three months is not enough. This time we will sentence you to three years."

Three years! His words rang like gongs in my ears.

CHAPTER

Thirteen

Once again I woke up on my back in cold darkness. This time the pain took my breath away. It seemed my whole body was throbbing with it. I couldn't tell where the door was. I remembered the beating I had just taken with the electric rods and shivered. The shocks had sent snakelike waves through my body, jerking me over the floor like the headless chickens I'd watched Amah butcher.

My throat burned with thirst, and my mouth tasted foul and sticky. I touched my cheek. Dried blood. I couldn't breathe through my nose, and each deep breath through my mouth brought a stabbing sensation to my ribs. I tried to breathe in shallow puffs to relieve the pain.

Am I going to die?

I allowed tears to trickle down my face, mingling with the dried blood and making my face itch. My body shook with pain and fear and tremors. The shaking brought more stabs of pain to my ribs.

Then a Scripture came to me: *Do you not know that your body is a temple of the Holy Spirit who is in you? Therefore glorify God in your body.*

In a husky, broken whisper I asked the Lord, "How can I glorify you in such a body as this?"

Lights turned on within my soul. The glory of God always follows suffering.

So there is some purpose in all of this.

A peaceful calm swept over me, causing the tears to subside. Immediately I knew how to pray. Slowly and with great effort, my mouth formed the words. "O God, I ask that you forgive the ones who beat me and put me here. Give me the power to forgive and the wisdom to know what to do. Help me to stay strong in faith."

More tears flowed freely. Only now they weren't so much for myself but for some deep joy I could not describe. I remembered Jesus hanging on the cross, mocked and bleeding and alone. I cried unashamedly for Him. My heart was bursting to sing. Lifting my hands I began to sing hoarsely,

> *I surrender all, I surrender all.*
> *All to you, my blessed Savior,*
> *I surrender all.*

I sang it over and over until strength filled my being, birthing glorious praise and worship. I was lifted to places in God far beyond the little dungeon I was in. Time was forgotten. My foul cell had become a holy sanctuary of fellowship with my Master, Jesus. Somewhere in the midst of worship, I felt I knew Jesus more intimately than I'd ever imagined possible. He became more real to me than the cell with its stench and filth and rats. He was even more real than my battered body.

Was this what it meant to share in the fellowship of His sufferings?

Humble, wordless worship continued to stretch out from my soul to heaven until, exhausted, I fell into a deep and peaceful sleep.

When I awoke I felt something at my head. Afraid it was a rat, I batted at it and knocked over the water flask. My head was at the door.

Lying on my side, I opened the lid, drinking slowly and deeply. The throbbing from earlier had transformed into a heavy ache. I knew I was not going to die, but this beating would take longer to heal from than the last. I was overjoyed that I had not denied my Lord.

Ten rice bowls later, I was sitting quietly singing a hymn when the Lord spoke to me. "This is to be your ministry."

"But I am all alone. Who is there to preach to?"

No answer. So I continued to pray for God to lead me in this ministry, whatever it was.

Many rice bowls went by, and my body was beginning to heal. Suddenly, an idea came to me.

"Guards!" I shouted, not knowing if anyone was out there or could hear me. A guard I hadn't seen before put his head in the door, flooding the cell with precious light.

"Sir, can I do some hard labor for you?" I asked.

The guard crossed his arms and looked at me in suspicious surprise. I'm sure no one had ever made that kind of request before.

I continued quickly, before he could shut the door. "This

prison is so dirty. There is human waste everywhere. Let me go into the cells and clean up this filthy place."

"Ah, the prison walls are known for changing counter-revolutionary thoughts," he answered, pulling a cigarette out of his shirt pocket.

"All you will have to do is give me a bucket of water and a brush."

"Labor has been known to reform the worst offenders," he replied, lighting his cigarette. "I'll tell the warden."

With that, he shut the door in my face.

I prayed that God would give me favor with the guard and the warden.

Several rice bowls later, I heard someone opening the door to my cell. I stood up and braced myself. As before, my eyes were blinded by the light, and I could hardly open them to look at the guard. My squinted gaze naturally moved downward, where I glimpsed a brush and a bucket standing beside him. My heart leaped for joy.

I couldn't stop grinning as I picked up the brush and bucket. What would Liko think of this? This ministry is not too glorious!

The guard led me down the hallway and opened the first cell. I entered with my bucket and brush, and then the guard thrust a lantern into my hand and shut the door.

"No, please, no!"

I whirled around as pitiful pleas for mercy came from a crumpled figure in the corner. I stared into the face of what appeared to be a man. He was barely recognizable as a human being.

"I am here to clean your cell," I said quickly, and set to work, scrubbing furiously on my hands and knees.

I left the lantern near the man to bring him comfort. He kept staring at me as though he wasn't sure I was real. When I sensed that the guard outside the door had left, I stopped scrubbing, looked into the poor man's eyes, and began to speak about Jesus. "I too am a prisoner. I asked permission to clean your floor so that I could tell you good news."

"Good news?" The lantern cast shadows across the man's sunken face so that he resembled a skeleton.

"Yes. No matter what crimes brought you to this awful place, you can be forgiven by God, the One who created the skies and the earth." By now my eyes were adjusting to the room.

The man leaned forward. "Forgiven?"

"Yes. The true God offers forgiveness and eternal life to all who believe."

"This cannot be true," said the man. "You must be the spirit of one of my late ancestors."

"I am not your ancestor. I am Kwan Mei Lin, and Jesus has saved me from my sins and promised to take me to heaven when I die." I continued to tell him the wonderful story of Jesus, about His birth, the miracles He performed, His cruel death on the cross, and His amazing resurrection.

"You can be forgiven too, if you repent of your sins and believe."

He looked astonished. "I can go to the good heaven with Jesus?"

"Oh yes! Tell God you are truly sorry for your sins of the past and believe in His son, Jesus. He will forgive you, and He promises eternal life with Him in heaven."

The man immediately got on his knees and prayed earnestly that God would forgive him. In the golden glow of the lantern light, I could see his skeletal face flush with the happiness of knowing he had the promise of eternal life.

"Dear lady, you are a *guiren*!"

"No, I am not a saintly person but a forgiven sinner like you," I replied. "Give thanks to God." Feeling strongly impressed to do so, I wiped off my wet hands and touched his arm. The only touch he knew was that of a rod on his back and excruciating tortures to his body and mind. I simply said, "God has forgiven you. Now you must forgive others. Even those who have tortured you."

"How do I do such a thing?" he asked. His dirty face looked thunderstruck.

"When Jesus was on the cross, He asked His father in heaven to forgive those who crucified Him because they didn't understand what they were doing. And when He taught His disciples, He said that we must forgive others just as God has forgiven us."

"I will do this," he said. Kneeling on his newly cleaned floor, he forgave his tormentors from a newly cleaned heart.

As I finished scrubbing the floor I quoted as much Scripture as I could remember. The man sat weeping. Finally I called the guard. It was hard to hide my joy as he escorted me to the next cell.

So this is my ministry!

From one cell to the next, on my hands and knees, I preached the Gospel of Jesus Christ.

After the guard had escorted me back to my cell and locked me in again, I couldn't help myself. I laughed out loud.

The months passed, and I developed strong muscles in my arms and back. The physical labor was good for me. It also helped me to grasp the time of day and develop a sleep pattern. After the daily routine of cleaning the cells, my evenings were spent praying for the ones I'd preached to before I fell asleep. Still, I was growing extremely thin. My labor had increased, but my rice bowl had not. Most of the time I felt hollow and sickly and weak. My stomach was beginning to swell, like the protruding stomachs of some of the prisoners I talked to.

Day by day, the response to the Gospel was much the same from these ruthlessly tortured prisoners. They were touched that my God cared so much for them that He sent me to them. They always wanted to know as much about Jesus as I had time to tell. And nearly all of them received Him as their Lord and Savior.

One day the guard opened a cell to find a dead woman. I was quickly escorted to another cell. Feelings of anguish swept over me. Did she know Jesus?

It seemed we faced a similar situation the next day as I entered a cell where a human figure lay motionless on the floor.

"Oh!" I held my hand over my mouth.

"He's alive," the guard said as he pushed me into the cell. "Just unconscious."

I couldn't preach to this man. I wanted to clean for people who could hear my message. But before I could protest, the guard left me alone in the room with my water bucket, my brush, and the lantern. The man was barely breathing, so I determined I would do what I could for him. If I couldn't minister to him spiritually, then I would minister to him physically. Putting his head in my lap and using the end of his coat, I dabbed cool water on his lips and wounds. I began to wash the cuts on his head.

The man groaned pitifully. I placed the lantern closer to his body and gasped when I saw his hands. His fingers were so swollen that they seemed to be meshed together. Dried blood covered his fingertips, which seemed somehow twisted and disfigured. What had they done to this man? What crime called for this type of punishment?

I knew that the dried blood under his nails would only cause more pressure to his already swollen fingers. I was afraid he would wake up and howl like a mad dog. Still, he needed his fingers cared for. Carefully, I soaked the end of his shirt and wrapped it around his hands, waiting for the water to dissolve the dried blood. It worked. The shirt was bloodstained, his hands showing now the ghastly purple fingertips left to him by his torturers. I was thankful that he did not wake up.

I soaked the end of his coat with fresh water, then quickly set to work on the floor. I was nearly finished and nervously prepared to leave. This man's pain would be excruciating when he woke up. I wasn't sure how he'd react if he saw me.

"Guard," I called out the door. This time no one came.

The man stirred.

"Ohhhhhhhh," he howled in pain. "Please, water."

"There is water soaked into your coat," I said, hovering by the door. "It is clean. I soaked it before I washed the floor."

Again, compassion washed my fears away, and falling on my knees, I offered the wet end of his coat to his lips.

"No, my fingers, please. I need water on my fingers. I cannot move my hands."

Quickly I wrapped the soaked coat around his hands once again.

"Ohhhhhhh," he groaned as he directed me in adjusting his hands into a more comfortable position.

"Thank you, dear girl. You have brought much comfort." His breathing was labored as he tried to conceal his obvious pain.

"I already called the guard. He will come any moment," I said. "Please, I wish to tell you of One who cares about you and sees us in this dark prison cell. He made the skies and the earth. He loved us so much He sent His son, Jesus, so that we can have forgiveness for all of our sins. He also gives the promise of eternal life to all who believe—"

"You are a Christian?" asked the man in a strained voice. He didn't wait for an answer. "Glory to God."

In all of my cell visits this was the first Christian I'd met.

"My name is Wong San Jun."

"I am Kwan Mei Lin." I told him the story of my arrest and my call to ministry in the prison. "What have they done to you?"

With labored breathing, he slowly told me his story. "I am a house-church pastor. I travel throughout China preaching the Gospel and teaching. They asked for the names of other pastors, church members, and foreign contacts. I would not give the list to them. They squeezed the ends of my fingers with pliers and broke them. I passed out. While I was unconscious, they must have finished the job."

"Oh, they are so heartless," I said, the old anger rising again.

"Forgive, sister," he said.

"Forgive them, Father," I prayed in earnest, my lower lip trembling.

"Mei Lin, endurance is the Gethsemane gift. You experience this gift when, somehow, God gives you supernatural strength to continue glorifying God."

Tears filled my eyes. "Even though you would rather die?"

He nodded.

It seemed a dam of tears burst from within me, and the suffering and grief I'd experienced all these months poured out of my soul and gushed down my cheeks. For the first time in my life, I wasn't ashamed to cry.

We wept together for some time. I wept over the woman who died before I told her about Jesus. I wept over the searing hunger in my stomach. I cried over the filth, the cold, the rats, and the beatings. I saved my most bitter tears for Liko and Ping and my family.

Pastor Wong began to pray. "Father, thank you for the honor of suffering for you. Please grant my sister the Gethsemane gift, that she would have your power and strength to go on. And bless her ministry here with many souls for your kingdom. In Jesus' name. Amen."

Finally I was cried out. There was a sweet release and the warm presence of Jesus in the small prison cell.

"Have you been to Tanching Village in Jiangxi Province?" I asked Pastor Wong, tears dripping from my nose. "Have you heard of the welfare of the church there?"

"Your home?" he whispered.

I nodded.

"I wish I could tell you I've heard news of your church. I do visit Jiangxi Province, but I rarely travel south of WuMa. I can only tell you that it is about the second week in August 1997. I know how much it helps to know that in this place."

"You've been here before?" I asked.

"Twice. Now I will quote Scripture to you before the guard returns."

I was so honored. I came to wash the floor and witness to this seemingly dying man. Now this saint with crippled hands was ministering to me.

" 'Even if you should suffer for what is right, you are blessed.

Do not fear what they fear; do not be frightened. But in your hearts set apart Christ as Lord. Always be prepared to give an answer to everyone who asks you to give the reason for the hope that you have. But do this with gentleness and respect. . . .' "

The words washed over me, the beautiful words of the Bible, offering strength and wisdom in my time of loneliness.

The guard was coming, shouting at some poor prisoner.

"Sister," said Pastor Wong, "Jesus said, 'I was sick and you looked after me; I was in prison and you came to visit me.' "

"Yes," I answered. " 'Whatever you did for one of the least of these brothers of mine, you did for me.' I will pray for you, Pastor Wong."

The guard opened the door.

CHAPTER

Fourteen

The verses Pastor Wong quoted gave me strength and hope. Just knowing he was in the same prison encouraged me in my faith. One morning several weeks later, I sat waiting for the guard to take me to the cells to scrub floors. I prayed, as usual, for those I would witness to that day.

My cell door finally opened.

"We're starting late today?" I asked the guard.

"We aren't starting at all," came the curt answer.

"Then where are we going?" I asked. His unusual manner alarmed me.

"The warden wants to see you. You've put me in a nasty struggle with him."

"I'm sorry. I didn't mean to trouble you. What have I done?"

"You nearly cost me my position, that's what you've done." It was strange. He really didn't seem to be very angry with me.

"I'm truly sorry," I repeated. "You've been very good to me. I'll try to explain to the warden."

"You'll do enough to save your own neck," he said.

Our conversation stopped. We were at the door.

"Here's the parasite," yelled the guard as he opened the door.

Again I was thrown into the chair facing the warden's desk; only this time the warden was already there. It was the same light-skinned, husky man who had sentenced me before.

"Kwan Mei Lin, you were given the privilege of hard labor with the hope that you were working to reform your thoughts. Instead, you've taken advantage of our good favor and spread your counterrevolutionary thinking throughout our entire prison."

"I'm not sure I understand," I said.

"Our prisoners no longer submit to our methods. We beat them and they say, 'I forgive you in Jesus' name.' "

"Oh." I tried not to smile.

"There is no way of controlling them. Your floor scrubbing could have given you a lighter sentence. I was soft and cowardly in permitting it. And the guard who took you—"

"The guard had no idea what I said to the prisoners," I interrupted. "He went elsewhere to perform his duties once I was locked in the cells with the prisoners."

"Likely story. You probably bribed him. A young girl like you could certainly find a way to bribe a guard now, couldn't you?" The warden was talking with lust in his eye, and I knew if I showed any fear, the flame could turn to fire.

Leaning forward over his desk, I answered evenly, "There were no bribes of any kind."

The warden leaned back on his chair and laughed. Finally he sobered enough to continue. "Kwan Mei Lin, if you sign a confession and stop believing in this Jesus Christ, you can go home right now. Today. Today you can have a big family reunion. Your grandmother's getting old. Perhaps you'd like to see her again before she dies?"

The warden's words seemed to come from the devil himself. Amah was nearly eighty. I wanted nothing more than to see her become a Christian before she died. Suddenly, I was strongly tempted to make up a false confession. Then I thought of the many souls who had come to Jesus in their cells over the last few months.

"You do not understand," I answered softly. "Jesus gave up His life for me. How can I deny Him now?"

The warden's apparent lust turned to seething hatred. "You cannot be redeemed. Your mind is rock. You'll need more time to reflect on your mistakes. You are sentenced to ten years in our prison. Without privileges!"

With those words, the warden got up and left, slamming the door behind him. I just sat staring in the empty office. The calendar said September 1997. *Will I be alive or dead in September 2007?* I stood to leave. My legs nearly folded under me. I couldn't imagine the sort of beating I'd receive for this "crime." To my great relief, the guard escorted me back to the cold, dark cell. Numbly I walked beside him, saying nothing.

Finding myself sitting in darkness again, I was thankful I had not received a beating this time. I felt even more thankful that I had received the Gethsemane gift and had not given in to the temptation to deny my Lord.

The rice bowl came, and I fought back the rats as usual. I could feel my anger rising as I threw the rodents against the wall.

"Lord God, please help me not to despair. And thank you for strengthening me so that I would not deny you. Please bless the food I'm about to eat. In Jesus' name. Amen."

I picked up the kaoliang and put a handful in my mouth. I spit it back into the bowl. The cold, sticky rice had sand in it. It was awful to chew.

"What now, Lord? Shall I fast?"

For the next week every rice bowl I received was mixed with sand. I tried to wash out some of it with my water, but afterward my meager water allowance left me thirsty, and the remaining sand in the kaoliang was difficult to digest. The worst part was having no one to preach the Gospel to. The black loneliness stretched on and on until the old enemy of depression began to search for me.

One morning a few days later, I sat in my cell, singing a hymn.

Amazing grace,
How sweet the sound,
That saved a wretch like me,
I once was lost, but now I'm found,
'Twas blind, but now I see.

The cell door opened, and I shielded my eyes, trying to see who was there.

"Get out, young girl, get out!" I could barely see the two guards. "The warden is dead, and we don't want you here anymore."

The men pulled me onto my feet and out of the cell. I was scared. Was this some kind of a trap? The warden had looked perfectly healthy last week.

"Where are we going?" I asked.

"The warden wanted you here. We don't want you. All your talk about your God has frightened everybody."

"You must leave now," said the second man, spitting on the floor.

I was escorted quickly down an unfamiliar hallway, then through several heavy wooden doors, each bolted and locked. One guard unlocked the last door and pushed me outside. I stood blinking at the daylight.

The door slammed behind us, and the guards led the way to the black iron gates. I stumbled behind them, dumbfounded. One of the men jingled his keys, searching for the right one. Finally, he unlocked the tall gates.

I walked through the gates, the sunshine warming my face. The guards said nothing. I heard the gate creak shut behind me and the sound of their footsteps returning to the prison. Cupping my hands around my eyes, I looked up. The sky was still blue, a wonderful brilliant blue, with white puffy clouds moving slowly in formation.

I stepped away from the prison entrance and onto the sidewalk, taking in a deep breath of fresh air. I was free!

"Thank you, Lord," I said aloud, smiling into the skies, but now through tears of joy. My prayer was short-lived, as the street in front of me commanded my attention. It was jammed with honking cars, impatient taxis, slow-moving buses, bicycles, and pedestrians. I had never seen so many people at one time. And I'd never seen so many cars in my entire lifetime!

Then I noticed that people who passed by me turned their heads and quickly walked ahead, as though not wanting to become contaminated by contact with me. I felt self-conscious— without having washed often or changed clothes in all these months, I was sure that I looked and smelled horrible.

Where will I go? I thought. *Which way is home? I have no money, and only these rags to cover my body.*

Across the road I noticed a middle-aged woman sitting on a bench by the roadside, a basket of cigarettes on her lap. Her clothing caught my attention. She looked very *yang* in her Western blue jeans and T-shirt.

"Cigarettes," she called to the passersby.

I slowly approached her and sat down beside her. I was surprised that she didn't seem to mind my appearance or my smell.

"Miss, would you care for a cigarette?" she asked me.

In Jiangxi Province she'd have addressed me as Comrade, I thought.

"No, thank you," I replied. "Smoking those little sticks can kill a person."

The woman nodded. "Yes, but it's a living."

"May I tell you a story while you're waiting to sell more cigarettes?"

"I am Chinese," said the woman as she took money from a customer. "How can I refuse a good story?"

Encouraged by her somewhat playful remark and excited that she seemed to accept me regardless of my appearance, I began, "I would like to tell you of the One who made the earth and the skies." I noticed that she looked disappointed, and I stopped for a moment, silently praying for God to give me wisdom.

"I thought you were going to tell me about what you endured in the prison," said the woman. "But I can see that its small rice bowl has not broken your spirit."

"I hope the prison served to strengthen my spirit, not break it," I answered.

She offered me a drink from her water bottle. Then hesitantly, she said, "I would like to know more. Tell your story."

Offering a quick, silent prayer of thanks, I told her the story of Jesus, drawing a cross in the dusty sidewalk to show her how He died. A short time later, right there by the side of the busy Shanghai street, a brand-new Christian was born into God's kingdom.

"You know," the woman said to me, "I really feel changed inside."

"Jesus can clean out any heart of all sin and hurt and make you feel new." It was exciting to see another person changed by Him—this time outside the prison.

"He's really alive now?" she asked. "And I will go to the good heaven when I die?" Her round face was glowing.

I nodded. "It's true. If I had a Bible I'd show you where it says so."

She looked at the prison and became serious again. "Did you really just come out of that prison?" she asked.

"Yes," I replied, staring at the building through the traffic. "I'm from Jiangxi Province."

"What did you do?" she asked quietly.

"I told people about Jesus," I said.

The woman scribbled on a piece of paper. "Here is my address with directions to my apartment building. Will you come and spend the night?"

"Oh, that's such a kind offer," I replied, receiving the address and directions. "I . . . I don't even know your name. And what about the rest of your family?"

"My name is Deng Su, but everyone calls me Mother Su. As for the rest of my family, there's only my daughter and me at home. It's four o'clock now. Come for dinner at six. But don't follow me—the police may be watching you. Walk the other way around the park and circle back into the city."

"I'll be there," I said. I was giddy with excitement from the events of this wondrous day. "God bless you."

The woman stood to leave. "I want you to tell my daughter of the One who made the earth and skies, and about the good heaven."

"Oh yes, I'd be glad to!"

"You'll come for sure?" asked the woman.

"For sure," I replied. "I have nowhere else to go."

Mother Su picked up her basket and left.

I turned to leave in the opposite direction, then glanced back at the prison. From the outside it was just a large gray-brick building with iron bars surrounding it—relatively harmless in appearance. Did people know that inside there were prisoners who suffered daily from darkness and starvation and torture? It blessed me to know that now many of them had the hope of going to the good heaven.

"Remember those new Christians still in prison, Lord," I prayed. "And Pastor Wong. Please fulfill his ministry there, and then release him as you have me this day. I believe you will answer my request. Thank you."

My legs were wobbly from hunger, but my heart was full of happiness as I started my journey around the park. Dark clouds began to hide the sun, warning of an approaching storm. The wind picked up, swaying the willow trees back and forth. They appeared to be greeting one another, bowing in the Chinese fashion and whispering secrets as their arms flailed wildly about. I was glad for the oncoming rain. It would provide good cover from police surveillance.

My legs seemed to gain a little strength with the exercise, and after a time I was able to pick up my pace. I watched several couples walking on the winding sidewalks and thought of Liko. I wondered if he still cared about me.

I was just beginning to relax when I saw something rustling in the bushes several yards ahead. There it was again. Feeling rather bold after so much good fortune, I casually changed my course and walked toward the bushes. I was surprised when a young child darted out from behind the bush, running toward the street. He had tattered clothing and unkempt hair that bounced in long spikes about his head as he ran.

"Wait!" I called. "I won't hurt you."

The strange little boy didn't seem to hear a word, but kept running as though his life depended on it. People pointed and stared, then moved ahead as the thunder reminded them of the coming storm.

I knew I was in no condition to run after the child, so I too stared, then hurried on my way to Mother Su's house.

CHAPTER
Fifteen

When I was certain I wasn't being followed, I left the park and entered the crowded, noisy streets of Shanghai. Mother Su's directions took me down Nanjingxi Lu. It was the street I'd told Liko about, the one that was one long shopping mall!

I was so hungry it was difficult to take in everything around me. Music, unfamiliar to me, practically screamed from loudspeakers, mingling with the rumble of big city buses and the buzzing sound of people talking all around me. The sidewalks seemed wider than the street, and there were so many people I couldn't tell where the sidewalk and street met. It amazed me to see no cars or taxis, only buses. Pedestrians jammed the rest of the street, leaving little room for the few bicycles trying to plow through the crowds.

Men and women in business suits hurried along, carrying briefcases and folders. Most people carried shopping bags. Flashing neon lights and "on sale" posters hung in beautifully decorated store windows stocked with cosmetics, fine jewelry, and

Western clothing and shoes. I saw television screens with writing and games on them. Immediately I remembered the computers I had heard about in school. Teenagers were gathered around these computer and video-game shops, pushing and crowding their way to the front. I felt as though I had been dropped on another planet.

I wanted to linger outside the restaurants teeming with the delicious smells of different Chinese cuisine. Vendors and peddlers could be seen everywhere, scurrying to cover their goods before the rain started.

I read the street signs, looking for Second Street. Some cyclists shouted back and forth to each other, and the pedestrians seemed to be going in all directions. I had no path to walk in and found myself pushing my way through the congestion like everyone else.

Then I saw Second Street. I turned the corner to find myself part of a large crowd of people gathered on the sidewalk. They were all staring at a disturbance in the back of the department store. I tried to pick my way through to go around them.

"Where did you find the baby?" asked a man from the center of the crowd.

"In that box," answered the man up front, pointing to a cardboard box inside the glass doors that led into the rear of the department store.

"Is it a boy?" asked another.

"A girl," came the answer.

"Oh, what a pity, poor thing. Left alone in a doorway of a department store."

I couldn't believe my ears! I quietly slid along the wall toward the front to get a look at the foundling. The baby had fallen asleep in the man's arms.

"She doesn't look to be a week old yet," said a woman in the front. "What are you going to do with her?"

"She's supposed to go to the police."

"Yes, and they'll take her to Shanghai Orphanage. You know how it is there."

"The newspapers said they've changed the orphanage into a better facility now," said the woman in the front.

"A better sightseeing facility," answered the man holding the baby. "Some say Shanghai Orphanage is a showcase, and a lot of the orphans are on Chongming Island now. That place is more like a prison."

"Chongming Island is for mentally retarded adults—"

"And orphans," said the man, passion rising in his voice.

It was as though the baby understood her fate, for suddenly she wakened and cried pitifully, so that the man holding her was totally engrossed in calming her again.

"What will you do with her?" someone asked, echoing my thoughts.

"You tell me, what should be done with her?" demanded the man who was bouncing the crying infant.

"You can't let her go to the dying rooms of Shanghai Orphanage or to Chongming Island. Do you know of someone who can keep her?" asked the woman in front.

"Why don't you keep her?" asked another.

"I don't know." The man thought hard. "My factory's family-planning office would not approve. We have one child, although he is grown now and in a university."

"I say you should take her home with you," the woman said. "It is your good fortune to have found her."

"Yes," a few others murmured.

I watched the man's face. He tenderly offered the abandoned baby his little finger to suck on, pacifying her hunger and lulling her back to sleep.

Lightning suddenly flashed, followed by a short rumbling of thunder.

"Perhaps your cadre can be paid off," the woman said. "What can it hurt to try?"

The man looked up and searched the crowd. "Is this what you all think?"

"Yes," several answered. "Take her home."

With that the man tucked the infant under his arm, mounted his bicycle, and rode off down Second Street. A light rain began to fall.

The woman in the front picked up the box, crumpled it, and threw it into the sidewalk trash can. The crowd dispersed quietly, some mounting bicycles and others walking. By now the light rain had turned to a heavy downpour. I lifted my head and drank from the sky, laughing. "Thanks for the drink," I said softly to the One who made the earth and the skies.

Second Street was less congested with people and traffic but just as crammed with buildings. The warm rain soaked my hair so that it stuck to my face and neck. My clothes hung on my body like limp rags. I walked along like a half-plucked chicken.

By the time I arrived at Mother Su's address, I felt overwhelmed by the day's events, as well as weak and sick from hunger. It took every ounce of strength I had to climb three flights of steps. I was glad she didn't live on the tenth floor! I followed the door numbers until I finally came to apartment 311. I wondered whether the Shanghainese called out to their friends outside the door before entering.

While I was debating what to do, the door opened and Mother Su motioned me inside. I entered quickly, leaving my wet shoes outside the door. The aroma of vegetables and rice filled the room.

"This is my daughter, Sun Chang," said Mother Su.

I was soaking wet and filthy, so I nodded respectfully at Chang. She was about my age, though shorter, and definitely prettier.

"Please forgive me. I don't normally call on friends in this attire."

"My mother has found your conversation most intriguing, Kwan Mei Lin," answered Chang. "I understand you were in Shanghai Prison Number Fourteen?"

"Yes, I was released this afternoon."

"Well, that explains a lot! Come, wash in here. Supper is almost ready."

Mother Su's daughter led me across the hard floor to a little room. Sun Chang stood on a soft mat and leaned over a large white basin that was almost as big as me. To my amazement, she turned a shiny knob sideways, and water rushed out of a spout as though it was the top of a waterfall. I thought my eyes would pop out! I had seen pictures of running water for kitchen sinks, but I'd never seen such a big sink. I stood entranced, watching the waterfall.

Chang left the room momentarily. While she was gone, I watched the water rise in the huge sink and sat wearily on the side of it. I reached down to dip my hand into the water and laughed when I felt how warm it was.

Returning with dry clothing and shoes, Chang told me, "I'll take your clothes when you're done. You can wear some of mine."

"Oh, you are so kind." I stumbled over my words, still unable to take my eyes off the water, which now filled half of the huge basin.

"Is this full enough for you?" asked Chang.

"Yes," I answered numbly.

"Here's a towel. The soap is in the corner there." She pointed to a little ledge on the basin and turned off the water. Then she left the room, shutting the door behind her.

Quickly I slipped out of my wet filthy rags and stepped into the white, smooth basin. I sank down into the water until my head was totally immersed, then came up a few seconds later. Grabbing the soap, I scrubbed my skin until it turned red. I nearly forgot my hunger as I lathered my hair and rinsed it in the beautiful water. I felt as though I were washing away Shanghai Prison, with its stench and filth and rats.

I stepped out of the large basin and picked up the towel, turning to find myself in front of a long mirror. I gasped. "Is that really you in there?" I asked myself. I touched my arm to make sure. My eyes were larger than they used to be, sort of sunken and giving me a skull-like appearance. My bones protruded, showing my entire bone structure covered only with skin.

I combed through my washed hair, trying to get used to the stranger in the mirror. My bangs hung down to my chin, and the rest of my hair was well below my shoulders. It was very thin and broke easily. My skin was translucent and had lost its elasticity.

"Dear God, I'm nearly starved, aren't I?" I said, touching my face.

I turned away, fighting back the tears. I didn't want to look anymore.

"Supper is ready," called Chang outside the door.

"Thank you. I'm coming," I answered with as much cheer as possible.

I quickly dressed in Chang's dark blue pants and T-shirt, rolling the pants at the waist so they would stay up. I stuck my head out the door. "Where do you dump the basin?" I asked.

Chang appeared from around the corner. "The basin?"

"Yes. I need to dump the dirty bath water," I said.

"Oh, the bathtub," said Chang, laughing and walking past me. "I don't think we could dump that if we tried." She pointed to a dark plug at one end. "See this?" she asked. "You pull this up and it sort of dumps itself."

"Amazing," I said, pulling the plug out of the hole. "I feel like such a *tu-bao-dz*."

Chang seemed amused. "Country bumpkin or no, you look refreshed."

"You're very kind," I said, feeling self-conscious. "I just saw myself in the mirror for the first time in nine months. I look like a skeleton."

"Come," Chang said gently, "my mother will take care of that."

We walked to the dining table, and I sat down with Mother Su and Chang, who immediately began serving the food.

"Here, eat this," said Mother Su, ladling a pile of vegetables onto my plate. "You need these."

My mouth began to water, but I hesitated to begin eating, wanting to thank God for the miracle of this day and the wonderful sand-free food set before me.

"Is something wrong?" asked Mother Su.

"Would you mind if I prayed before I eat?" I asked.

"Of course not! Please do."

I bowed my head, but I suspected Mother Su and her daughter were just watching me. "Lord Jesus, I thank you for this wonderful meal. I ask you to use it to make our bodies strong and healthy. Thank you for releasing me from prison today. Please bless my new friends, Mother Su and Sun Chang, for opening their home to me. In Jesus' name. Amen."

Mother Su began to eat her rice and vegetables.

"Please just call me Chang," said Sun Chang.

My mouth exploded with the tiny bite of the sweet-and-sour vegetables, overpowering my taste buds so that I couldn't swallow. I began to choke, quickly putting the unwanted bite back on my chopsticks and taking it out of my mouth. I drank water, trying to drown the burning sensation in my mouth.

"I'm so sorry," I said, choking and apologizing all at once. I felt so embarrassed. "After so many months of just kaoliang, I'm afraid I'm not able to enjoy your delicious cooking."

"It's all right," said Mother Su. Undaunted in her venture to nourish me, she got up and walked over to the kitchen counter. "Here, try some plain steamed rice."

The white rice had no spices or salt, and I found it went down easily. I savored each bite, eating slowly as I'd trained myself to do in prison.

"It must have been terrible in prison," said Chang.

"What were your meals like?" asked Mother Su.

"Meals?" I asked. "They fed us a small bowl of cold kaoliang once a day."

"That's all?" asked Mother Su.

"My last week there, they put sand in all of my food."

"That's awful!" exclaimed Chang. "How long were you there?"

"I'm not sure," I answered. "What month is it?"

"You don't know? It's Friday, October 4, 1997."

"That makes it almost ten months, then," I said. "Only the Lord Jesus sustained me. Most of the prisoners look worse than I do."

"You were able to meet the other prisoners?" asked Mother Su. "That is more than we had hoped for."

"More than you had hoped for?" I asked, curious.

Mother Su looked at Chang and nodded.

"My father is in Shanghai Prison," said Chang. "We miss him terribly. He's been there over two years now."

"Oh," I said, "is that why you sell cigarettes outside the prison?"

"Yes, I've sat on the curb every day for two years," said Mother Su. "I have a real job at a dress factory, but we need the extra money, and I try to get the guards to tell me of the welfare of my husband. I've heard very little for the amount of cigarettes I've given away."

"My father is a driver," said Chang. "He drove a taxi to pick up extra money. Technically, he was sent to prison for embezzling money from foreigners and diplomats he had driven through Shanghai. In reality, he knew too much. He was the driver for Shanghai Orphanage. He saw pictures of malnourished orphans taken by one of the orphans there. He also saw crematorium workers sometimes taking away the bodies of dead babies."

"You're not serious?" I was horrified.

"It's true," concurred Mother Su. "He said that sometimes the bodies were so decayed from sitting at the orphanage for days that the crematorium workers refused to take them. Then the workers began leaving small boxes of juice just outside the orphanage morgue as an incentive for the workers to take the bodies. One food item for each little body that was to be removed and cremated."

"How awful!" I exclaimed. "Why were there so many dead babies?"

"We aren't sure," said Chang. "Father assumes it's because of the one-child policy. Maybe even the orphanages have a birth quota and can only keep a small number of babies. There are plenty of workers and food, but the babies were dying from starvation."

"My husband knew far more than Shanghai Civil Affairs Bureau wanted him to know," said Mother Su. "He was questioned about what he saw at the orphanage by both Chinese press and foreign journalists. There was a big investigation in 1993 and 1994. Many times people from the foreign press hailed Tao's taxi. They got in and paid him to drive them around while they questioned him about what he saw at the orphanage."

"When the authorities found out about my father's involvement with the foreign press, he was dismissed from his orphanage route," said Chang. "Then they made up a story that he overcharged foreigners for his taxi services, embezzling money. They wanted him to be put quietly out of the way. He was sentenced to eight years."

"The pictures that an older orphan showed him one time were of babies and children who were near death. They were malnourished, some tied to their beds. I didn't see the pictures, but my husband said they did not do justice to the flies that clung to open sores and the stench of human waste in every room. He stepped inside the orphanage several times to assist the orphans being transported."

"Let me guess," I said. "He was transporting them to Chongming Island."

"Yes, to Chongming Island and to Shanghai Number One Social Psychiatric Rehabilitation Institute. How did you know?"

I suddenly felt overcome with grief. The Shanghai orphans seemed to be in a worse prison than the one I'd just come out of. "I just witnessed an abandoned baby left outside a large department store on Nanjingxi Street," I answered. "The man who found her took her home under his arm. A crowd of people there encouraged him to do so."

"The Chinese people of Shanghai are mostly good people," said Mother Su. "You saw an example of their good hearts today."

"And the orphanage workers?"

"The few who were good-hearted people have either fled or were forced to retire early. Now Shanghai Orphanage permits and even encourages foreigners and high government bureaucrats to visit. It is set up like a model orphanage for the officials to take pride in. Most of the abandoned orphans who live there are now transferred to Chongming Island. And I understand there are many abandoned babies."

"Why are there so many?" I asked.

"Certainly you know of the one-child policy?" asked Chang.

"Of course." I thought of An and wondered whether she was able to keep her baby.

"Babies are abandoned every day in Shanghai. Most of them come into the city from the countryside. Because everyone wants a boy to care for them in their old age, most of the babies they abandon are little girls. A few handicapped babies are left as well."

"How could a mother do such a thing?" I asked indignantly.

"The mothers who abandon their babies are actually the brave ones, who give birth in secret," Mother Su answered. "Most are forced into abortions. The ones who have their babies at the clinics and hospitals give birth to their second child only to have the nurse or doctor inject iodine in their soft spot and kill them."

I felt sick, and remembered Amah's story about Aunt Te and her firstborn baby girl. After my prison experience, these atrocities were very real and very personal.

"Please, Kwan Mei Lin, do you know if you saw my husband, Sun Tao?"

"I rarely asked the prisoners their names," I answered. "I just scrubbed their cell floors and told them of the God who created the earth and the skies. Many of them became Christians."

"I have something that may help," said Chang. She left the table and soon returned with a picture. "This is my father, Sun Tao."

I stared at the picture, trying to piece together the faces of the many prisoners I'd talked to. "It's difficult," I said. "I met no one who looked this healthy. Everyone was thin and half starved."

"Oh no," said Chang, and she turned her head to hide her emotion.

"I'm sorry, Chang," I said. "I can't imagine how I'd feel if my father were in prison." Seeing her pain made me think of my own father. "Please, is there any way I could do some work for you? I'd like to pay for postage to write to my father and Amah. They must be as worried about me as both of you are about Sun Tao."

"I'd be honored to pay your postage," said Mother Su. "And Chang has plenty of paper."

"Thank you," I said as I placed Sun Tao's picture on the table.

After supper Chang took me on a tour of the apartment. Mother Su and Chang had two bedrooms and a kitchen inside the house with a stove and refrigerator.

"Your apartment is beautiful," I said. "It's about three times as big as my home in Tanching."

"Yes, but we have no land. Do you have land in Tanching?" asked Chang.

I smiled. "We are each given a portion of the rice paddies to farm. Part of our family's harvest goes to the government, and we keep the rest. Behind our house we have about half an acre of land. We have a small fishpond, a garden, and some ducks and chickens."

"Oh, it sounds wonderful," said Chang. "I'm almost envious."

"Envious?" I asked. "It is I who have been envious. I've wanted to live in Shanghai since I was a little girl."

"You sure picked a hard way to get there," said Chang, smiling.

"We'll set up a cot for you in here, Mei Lin," said Mother Su as she walked into the living room with a folded bed in her arms.

While Mother Su worked about the apartment, Chang and I walked to the roof of the apartment building. It was dark outside now, and I was quiet for a few minutes once we reached the top. I could look at the city from each side of the building. Lights were everywhere, casting an orange glow about the streets. The only true darkness above me seemed to be hiding the stars instead of revealing them. On the street below, cars and pedestrians still moved about as though it were daytime, hurrying here and there.

"I remember telling my friend Liko how I wanted to climb the highest building in Shanghai and look at the city lights at night," I said to Chang.

"You would have to go to the Bund to find the highest building," said Chang. "But you can see Nanjingxi Lu from up here." Chang pointed to the bright white lights that ran in a long line a few blocks away. The road went on as far as my eyes could see.

"That's the road I walked to get here," I said. "There weren't any cars. Why not?"

"Nanjingxi Lu is the biggest shopping center in Shanghai," answered Chang. "There's no room to park anywhere, so only buses and a few bicycles try to push their way through."

"Is it always so jammed with people?" I asked.

Chang nodded. "Always. The last few years they even sold Christmas ornaments in December."

"What?" I nearly shouted at Chang. "Christmas celebration is forbidden in Tanching."

"It's all economics, Mei Lin. The people are almost as happy at Christmas as on Chinese New Year, and the shops are glad to make the increased sales. Everyone profits."

"Anything to make money, hmm?" I asked thoughtfully.

"China's prospering. Do you know that Hong Kong became part of China again in July?"

"I knew it was coming," I replied. "My history and political science teachers were very proud of the upcoming change. Great Britain would no longer fly her flag over Hong Kong."

"Everyone's excited," said Chang. "You should have seen the celebrations on National Day a few days ago."

"A happy day, yes?" I asked.

"Very happy," answered Chang. "Shanghai has changed in the

last ten years. We have gone from poverty to a thriving economy. And the housing problem has softened. My father's extra taxi money bought us this apartment. Many Shanghainese have moved out of the city into the new housing developments in the suburbs."

"Perhaps my desire to come to Shanghai was just a childish dream," I sighed, still deep in thought.

"It's getting chilly out here," said Chang. "The wind's picking up."

"We can go back now. I've seen the lights of Nanjingxi Lu," I said proudly. "Now I'll have a story to tell my family."

———————

Later that evening I sat under the beautiful electric lights at the table and stared again at Chang's picture of her father. "Mother Su, I think I do remember Sun Tao," I said cautiously.

"Oh, tell us what you remember, please," said Chang, coming out of her bedroom.

"He looks like the first man I talked to in the prison. Except he has less hair now."

Chang laughed. "He was just starting to lose his hair when he was imprisoned."

"Well, I will tell you the truth," I said. "He was very thin but very much alive."

"And you talked to him? When? Was he sickly?" asked Mother Su, her questions gushing out all at once.

"When I came into his cell he begged me not to beat him." Mother Su and Chang sat spellbound as I told them the story. "His face brightened when I told him he was allowed to go to the good heaven. He prayed and asked Jesus to be his Savior. He also forgave the ones who'd beaten him, just as Jesus forgave those who tortured Him.

"At first he thought I was the spirit of one of his ancestors," I continued. "I told him I was just a plain person who wanted to tell him about Jesus."

"This Jesus was a fairy-tale story?" asked Chang.

"No, Chang. He really lived on the earth two thousand years ago. I told your mother that I'd read the story to you myself if I had a Bible."

"Now that my mother and father have received Jesus, they have put their lives in further danger," said Chang. She was obviously unnerved. "It will be best if one of us stays true to Buddha. Perhaps the evil spirits will not be so angry at us if I remain a true Buddhist."

I glanced quickly at Chang's mother. Mother Su shook her head slightly, telling me to let the subject drop.

"Mei Lin, please stay with us until you're able to return to Jiangxi Province," said Mother Su.

"I don't want to take advantage of your wonderful hospitality," I said. "But I must admit, I'm very tired. I keep wondering if I'm going to wake up and find myself in the cold darkness. I can't tell you how much I welcomed the sunshine today."

"It helps me to hear you tell how it is in the prison," Mother Su said. "At least I know now what my husband is facing every day."

"We will pray for his quick release," I answered.

She gestured toward the living room. "Your cot is ready. Let's go to bed."

Instead of a cold dirt floor, I lay on a cot that night. Instead of hunger pains, I had a stomach full of rice. And Mother Su, the wife of the first prisoner I'd brought to Jesus, had come into the kingdom of God.

"Lord, how can I say thank you enough?" I prayed quietly in the dark. I imagined my homecoming. Father would be so glad that I wasn't near death like Mother. And Amah, she would try to fatten me up my first day home! Then I thought about Liko. How would Liko react when he saw his old friend just skin and bones and thinning hair?

Before drifting to sleep, I released my concerns to God and prayed again for the prisoners I'd led to the Lord, especially Sun Tao.

★ ✱ ★

CHAPTER

Sixteen

I spent the weekend resting at the apartment. Although I still ate nothing but rice, I was working toward eating three meals a day. When Monday morning rolled around, I felt refreshed and strengthened. By the time I woke up, Chang had left for her job at Park Hotel, and Mother Su was about to leave for her job at the dress factory.

"Make yourself at home here, Mei Lin," said Mother Su. "Lunch is in the refrigerator. Chang and I usually get home around five-thirty."

"Thank you," I said, sitting up on my elbows.

"Chang left a house key and directions to the post office on the table. Don't forget to take those directions I gave you to the apartment in case you get lost on the way back."

"I will," I said, rubbing my eyes. "Thank you."

"Breakfast is on the table," she said as she walked toward the door.

"May God bless you today," I said with great feeling.

She smiled. "My heart is so happy now that I'm a Christian. I'll see you tonight." Mother Su left, locking the door behind her.

After using their indoor bathroom, I lay in bed and talked to God. I felt so thankful, yet I couldn't shake the feeling of still being in possible danger.

What if the police follow me to the post office? I thought. Who would know what happened to me if they arrested me and took me back to prison?

I got up and decided to write two letters to Father and Amah—one to take to the post office and one to leave with Mother Su and Chang in case the first one didn't make it through.

Monday, October 7, 1997

Dear Father and Amah,

Something happened, and I happily left prison on Friday, October 4. I am staying with newfound friends in an apartment in Shanghai. You can send a return letter to Deng Su, Song's Dress Factory, Shimen Lu, Jiangsu Province, Shanghai.

After sending this letter I will look for some type of work to earn money for a train ticket back to Jiangxi. I long to see both of you. I miss Tanching Village!

Please do not worry. I am well. Send greetings to the Chen household. Wishing good health and success to both of you.

Your daughter,
Mei Lin

Quickly I placed the duplicate letter on the table. I folded the first letter and held it in my hand for a while. It all seemed like a dream. Three days ago I was in the total darkness of Shanghai

Prison. Today, Monday, I sat at a stranger's table, writing a letter to my family.

I smiled and looked up. "God, you are really amazing!"

The smile never left my face as I grabbed the little paper with directions and went out of the apartment building onto Second Street.

I felt stronger than ever. The sunshine seemed to soak right into my skin. My muscles felt sore for some reason, but my legs were not so wobbly and my lungs lustily inhaled the cool morning air.

The post office was close to the park, so I found myself walking within its perimeters again. Old men and women were practicing *tai chi*, Chinese exercises, to traditional Chinese music. Their eyes were half closed in meditation, seemingly oblivious to the traffic's blaring horns and roaring engines.

I kept feeling strange, almost scared, as if I were being followed. I scolded myself for being afraid. "God didn't give me a spirit of fear," I quoted under my breath. Still, I couldn't shake the feeling that I was being watched. I glanced around at the park's shadowy walkways.

On an impulse, I whirled around and saw a small figure dart behind the bushes. Instantly I thought of the little boy who had run out from the bushes on Friday. I wondered what he was doing, lurking in the park again. I decided not to scare him away by confronting him this time.

I walked on until I came to a park bench, where I sat for a few minutes, pretending to watch the birds in the poplar trees.

"What is your name?" came the voice from behind me. I jumped in spite of myself, turning to look at the child who'd been following me. He appeared to be about six, his clothes worn and tattered. His black bangs needed to be cut, and the rest of his hair still seemed to stand on end, as though he had little horns sticking out everywhere. He looked frightfully thin, but otherwise clean.

"Mei Lin," I answered. "And why do you keep sneaking up on me, watching me in the park?"

"I'm hungry," he answered.

I could certainly sympathize with that.

"Come here and sit down," I said. The boy stepped back.

"I won't hurt you," I said gently. "When did you eat last?"

His eyes searched my face. "Three days ago."

"Three days? Oh, I wish I had food with me, but I have nothing. Will you be here at lunchtime?"

He nodded.

"Then meet me here at this park bench at noon. I'll come alone, and I'll bring some lunch for you, okay?"

The poor boy hung his head and began to walk away.

"I will come, little friend," I said in my firmest, most reassuring voice.

"I'll be here," he said. Then he walked past the bushes and disappeared as fast as he'd appeared.

I found the post office easily. After mailing my letter, I quickly made my way back to Second Street to salvage some lunch for my new friend. I wasn't able to eat most of what Mother Su left for me anyway. I put the lunch into a basket and headed for the park.

Once in the park, I strolled along the raised sidewalk where sweet-smelling flowers were still in bloom. I watched the velvety grass move under the breeze while mist from a fountain sprayed my face, cooling me from the midday sun.

I sat down at the same park bench and placed the basket in

plain view so that the child would know that I'd kept my word.

"Why are you doing this for me?"

The words seemed to come out of nowhere.

"Why do you like to startle me?" I countered, turning around to find him behind me again. "Come here and sit down."

His eyes never left the food basket as he walked around the park bench and sat down on the other side.

"I am doing this for you because I am a Christian, and God says we're to love people. And I'm doing it because I know how it feels to be very, very hungry. May I pray over your food before you eat it?" I asked him.

The boy just kept staring, so I went ahead and prayed. "Father, I thank you for bringing food to my new friend. Please help him know that I care about him, and so do you. In Jesus' name. Amen." I looked up, and he was devouring the dumplings and rice.

"Now you know my name. What's yours?"

He hesitated. "Yatou."

"Yatou?" I asked, sure that he was trying to hide his real name. "*Girl?* That isn't a name; it's a gender, and not even your gender. Why would anyone call a cute little boy like you Girl? Surely you have a better imagination than that."

The little face looked up at me, cheeks still stuffed with dumplings. "I am a girl," came the muffled answer.

I was stunned. "But your hair," I said. "I guess I . . . oh, I'm sorry."

"My hair is a mess," said the child. "I don't have a comb to comb it, but I wash it in the park fountain. I am a girl, and everybody calls me plain old Yatou."

"Oh. How did you get your name?"

She answered me with her mouth full. "My mother and father didn't keep me. An old woman found me at a bus station in a trash can. I think I had a name, but she always called me her little Yatou and she took care of me. I called her Mother, but then she died when I was in kindergarten. So the aunties and uncles—I mean . . ." The poor little thing turned ashen. She nearly dropped her food and quit chewing.

"It's all right," I said, taking her hand in mine. "Did you know that the One who made the earth and skies especially loves little children? My mother and father told me about Him when I was a very little girl. Maybe I can tell you a bit about me, okay?"

The girl nodded.

"My name is Kwan Mei Lin. I am a country girl from Jiangxi Province. Do you know where that is?"

Her mouth was still full, so she shook her head.

"It is southeast of Shanghai—and far enough away for me to be very lonely for it."

I wasn't sure that she was even interested. But somehow it helped that she just sat there and listened, eating my lunch.

"My mother died when I was only two."

Now the little girl's eyes locked on mine.

"Is that why you were bad? I saw you the other day. I know you came out of that jail."

"No, I was not a bad child because my mother died. I was fortunate enough to have Amah, my grandmother, and my father caring for me."

She seemed perplexed. "So what happened?"

"I told some people in my high school about Jesus, and the authorities didn't like that. They told me to stop believing in Jesus, but I wouldn't do it. So they beat me and put me in prison."

"You must really like Jesus to do that."

I couldn't hold back a good laugh. "Yes, I'd say I like Him an awful lot. And I believe in His power too."

"Is He the one who wouldn't give you food?"

Inwardly I smiled at Yatou's inquisitiveness. "No, the prison is set up so that none of the prisoners get to eat very much. Jesus is the One who made the guards want to set me free. It was a miracle that I got out of there. I was supposed to stay for many more years." I was trying to explain things as simply as possible, but the child appeared to be only five or six years old.

"Do all the prisoners look so skinny?" came the question.

"Like me?" I asked.

She nodded.

I tried not to, but I felt self-conscious again about my bony frame. "Yes," I said, sighing. "Some looked worse."

My new little friend chewed quietly. She seemed to be trying to sort everything out.

"How old are you?" I asked her.

"Nine."

I didn't mean to stare at her or to go so long without answering, but it seemed impossible. This girl who looked like a boy appeared to be barely six years old. "You can't be ... I ... are you sure?"

She nodded, swallowing her mouthful of rice. "Do I seem like a baby to you?"

"Oh no. In fact, you've been asking some pretty grown-up questions. It's just that you look, well, younger than nine."

The girl hung her head.

"You're in trouble, aren't you?" I asked.

The lunch basket was empty, and Yatou leaned over, resting her head in her hands.

"You know," I said, "you can't live out here in the park for the rest of your life. You need shelter, a home, and people who care about you."

Tears seeped out of the girl's eyes now, sliding down her hands and chin.

"Please," I started, feeling awkward. "I know you don't know me very well, but I'd like to just hug you right now. Would that be all right?"

She didn't look up. Her head sank between her knees. I gathered her trembling form close to me and circled my arms around her.

Holding her tightly as she broke into sobs, I looked to the heavens. "Father, I cry out to you in Jesus' name on behalf of my newfound friend!" Sobs caught at my own throat, but somehow I continued, "God, Yatou has no father or mother. And I remember you said in the Bible that you would be a father to the fatherless. I'm taking you up on that promise. I believe that from this minute you will be Yatou's father. And please, help us think of a good name for her. Thank you. Amen."

Very un-Chinese-like, I thought. Crying and hugging, not to mention praying, at a public park. But the prayer helped me to gain control of my own emotions. I felt lucky to have somewhere to put them. "Yatou," as she called herself, needed a little more time.

Finally a calm came over her small frame.

"Yatou, I met a woman on Friday who became a Christian, like me. She let me stay at her house last weekend. I'll ask her if she will allow you to stay for a while. Just until we can work out something else, okay?"

"She will not let me stay."

"How can you say that? You haven't even met her."

"She would put herself in danger to keep me. I . . . I'm . . ."

"Tell me, Little One. You're safe with me."

"They decided I needed to be transferred to Chongming Island. Everybody's afraid to go there. About six weeks ago we got into the van at the orphanage gate. Most of us were little, but the one big teenager was put in the backseat and held down by two of the uncles. They stayed back there the whole time. It was an awful struggle."

"And then?"

"And then when we were driving through Shanghai, the driver stopped at an intersection. I knew the uncles were struggling in the back, so I took a chance. I was so scared. I unlocked the door and jumped out. I ran fast, down the street, then hid inside a department store under some clothing racks."

"That was some escape!" I was quite impressed at how much this child had accomplished.

"After a while I came out and stayed in the park. People were friendly, and there was plenty of water."

I saw fear cross Yatou's face. "Please don't tell. I'd rather die than go back there. It's just . . . so bad . . . I . . . they're still looking for me. I . . . I just can't go back."

Yatou broke into sobs again, and I held her for a moment, then took her by the shoulders and locked eyes with her. "Yatou, if my friends don't want you at their house, then I'll come to the park and stay with you tonight. All right? Either way, you will not be alone."

Yatou's eyes widened. "You will sleep outside in the cold with me? Why would you do that?"

"Because you need me. And I think that's exactly what Jesus would do if He were here. He'd stay or find a place for you to stay. Okay?"

"Okay." She began wiping her face with her sleeve.

"Here, use the lunch napkin," I said. I tried to think of how to work a plan to get Yatou to the address unnoticed.

"Do you know your way around Shanghai?" I asked.

"I'm learning," she answered. "It's a very big city."

"Tell you what. My friends will be home by five-thirty. Meet me behind the department store on the corner of Second and Nanjingxi. Nanjingxi is right over there. See it?"

"I'll be there. What time shall I come?"

"Better make it seven o'clock. That'll give me enough time to talk to my friends—and enough time to say good-bye to them if I need to." I looked down at her.

"You'll come?" she asked. "For sure?"

"I'll come. Seven o'clock." I gave her a quick hug. "See you then."

CHAPTER

Seventeen

I made supper for Mother Su and Chang from the vegetables in the refrigerator. I was intrigued by the stove that produced fire without matches or wood. I smiled and thought of Amah. What would she say about all this?

When Mother Su and Chang arrived, they were tired and very pleased that dinner was ready. They chatted about the events of their day, and as we finished eating I glanced at the clock. It was just a little after six. Mother Su poured tea, and we sat at the table like old friends. I prayed that this good feeling between us would not be ruined by what I was about to ask.

"I need to talk to you both about something," I began. "Unfortunately, it's very urgent."

They exchanged puzzled glances.

I took a deep breath. "I met a little girl at the park today. She is very troubled. I gave her my lunch; I hope you don't mind. I wasn't very hungry after that big breakfast. She had eaten for three days, and I know how that feels."

"Who is she?" asked Mother Su. "What's her name?"

I felt rather silly telling them. "Yatou."

"Yatou? She told you her name is Girl?" asked Chang. "That's ridiculous."

"That was my first reaction," I agreed. "Maybe she was afraid to tell me her real name, or maybe that really is her name. I can't be sure."

"Where does she live?" asked Mother Su.

"Right now she lives in the park. She's from Shanghai Orphanage. She's afraid of being discovered."

"She's a runaway?" asked Chang.

There was a testy expression on Chang's face, but I continued. "She was afraid to tell me very much, poor thing. Her hair is a mess and her clothes are in tatters. I . . . I don't know how to ask this, but—"

"Don't. It's out of the question," said Chang, leaning back in her chair as she tapped her fingers on the table.

"Chang, don't be so hasty," said her mother. "Listen to Mei Lin. She is our guest."

"Mother, we are in enough danger as it is," Chang argued, gesturing wildly in the air. "Surely this Yatou will bring bad luck to our apartment. We may have angered the gods already with you and Father becoming Christians."

I could see that Mother Su's anger was now aroused. "Your father was sent to prison for what he believes. He believes there is evil going on in Shanghai Orphanage. And he was put in prison before he became a Christian, remember that. Maybe . . . maybe this is a way we can take a stand with him. He would want us to do this."

I looked at both of them. "I'm sorry to cause strife between you." I stood up to leave. "I am very grateful for your hospitality, and—"

Chang softened some. "Look, it's not that I want you to leave, it's just so . . . so . . . sudden. I mean, we could get in big trouble. And for what?"

I looked at the mother and daughter. At that moment I saw the great risk I was asking them to take.

Mother Su interrupted my thoughts. "Please tell us. What is it you need?"

I hesitated. "I'm meeting Yatou at seven o'clock. But Chang is right. It may be too risky to bring her here. I can stay with her in the park."

"And sleep there?" Chang demanded. She was nearly yelling now, getting red in the face. "Why would you go sleep in a park with a child you don't even know? Are you crazy?"

Chang's anger reminded me of my clashes with Cadre Fang, the warden, and the prison guards. It didn't scare me.

"Why are you so angry?" I boldly confronted her, taking my seat again across the table.

"Why? Why?" Chang repeated, leaning over the table. "It's bad enough that my father is in prison. Now he has made the gods angry by believing in this Jesus. And now Mother believes in Jesus. It is bad luck, I tell you. One day my mother becomes a Christian because of an ex-convict and brings her home to stay—"

"Chang," scolded Mother Su.

"It's true! Then the next day we decide to take in a runaway orphan! What's next, a human rights march on Tiananmen Square?"

She's afraid, not angry, I thought. *I wonder if that's how the cadre and guards felt?*

"Don't be afraid, Chang," I said. "God can work a miracle to set your father free from prison. Or He can give him the Gethsemane gift, to help him withstand the time he spends there."

"The what gift?" she asked. "Oh, never mind."

Mother Su spoke. "Chang, I know you're concerned for our protection, but I have to stick to my original thoughts on the matter. If your father were here, he would take in this orphan girl"—Mother Su looked over at me—"and Mei Lin, ex-convict or not."

"Mother, I'm really not opposed to Mei Lin being here. She's brought the first bit of real news we've heard about Father. And if you want the little girl here, that's fine. We'll see if this Jesus can help to feed all these mouths." Chang folded her arms as if to challenge me.

I can't wait to see how Jesus meets her challenge, I chuckled to myself. Then I looked at the clock again. Six-forty. Just enough time to meet Yatou.

Mother Su smiled at both of us. "It's settled, then. Go get her, Mei Lin. I'll warm the leftovers."

I jumped up and smiled. "Thank you both. I cannot tell you how grateful I am that you are doing this!" And with that I ran out of the apartment and down the stairs to the street below.

I had no trouble finding Yatou, who seemed a little surprised to see me. She was even more amazed that my friends had agreed to take her in.

Her eyes sparkled as she surveyed every corner of the beautiful apartment shared by Mother Su and Chang. "You're rich, aren't you?" she whispered to them in awe. She looked around the room with a look of bliss on her little face, scanning the couch and simple wooden chairs.

"Hardly," answered Chang, scurrying around the apartment, apparently looking for something. "We had to sell some of our furniture and Father's taxi so we could keep this place. Besides his jail term, he had heavy fines to pay."

"Your father was in prison too?" asked Yatou.

I smiled down at my new little friend. "You're a mountain of curiosity, Yatou. Listen, let's save our talk for later, okay? Eat some dinner. Then we'll get you into a bath basin, okay?"

Yatou just looked up at me.

"She's your little project tonight," Chang said brusquely. "I'm going shopping." She grabbed her handbag and was gone for the evening.

Yatou quickly gulped down her dinner.

"Let's work on that hair," I said, mussing the top of Yatou's head.

Yatou fingered her hair carefully, stroking the short, matted locks.

Mother Su appeared from a back room. "Here are some of Chang's old clothes. I've been meaning to get rid of them. I'm afraid they're the old *qipao* style, not very Western."

"They're perfect," I said. "Do you want to help me do this? I'm not sure I have the motherly talents it's going to take for this project."

Mother Su laughed. "It's been a while since I had a little girl to take care of. I'd love to help."

As we washed Yatou's hair I thought about my own long strands. "Do you think I could cut my hair tonight?"

"Why not?" answered Mother Su.

"I can do my bangs, but I'm not sure about the back."

"I'll do it for you," said Mother Su. "Shoulder length?"

"Please."

Yatou dressed and watched as Mother Su cut the back of my hair. "Someday I want my hair to be that long," she said earnestly. "And I'll never cut it off."

I smiled at Yatou and looked at the tough job we were about to get into, combing out all of her tangles. "You can have long hair someday, but right now we need to cut your hair too, okay?"

Yatou reached up and fingered her wet little spikes of hair. "Do I have to?" she asked, tears springing to her eyes. "My hair has never been this long. At the orphanage, they made us get our hair shaved off every month or two, and all of us girls hated to have bald heads. Sometimes we would lie on the floor and talk about how someday we will let our hair grow down our backs and plait it into long black braids."

"Hmmm. You say all of the girls have their heads shaved?" I asked. "So the police will be looking for a little orphan with her hair growing out, right?"

Yatou nodded. "I've hidden from the police for about six weeks now."

"Mother Su, the orphanage people and the PSB are looking for Yatou, right?" I asked. "Well, what if the orphan girl just disappeared?"

"Ah, I see what you're saying," said Mother Su. "Maybe we don't have an orphan girl here after all, eh?"

"I don't see a girl here at all!" I said.

"Yes, you do. I'm right here, under all this hair," said Yatou, wiping the wet strands from her eyes.

"Yatou," I said, leaning down to talk to her face-to-face.

"How would you like to be a boy—say, my cousin who's come to visit?"

"A boy?" Yatou made a crinkly face.

"Yes! A clever, handsome, smiling boy. No one's looking for a runaway boy orphan. It's the perfect disguise!"

Yatou hesitated. "Can I be a girl with long hair sometime?" she asked.

I laughed and mussed her cold, damp hair. "Of course! As soon as we get you to safety, you can be a girl again. Then you can grow your hair down to your ankles if you'd like." I stood back and let the more experienced Mother Su take over.

Yatou sat on the wooden stool, trying very hard not to wiggle. She squinted under the falling hair. "I love to pretend! But I always pretended to be a pretty girl with long hair, not a boy!"

Mother Su and I smiled at each other.

Mother Su said, "You two are so skinny—you actually do look alike! I think you'll pass for cousins."

"But you won't really be a boy, Yatou, you'll just look like one. Okay?" I said.

Mother Su crossed her arms and stood back, sizing up her little boy. "I have a friend who owes me a favor. I'm sure she'll gladly give me some of her son's old clothing."

"It's settled, then. Our cousin has come to visit—Cousin . . . hmm, we'll need a name."

"How about Cousin Sam from the United States?" asked Mother Su.

"Sam?"

"Uncle Sam? United States? Get it? Then people wouldn't ask so many questions."

I grinned. "Oh, that would work—until someone tries to

speak to Yatou in English. Then we'll all be discovered."

Mother Su frowned, pretending to be hurt. "Well, since Yatou doesn't have a girl's name, maybe we should let her pick her boy name, what do you think?"

"Okay," I agreed. "What'll it be, Yatou?"

Yatou sucked in her bottom lip, thinking hard as she stared at the bathtub. "How about Zhu? I could have the same last name as you do, Mei Lin, since we're cousins. Kwan Zhu."

"It's a fine name," I said, clapping my hands. "Now, tomorrow we'll give our Zhu some real boys' clothing."

Yatou was still sitting on the stool. I looked down and saw a grief-stricken expression on her face.

"Don't you like our idea? Being a boy isn't too terrible, is it?"

Tears began slipping down her face.

"What is it, Yatou?" I asked.

She looked over at Mother Su, as though afraid to speak.

Mother Su was quick to get the message that Yatou needed privacy. "I'll go get your cot ready, Yatou. I'll set it up beside Mei Lin's, all right?"

Yatou nodded her head slightly, and Mother Su left.

"Why are you crying?" I asked, wiping the excess hair out of her face with a towel.

"Zhu . . . he . . . Zhu is a real person. A real live person."

"A friend?"

Yatou nodded. "He came to the orphanage right after I did, when I was five. He was six. His foot was lame, and his grand-parents said they couldn't care for him anymore. He became like my own brother."

Now Yatou smiled. "We talked sometimes after the aunties turned off the lights for bed. We imagined what it would be like to have parents, and a real family. We decided that if someone wanted to adopt one of us, we'd ask if the other could be adopted too, so we'd always be together. We knew it would never happen, but it was fun to pretend."

"Is Zhu at Chongming Island now?" I asked.

"I'm not sure. I heard one of the uncles say they were taking him to the, um, I can't say the word . . . the sikitakik hospital."

"Psychiatric hospital?" I asked.

"Yes. I said that I'd always remember that hospital word the uncle said, so when I got out of Shanghai Orphanage I could find Zhu."

"Is that the last you heard about him?"

"Yes. What is a . . . a . . . you know . . ."

"Psychiatric hospital?"

Yatou's little face looked up at me. She was so tender. So vulnerable. I was awestruck at how she had escaped Shanghai Orphanage. And I wondered what made her decide to do it. But I decided to hold my questions and answer hers.

"A psychiatric hospital is to help people who are sick in their minds. It's like they can't think clearly, so they need a doctor to help them."

"But Zhu wasn't sick minded," said Yatou, her voice rising with despair. "He was lame in one foot, but he could think all right!"

"Then perhaps it's best that a doctor looked at him, Yatou. Just in case there was any question. Your aunties and uncles may have noticed something was wrong and—"

"The aunties and uncles did not care!" she yelled. "They hated Zhu and me, but especially Zhu." Now Yatou was sobbing again, hitting her knees with her fists.

"How do you know they hated Zhu?" I asked.

Yatou hit her knees in rhythm to her words. "They made him ride the motorcycle and gave him *qiang shui*. They did it again and again. I hate them."

Yatou was losing control. Quietly and desperately I asked God for help. "Yatou," I said, taking her shoulders in my hands. "Yatou, no one's hurting you now. You're safe here. Calm down. I want you to stop crying, then tell me what the motorcycle and qiang shui are."

Yatou looked up. Her hair was half cut, and her eyes were puffy and swollen.

"Here, little one. Blow your nose. Start over again."

Yatou's voice was quiet and quaking. "The motorcycle is when we had to squat halfway with our arms out in front of us for a long, long time." She looked up at me. "Sometimes they made us balance a bowl of scalding hot water on our head or wrists or knees while we did the motorcycle. Sometimes they made us squat over the boiling water so we'd get burned when we fell."

I tried not to show the anger I felt rising in my chest. "Why would they make you do that?"

"Because we were bad. Or because they didn't like us."

"And the qiang shui—what is that?"

"I . . . I . . . we all hated it. We were more scared of that than anything else they did to us." Her voice was rising again, and I wondered if it was wise to continue. But Yatou hurriedly told the rest.

"They hung me upside down with my head down in the water for a long time. I almost died a lot. My nose bled, and I couldn't breathe. I was choking and couldn't breathe, and they'd do it again. I just couldn't stay there anymore. And if I go back it'll be worse than ever. Please, please, don't tell. I'd rather die than go back there." She was clinging to me now, sobbing.

Anger raged within me, and it was all I could do to control it. Once again I gathered my little friend in my arms, sat on the floor, and held her, stroking her hair, rocking her as if she were nine months old instead of nine years. She clung to me as if her life depended on it—for the first time I realized it probably did.

"Yatou, I will never tell. I promise. And I don't know how, but I'll do everything I can to make sure you never go back to that awful place. Those people were filled with evil hatred, God help them, and they were wrong to do that to you. Do you know that?" I asked, cupping her face in my hand and forcing her to look at me.

The wounded look on her face broke my heart as she nodded feebly. I held her close again and continued rocking her, all the while praying from the bottom of my being, "God, help us forgive them. God, help us forgive them."

CHAPTER

Eighteen

"What happened to you?" Chang asked as we all sat around the breakfast table. "Mom, is that one of your haircuts?"

Mother Su had a twinkle in her eye. "Yes, it's the new Western style. Like it?"

"No offense, but I'm glad I get mine done at the hair-dresser's," said Chang.

"Yatou is no longer a yatou," I announced. "Chang, I would like to introduce you to Kwan Zhu, my visiting cousin."

Chang looked at each of us, one by one, digesting the information I just gave her.

"Okay, I think I'm with you now. Kwan Zhu, where are you from?"

"Uh, I don't know for sure, I . . . Mei Lin?"

"Hmm. We'll need to come up with a place, and the work your family's involved in, and why you're not in school."

"Why not make him from Jiangxi Province, like you?" asked

Chang. "You know all about that area and can help Zhu here explain it when asked."

"Good thinking. Only I'll make him from DuYan, the village we had our second house church in. That way it won't be too obvious."

"And his parents, what are they doing?" asked Mother Su.

"Hmmm. His father could be the village cadre and his mother involved in the Family Planning Office with the Women's Federation. The Women's Federation is well respected by government officials. They'll probably ask fewer questions."

"Oooh, is DuYan a big village? Like Shanghai?" Yatou asked. "What does my house look like?"

"You like this pretending game, don't you?" I teased.

"But why isn't he in school?" put in Mother Su, who was clearing the table for tea.

"That's easy. It's fall, and we do not have school during certain weeks in the fall to help with harvest."

"So what are you cousins going to do all day?" Chang asked. She still had an air of distrust about her from the day before.

"We're going to pray first, then head out to see Shanghai. I'm planning to look for a job—something I can do for straight cash. Maybe Zhu and I can do a little sightseeing on the way. What do you say?"

"You mean walk around right out in the open?" asked Yatou, clutching the end of the table.

"Sure. Shanghai is a big place," I said. "We'll be fine as long as we don't make a spectacle of ourselves. We don't want to do acrobatics in the park or talk about the orphanage in public."

"Try to blend in," Chang added. She looked at me. "Don't give out our address either. You can tell them you have friends at the Park Hotel, where I work. People go in and out of the old hotel all the time. It's a good cover."

Chang went to her room and came back with a paper in her hand. "I picked this up at the hotel. It's a tourist map of Shanghai. Don't mark Second Street, okay? It's not even listed on the map, but we're right here. And the orphanage is here. I guess I don't need to tell you not to go in that direction. But you could go see the Children's Palace—it's an after-school training program center for children. They learn music, art, ballet, gymnastics, and computers. North of there is the Temple of the Jade Buddha."

"I've heard of that," Yatou said.

"You can visit there, although it may not be of great interest to a Christian," said Chang, looking at me. "Then there's Yu Gardens, a beautiful spot, and Old Town, which is a good place to see how Shanghai looked four hundred years ago."

"Our ancestors would roll over in their graves if they could see it now," said Mother Su, pouring tea. "Shanghai has been very Westernized in the last fifteen years."

"Are there many activities on the waterfront at Huangpu River?" I asked. "It seems like a logical place to look for a non-government job."

"There's Zhongshannan Street that runs right along the waterfront. It's busy, that's for sure. Lots of business people, docks, fishing boats."

"I don't think we can see it all in one day, but we'll get a good start. Thanks for the map, Chang. It's a great help."

Chang looked at Yatou. "And from now on we'll call you Zhu, in the apartment and out, okay? It'll keep us from slipping up when we're in public."

"I'm Kwan Zhu, inside and out," Yatou announced.

"We'll be careful. And prayerful," I said to Chang.

"Yeah. Look, I'm sorry about yesterday, okay? I really don't mind your staying here. I just don't want my whole family in jail, all right?"

"I understand," I said. "We won't put you in any danger. We'll not use the front entrance in the apartment building either. And if we're asked, we're cousins visiting Shanghai from Jiangxi Province who have friends at Park Hotel."

"Okay. I'm off to work. See you all tonight. 'Bye, Mother."

Mother Su kissed her daughter's forehead. "See you tonight, Chang."

"Would you like to join us for prayer, Mother Su?" I asked after Chang had left.

"Oh, could I?" Mother Su pulled up a chair, and we talked to God over teacups. Afterward, she got up to leave for work. "You can ride my bicycle if you think you're strong enough to pull both you and Zhu around on it."

"Oh, don't you need it?"

"No. It's yours for the day."

"A real bicycle!" exclaimed Yatou.

Mother Su and I smiled.

The way that God provided a map, a bicycle, and a little partner so quickly encouraged me to believe that He would watchfully guard us during our Shanghai tour that day. Yatou sat on the rack over the back tire. My legs stretched to push the pedals, every muscle straining as we rode down Second Street. I was glad that the bucket-and-brush ministry had done me the favor of keeping a few muscles on my frame. We rode down Second Street until we came to Fuxingzhong Street, which led to Old Town.

I couldn't tell where the street and sidewalk met. The street was an incredible sea of cars, taxis, buses, and people on bicycles. The sidewalks were crammed with pedestrians, many who were probably reporting to work at department stores and business offices. The buildings were so tall that the sky above them appeared to be a narrow blue path.

"Having fun?" I shouted behind me.

"I've never done this before," Yatou shouted back.

"You'll be a pro by the time we eat supper tonight!"

As I weaved in and out of the traffic, I thought about Old Town. I'd read about it in school, and it was one spot I'd always longed to see.

We stopped at a traffic light. I tried not to stare as Shanghai girls my age gathered in front of a shopping plaza, lured to a counter by free perfume samples. Their hair was long and shiny. Their short, tight dresses revealed their youthful, feminine figures. I felt embarrassed for them and looked away. Yatou nudged me and pointed at them, so I knew she had noticed them too.

I saw a few mothers carrying babies or pulling the hands of small children behind them, probably off to day care before their workday began. I had never seen such huge masses of people. They were everywhere, walking fast, talking, chewing gum, looking in shop windows before the stores opened, and laughing at what appeared to be nothing. They all looked the same, as though they had all come from the same big family, wearing the same styles of clothing out of the same closets. And these department stores were the closets.

At each stoplight we watched. The young and old alike seemed to walk to one clamorous drumbeat—buy, have, use, indulge, forget, got to have this, got to have that, it's new, it's you, don't let it go by you!

So this is the Shanghai I dreamed about, I thought.

We finally pedaled into Old Town. I felt as if I were going back in history. The narrow, winding alleys were a bustling bazaar of old Oriental times, lined with exquisite restaurants and small shops that sold Chinese embroidery, antiques, scroll paintings, and beautiful handicrafts. We slowed down to pass the gardens, teahouses, pavilions, ponds, rocks, bridges, and stone dragons. All the sites were in the Manchu-Qing style, forming a perfect harmony with one another.

"Let's go over that bridge," said Yatou, pointing to a small arched stone bridge. I guided the bicycle slowly to the bridge and stopped.

"What do you say we walk over, Cousin?"

"All right."

"Look down there," I said, pointing in the water.

"Goldfish!" exclaimed Yatou, delighted with the find.

I pushed the bike, Yatou leading the way across the bridge.

"Wow!" said Yatou. "Look at that!"

Yatou was pointing to a large Buddha statue that appeared to be at least three stories high. Several people were lighting incense and praying in front of it. I shuddered, thinking of Amah and Old One Tooth.

"Is that the Temple of the Jade Buddha?" asked Yatou.

"No, this is just another Buddha statue. I can hardly believe it's here."

Yatou started back to the goldfish under the arched bridge.

"Wait, Zhu. I must say a prayer too." I held the bike with one hand and put the other around my new little cousin. I looked to the skies and talked to the One who made them. "Jesus, you are Lord. Please free my Amah and our people from idol worship. Please show them this Buddha is no more than a fat, voiceless, earless god. Thank you. Amen."

Yatou giggled. "You're funny. You told your God that Buddha is fat and earless. I'll bet He thought that was funny too."

I couldn't help but be amused by Yatou's childish observations. "It's true, you know. Jesus is the only living God who can hear us. All the other ones are dead—just people who died like other people."

"The Buddha makes you sad," said Yatou, using her hand to shield the sun so she could look up at me.

"Let's go. I don't want to feel sad today." I took Yatou's hand and then glanced one more time at the site of the statue with people worshiping and praying around it. "I just can't believe that idol is standing there, bigger than life. Our Buddhist temples in Tanching Village are just work offices now, where the cadres manage the village business. They'd never let something like this stand in our town."

"This statue wasn't standing during the Cultural Revolution, you can be sure of that." It was a man's voice from behind us. I whirled around, jolted that someone had been listening to our conversation. The man was short and slim, not much taller than I. His hair was cut short on the sides and the back and graying at the temples. He wore silver wire-rimmed glasses. From the neck up he looked like a college professor. But his dress was definitely outdated by Shanghai's standards. His high-collared blue shirt and baggy gray pants, although neat in appearance, bore testimony of the more traditional Mao fashion.

"I . . . I . . . didn't see you behind us," I said. "You startled me."

"I apologize. I couldn't help but hear your prayers and your viewpoints of this idol. I'd—"

"I think you were right, Zhu; we need to go now." My legs felt heavy, like iron. I wanted to ride out of there as fast as I could, but the way I was shaking, I could only push the handlebars and turn to leave.

"Please, wait. It's all right. I'm a Christian too."

"You are?" asked Yatou, her face an incredulous question mark.

This may be a trap, I thought. I laid my hand on Yatou's shoulder to signal her to silence.

"I'm sorry, you are shaking. I didn't mean to frighten you."

Yatou and I exchanged glances. I knew our first test had come. I tried to sound casual.

"We're cousins, just visiting Shanghai."

"You have a southern accent," said the man. "Guangdong Province?"

"Uh, no, Jiangxi."

"I see. Well, Shanghai's changed in the last twenty years," he said, looking at the Buddha statue. There was something trustworthy in the man's eyes as he began to reflect on his Shanghai heritage.

"We still wear the blue and gray Mao jackets in Jiangxi," I said. "And I could count on two hands the number of cars I saw in Jiangxi in my whole lifetime."

"Ah, Shanghai is a wonderful old city. May she prosper in Western wealth without adopting Western morals."

I knew what he meant. I thought of the girls in their short

skirts on the corner, the stores packed with people, the abandoned baby.

"Only God can keep Shanghai from falling," the man continued.

"What did you say?" I asked. I wondered if I heard him right.

"Shanghai is brimming with prosperity. But this kind of wealth was a trap for the Western continents."

I looked at this man, who was barely above my eye level, and decided to take a chance.

"Are you really a Christian?" I asked.

"Mei Lin!" said Yatou, her eyes glazed with fear.

"Pleased to meet you, Mei Lin, and cousin of Mei Lin," said the man, shaking our hands as he introduced himself. "All my friends call me Tom. It's an American name. I've never been to America, but they call me that because I have quite a few American friends. And, well, I hope you don't report me, but yes, I am a Christian."

"How long?" I asked.

"Ah, only three years," Tom replied, shaking his head sadly. "I wish I'd have known the Lord Jesus when I was young, like you two cousins." He had a tease in his smile when he called us cousins. I could tell he suspected we weren't really related.

"I was blessed to hear you pray as you did. I have to admit, though, I had to hold back a laugh myself when you called old Buddha a fat, voiceless, earless god."

Now I laughed. "I guess God doesn't mind our picking on old Buddha. It's hard to believe people pray to that thing." I took one last look at the statue and again felt sad.

"Would you like to visit our house church?" asked Tom. "We would love to hear about what God is doing in Jiangxi Province.

Our house-church people really love the Lord. I think you would enjoy yourselves there. That is, if it's all right with your parents."

"I don't—"

I cut Yatou off. "Our parents won't mind. Where is your church?"

The man wrote down directions for us, then showed us where it was located on our tour map. "Please come. Of course, we cannot guarantee that we will not have a police raid. But we haven't had one in more than six months."

"I'll pray about it," I replied, although deep inside I knew I wanted to go.

"Oh, and . . ." The man stalled, pulling something from his back pocket. "Do you have a Bible?" he asked.

I felt my heart leap as I stared at his precious book.

"Here, you may keep this one," he said.

"Oh," I cried out. People walking toward the statue looked over at us, and I quickly tucked the little New Testament under my arm. I tried to control myself for the joy I felt, but I couldn't. I began to giggle, springing up and down right there in public in spite of myself. I'd promised Chang I wouldn't make a spectacle of myself. But a Bible!

"Oh, how can I ever repay you?" I asked.

The man seemed both amused and pleased, then looked around to be sure no one was listening. "I've never had anyone react quite this way when I gave them one. It's only a New Testament, but if you come to church Saturday night, I'll make sure you both get your own Bibles. The whole Bible, okay?"

"Oh, do you mean it?" I asked. "May I bring a friend with me? She's a new Christian."

"By all means. Only, remember to come in the back entrance.

There are stairs outside. It's on the third floor, room sixteen. Knock twice, then four times. Then we'll know it's a friend. Got that?"

"Twice, then four times," said Yatou, knocking out the code on the bicycle seat.

"I'm so grateful," I said. My excitement gave way to a deep reverence for what I held under my arm.

"Keep it tucked away, now," said the man, grinning. "I'll see you Saturday night at eleven-thirty."

★ ✱ ★

CHAPTER

Nineteen

The narrow alleyway led us deep into the heart of the poorer section of Shanghai. The three of us walked together, picking our way through the cyclists and pedestrians. We finally found the right address and climbed three flights of rickety steps to the back door.

"Room sixteen," Mother Su read.

"It's eleven o'clock. I guess we can come a little early," I said. I took the New Testament out of my jacket pocket. "Ready?"

They nodded.

Yatou had practiced the code all week. Knock, knock. Pause. Knock, knock, knock, knock.

An elderly woman opened the door slowly and hesitated, looking over the three of us. "Ah, Brother Tom's friends," she said, opening the door. "Come in, come in. Welcome to our little church."

I stepped into a huge room that was packed with benches with backs on them. They were shaped very much like the ones in the park, only these were wooden and had bookracks on the back. The racks held books that appeared to be handmade. About ten people stood around, sipping tea and talking. I couldn't resist picking up one of the books.

"What are these?" I asked the elderly woman.

"These are our hymnals," she told us proudly. "Hand stenciled, to be sure, but full of wonderful songs."

Mother Su opened the pages, running her hand gently over the words, saying them to herself. "I've never read such beautiful words," she said. "It fills me with happiness to read them."

Yatou tagged along as I walked around the room. I tried to memorize everything there so that I could tell Liko and Father later on. The room was large for an apartment in this sort of neighborhood. I guessed that someone must have torn down walls to the bedrooms and kitchen to make room for everyone.

Various scrolls with Bible verses on them hung here and there. I didn't see Tom yet. The two front benches were filling up quickly. Yatou and I chose our seats on the third row.

"Being a Christian is a lot of fun, isn't it, Mei Lin?" She didn't give me time to answer. "It's like you're special, and you kind of belong with other special people. Know what I mean?"

"It's a family, Zhu. That's what you're seeing. And that's just what God wants. A family of His own."

"He does?"

"Sure."

Yatou was quiet for a minute. "Wow! I'm just like God, you know that, Mei Lin? I want a family too!"

I smiled at my new little cousin. I had grown very attached to her the last few days, and nothing could have made me happier than to see her born into the family of God. So I tried to explain salvation in the simplest of terms. "God made Adam and Eve, the first people, because He wanted a family. They sinned, and all their children sinned, so God sent Jesus to save us from our sins. Jesus died for all of our sins so God could get His family back."

"He must have wanted a family really bad," Yatou said soberly. "Like me."

I squeezed her hand. "He wants you to be in His family too, Zhu. Look, the meeting is about to start."

The people were settling into their seats. Mother Su sat in the back with the woman who had met us at the door. A high sort of desk was at the front. I assumed the speaker would stand or sit behind it, the way Pastor Chen used to stand behind the desk at our house church in the barn. My eyes locked on to a scroll that hung on the wall behind the desk. It read, *Be faithful, even to the point of death, and I will give you the crown of life. Revelation 2:10.*

I fumbled for my Bible. *Is that really in here?* I wondered. I found the verse, and all of the memories of prison came rushing back to me—things I had been trying to forget for the last week, pushing them into the back of my memory. The darkness, loneliness, hunger, rats, human waste, beatings, the electric cattle prod. I felt that sorrow would overtake me, and I clenched my fists. Then I remembered Sun Tao, Mother Su's husband, and the other prisoners who came to believe in the One who made the earth and skies, the One who gave His life for them.

"Lord, did you find me faithful?" I whispered quietly.

Yatou noticed my somber mood and moved closer to me, resting her head on my arm. I kissed her beautiful boyish hair. "It's okay," I whispered, amazed at how easy it was for me to show her affection.

Then I bowed my head, my hands folded in front of me, and worshiped the Lord. I felt as though He was catching every tear that fell from my chin. I thought of the woman in the Bible who poured her expensive perfume on Jesus' feet, and I prayed quietly, "Please receive my tears, Lord, as you received the perfume from the lady who gave you her very best ointment. I desire to worship you as she worshiped you that day."

Suddenly a woman in the second row began softly singing.

Take my life and let it be
Consecrated, Lord, to thee;
Take my hands, and let them move
At the impulse of thy love,
At the impulse of thy love.

Take my love, my God, I pour,
At thy feet its treasure store;
Take myself and I will be
Ever, only, all for thee,
Ever, only, all for thee.

My heart swelled within me. "Ever, only all for thee, ever only all for thee," I told Him over and over from the depths of my being. Once again, as within the dark prison cell, I felt like I was sitting at the feet of Jesus as He hung on the cross for me. This time I was not called to know Him in His sufferings, but to worship Him with my whole being.

Beautiful four-part harmony whispered about the room as the people sang:

See from his head, his hands, his feet,
Sorrow and love flow mingled down;

Did e'er such love and sorrow meet,
Or thorns compose so rich a crown?

Father's favorite hymn. I wasn't sure what else was sung after that. Time escaped me. I couldn't leave the cross. I touched it. I cried on it. I clung to it as if it were the only rock in the middle of a stormy sea. I felt the raging sea within me surrender to the power of the cross, until it was transformed into calm waves of blessing, rolling over me, filling me, washing me clean.

When I finally looked up, the whole room had fallen silent. All that was visible around me were the tops of people's heads—some dark, some graying, bowed in worship and prayer. Yatou was sitting up now. Her head was bowed too, and I prayed quietly that God would touch her.

After some time of silence, a man who seemed to be in charge of the meeting went to the high desk. "Brothers and sisters, God has graciously met us in this place tonight. Let us offer silent praise." With that heads and hands were uplifted, many stood noiselessly to their feet, and without so much as a whisper the whole room tingled with praises and thanks. I assumed they were quiet to protect themselves from being discovered by the PSB.

I'd never been in a meeting like this one, and I found myself joining in the enthusiasm. *God deserves this kind of thank-you,* I thought.

The praises went on for about five minutes. It was electrifying—like lightning without the noise of thunder. I closed my eyes and absorbed all that I could hold.

The man up front finally stood up to speak. "Brother Tom has invited a special friend tonight." I slowly sank in my seat. I wanted to hide under it. Was I the friend he was speaking of?

Were they going to want me to say something?

"As most of you know, Brother Tom has been involved in a special prison ministry in Shanghai. He works hand in hand with organizations from the United States to free our Christian brothers and sisters who are in prison for their faith."

Several "ahs" went up around the room. I thought, *What in the world is this man talking about?*

"Today I'd like to introduce to you our special speaker, who was released from Shanghai Prison Number Fourteen just a few days ago through Brother Tom's ministry. Please come and share with us, Pastor Wong."

I gasped and turned around to see Pastor Wong walking down the aisle toward the desk. He held his hands to his chest, his broken fingertips wrapped in white bandages. Forgetting there was anyone else was in the room, I cried out, "My God! My God, you are faithful!"

Pastor Wong was standing at my row. Our eyes met.

"You . . . you're . . . you're Kwan Mei Lin," he said with the same disbelief I felt.

My lower lip quivered, and I couldn't take my eyes off of him. "Yes, yes," I answered, clenching and unclenching my fists. "My God is faithful!"

A murmur arose among the people around us. "Come," said Pastor Wong, tears springing to his eyes. "We will share our testimonies together, sister."

I squeezed Yatou's hand, then joined Pastor Wong at the desk. I just couldn't believe I was in the same room again with this holy man of God. Hanging on to the desk to steady myself, I bowed my head, shaking it in disbelief. "My God is faithful," I muttered again under my breath.

Standing beside me, Pastor Wong began to speak. "I was speaking at a house church last month when the PSB raided our meeting. They arrested me and bullied some of the others. When I was interrogated, the officers asked me for the names of my church members and foreign contacts. When I refused to give them the information, they—well, they took pliers and broke the ends of all my fingers."

At this we all wept, including Pastor Wong. Then he led us out of our weeping by raising his bandaged hands and praising the Lord, saying, "Worthy is the Lamb, worthy is the Lamb, worthy is the Lamb." We joined him in what became the most sacred offering of praise I had ever experienced.

When the time was right, Pastor Wong continued. "When I was in prison, God sent someone to me to nurse my wounds and encourage me in my afflictions. I wondered later on if it was only a dream, but the evidence was there. My broken fingers were soaked in cold water. I wondered if God had sent an angel. This is the sister that God sent to my room. I had no idea, and it appears she didn't know either, whether we would ever see each other again."

A silent reverence filled the room. Several of the older women quietly raised their hands in praise. Pastor Wong went on. "The Bible says, 'When I was in prison, you visited me.' Kwan Mei Lin visited me, a thin, frail girl not twenty years old." He turned to me. "Would you please tell them how it came about that you were in my prison cell with a bucket and brush?"

I felt awkward. A bucket and brush somehow didn't seem to fit into such a spiritual meeting as this. I hesitated.

"It's okay, Mei Lin," said Pastor Wong. "Tell them about your ministry."

"I . . . I'm from Jiangxi Province," I started. "I always wanted to come to Shanghai—it was my dream to come to the university here." I couldn't look up. I felt so skinny and small. "I was put in prison because I wouldn't deny Jesus as my Lord.

"One day I sat singing a hymn in my cell, and the Lord gave me a message: 'This will be your ministry.' I objected and said, 'I am all alone. Who can I preach to?' And then there was silence. I did not understand what the Lord meant, but I continued to pray that my ministry would be fulfilled. Then suddenly an idea came to me. I stood up and called the guards.

" 'Sir, can I do some hard labor for you?' I asked. The guard looked at me with contempt and surprise. I'm sure no one had ever made that sort of request before. I told him, 'Look! This prison is so dirty. There is human waste everywhere. Let me go into the cells and clean up this filthy place. All you will have to do is give me some water and a brush.' I told him hard labor would help me to rehabilitate myself."

There were a few giggles, and I smiled.

"Permission was soon granted, and I found myself on my hands and knees, going from cell to cell. I saw people who were barely recognizable as human beings. But, oh, when they discovered they could have eternal life, they would get so excited. They would fall down on the dirty floor and repent of their sins. And do you know that soon nearly all the prisoners believed in Jesus Christ?"

"Ahhh," came the reaction from the people. I heard a soft "Hallelujah" and "God is faithful."

Telling the story brought back the joy I had in the prison ministry. I stole a glance at little Yatou. Her eyes were wide with wonder, as though she'd never seen me before.

"One day I was taken to Pastor Wong's cell. At first I thought he was dead. He lay still and lifeless. I wanted to leave because . . . well, I couldn't witness to a dead man."

A quiet laughter rippled across the room again.

"But the guard said he was alive and then just left me alone with him. With the lantern light I could see that his hands were horribly swollen and dried blood was everywhere. I'd . . . I'd never seen such a thing." Tears sprang to my eyes, and my voice cracked with emotion as I tried to share the rest. "I soaked his hands in the clean water while he was unconscious. When he woke up, it was I who was ministered to. In his great pain he encouraged me, quoting Scripture to me."

I looked up at Pastor Wong. "I was most honored, and greatly strengthened."

Many of the people sat on the edge of their benches, listening. I was finished, so I moved to sit down.

"Wait, Mei Lin," said Pastor Wong. "How were you freed?"

"I really don't know," I answered. "The warden found out about the bucket-and-brush ministry and was very angry. He said that when they yelled at or beat the prisoners, now they just cried out, 'I forgive you in Jesus' name.' He said he was losing control of the prisoners and that I wasn't allowed to clean any more cells. They put sand in my meals that week. But at the end of the week, two of the guards came to my cell and said that the warden was dead. They didn't want me there anymore, and some of the other guards were afraid of my God. They hurried me down the hall and escorted me out of the prison."

With that the whole room stood up, offering praise, a little less silent than before. Now it was Pastor Wong who shook his head in disbelief. "Our God is faithful!" he proclaimed, raising his bandaged hands into the air. "Glorify the Lord!"

All fear and restraint were abandoned in an instant. "If we don't praise Him now, these benches are going to do it for us!" declared the man who'd been in charge of the meeting.

Shouts went up all over the room.

"Glory!"

"Hallelujah!"

"Praise Jesus!"

I closed my eyes and thanked God quietly. Telling about the bucket-and-brush ministry seemed odd. I'd left out so much—the pain, the torturous beatings, the rats, the loneliness in the thick unrelenting darkness. Yet now, after telling it, I could see the whole picture. *It is amazing!* I thought.

After the praise subsided, Pastor Wong asked, "Were you beaten, Mei Lin?"

"Yes," I answered simply.

"How many times?"

"Twice."

"Can you tell us what God showed you during those times?"

"Yes . . . He . . . He . . ." Again I choked, trying to clear my throat to keep from crying. "He showed me the cross. The precious cross. That I may know Him and the fellowship of His sufferings."

I looked over at Yatou. This was the first time she'd heard any of this. Her face was wet with tears, and my heart went out to her. I returned to my seat, and she reached over and hugged my neck.

"Oh, Mei Lin," she whispered. "I didn't know. You hurt too. Just like me. I didn't know."

After the meeting Pastor Wong introduced me to Tom.

"Mei Lin and I have already met," said Tom. "Although I

must admit, I didn't realize what a young woman of God I'd invited here tonight!"

"I prayed you'd be released," I said to Pastor Wong. "How did it happen?"

"Tom was responsible for my release," replied Pastor Wong. "He has contacts."

"Foreign contacts?" I asked, remembering that's why they'd nicknamed him Tom.

Pastor Wong nodded. "Really, Christians in the United States are responsible for my release. You can explain it better, Tom."

Tom adjusted his glasses. "People in the States pray for our house churches in China. These Christians send money to various organizations in the States who help persecuted Christians from many countries, including China. The money comes to us through a mutual contact."

"Really?" I asked. "You mean, the Christians in the United States know that we're being persecuted?"

"Some of them. There are many Christians in the United States and other countries who care. They pray and they give."

"I didn't know that," I said slowly, lost in the thought of realizing we were not isolated in our persecutions. Others knew about the madness we endured, and they cared. "That's wonderful! So what you're saying is that you paid off the prison, right?"

"Right," answered Tom. "You know how it is in China—money can buy just about anything."

"But you didn't pay for my release?" I asked.

"No. We didn't know anything about you until Thursday when Pastor Wong was released."

I felt Yatou tugging at my elbow from behind. "Oh, this is

Zhu, my little—well, I guess I should say . . ." I looked down at my little friend.

"It's okay," she said.

"This little one is known in the greater Shanghai area as Zhu, my cousin from Jiangxi Province. However, Zhu really isn't a boy. Her name—I feel so bad saying it—her real name is Yatou. Just Girl." I told Tom and Pastor Wong Yatou's story, about her escape from the orphanage and our finding each other.

"Remarkable," said Pastor Wong.

"Please, do you think you can find my friend Zhu? He was taken to the sikitak—" She looked to me for help.

"Psychiatric," I said.

"They took him to the psychiatric hospital."

The two men suddenly had a funny expression on their faces.

"No, no," cried Yatou, reading their faces. "He can think clearly. They sent him there because they don't like him. He's lame in his leg, but really, his thinking is good!" Yatou was excited, pleading with her eyes for a ray of hope for her friend. "Please, don't the Christians care about children too? I can make Zhu a Christian when we find him. He'll do it! Please!"

I hadn't seen Yatou this upset since the day we cut her hair. "Yatou, these men are good men. But we must believe God to help Zhu. And to help all those other children."

Pastor Wong squatted down, eye level with Yatou. "Yatou, we have a mighty God. We will pray." With that Pastor Wong took her little hands in his bandaged ones and prayed a simple prayer of faith that God would release Zhu from the psychiatric hospital.

———

Mother Su and Yatou and I lingered until most of the people had left.

"It's time to go, Yatou."

"Do we have to?" she asked, yawning.

I smiled and hugged her again. "Yes. Look. It's three-thirty in the morning!"

"Mei Lin," said Tom. "I brought Bibles for all three of you. Here."

"Oh, Tom, thank you. Here's your New Testament."

"No, you keep it. See me before you go home. I'll make sure you have more Bibles for your house church in Tanching Village."

Oh, Liko was right! I thought joyously. *They do have Bibles in Shanghai!*

Mother Su, Yatou, and I walked home in the early-morning darkness. I was both exhilarated and exhausted.

"I felt so honored, tonight, Mei Lin," said Mother Su, "to know that God sent you to live at my house, out of all the people in Shanghai. It made me feel so special."

"Me too," said little Yatou.

"I am the one who is honored. And well taken care of, Mother Su!"

I took my new Bible to bed with me that night, fingering the new pages in the dark. As I lay on my cot next to Yatou, I rehearsed the whole meeting again in my mind.

"Mei Lin?" said Yatou. "Are you awake?"

"Yes, are you awake?" I teased, smiling in the darkness.

"Mei Lin, tonight when everyone was singing, I became a Christian. Just like you."

My heart soared. I reached my hand down to her floor mat and squeezed her arm.

"Welcome to the family, Yatou. My little cousin Zhu has just become my little sister Yatou."

"Mei Lin?"

"Yes, Yatou?"

"I like being your little sister."

"I like being your big sister. Good night, little one."

"Good night."

CHAPTER

Twenty

It was Monday, and I was more determined than ever to find a job. I longed to see my family and Liko and take Bibles back home to my village. Now I needed one more train ticket. I knew I could never leave without Yatou.

"Chang, what's the back way to the train station?" I asked at the breakfast table. I laid out her hotel map in front of us.

"The train station is here," she said. "You'll be able to take the back way only so far." She mapped out the route.

"And which back street goes to the river?" I asked. "I'd like to ride over there to try to find a job."

"Can I go?" asked Yatou. "And why are you going to the train station? Where are you going?"

"Yes, you may go, and we are both taking a train to Jiangxi Province as soon as I can make enough money to get us there."

Yatou grabbed my arm and squeezed it until it hurt. "You mean it? You're really going to take me with you?"

"How could I leave behind my cousin Zhu or my sister Yatou? Of course I mean it."

Yatou leaped out of her chair and hugged my neck hard. "Oh, thank you, Mei Lin. I'll try to be a good sister, really I will."

"Now, I don't know if I can bribe the cadre into letting you stay permanently in my home or not. I'll certainly try. But we'll try to find a home for you in the same town. Okay?"

Yatou had fire in her eyes and her hands on her hips. "No matter where I live, I'll always be your sister, right?"

"Right. I've always wanted a sister. Now here you are!"

Mother Su rushed around the house, running late for work. "I gave Brother Tom our address Saturday night. He and Pastor Wong are the only ones who have it."

"Mother—" Chang objected.

"It's all right, Chang," said her mother. "We know these men. And they have foreign connections. Right, Mei Lin?"

"Foreign connections?" Chang was yelling now. "Do you know what that means? They're probably being watched by the Public Security Bureau. That means they're doing some big business—black marketing or something. Surely, these Christians are not businessmen!"

"Chang, you're jumping to conclusions. They are good men. Better than I've ever invited to our home. You make sure you show honor and respect if they come to visit."

"Well, I—"

"Chang," warned Mother Su, raising her eyebrows.

"All right, I'll honor them. If I'm here. But I'll do my best not to be here. I'll find something to do. I'll go shopping or something."

"I'll see you all around five-thirty," said Mother Su with her all-knowing smile, and she hurried out the door.

"See you later," mumbled Chang, leaving right behind her mother.

Yatou and I spent the next hour cleaning up the kitchen and the apartment. When we were finished I glanced at the clock. "It's nine o'clock. The traffic shouldn't be so heavy now," I said. "Let's go find out how much money we'll need for a train ticket."

Yatou and I practically flew down the stairs, then pulled the bicycle out from under the stairwell.

"Sister Mei Lin!"

I turned to see who was calling me. Tom was walking quickly toward us.

"Brother Tom!"

"I'm glad I caught up to you before you left."

I explained our day's plans to him, and he asked if we could speak in a more private place. After we were safely back in Mother Su's apartment, he handed me an envelope. "Perhaps you'd be interested in this."

I carefully opened it. "Train tickets! And all this money, Brother Tom. What is this for?"

"It's for you," he said, smiling. "And as for where it came from—you know, contacts."

"I hadn't even thought of other expenses. Oh, thank you! Thank you! This is more than enough to get us home." I turned to Yatou, so excited I felt I would burst. "Yatou, we can go home!"

"That's not all, Mei Lin. I just took Pastor Wong to the train station. It's not safe for him to stay in Shanghai. He'll be going to other house churches to preach."

"I'll miss him," I said sadly.

"Well, there are two things. First of all, he'd like to meet you both in WuMa."

"WuMa?" I asked. "In Jiangxi Province?"

"Yes. He'll meet you at the train station in WuMa. He's not sure, but he thinks your village is about fifty miles south of WuMa."

"That sounds about right," I said, excitement rising in my voice.

"He may accompany you to your house church in DuYan. He wants to minister to the people there. The second thing concerns you," said Brother Tom, looking down at Yatou.

"Me?" asked Yatou.

"I have connections at the psychiatric hospital. Your friend Zhu is no longer there. He's been transferred to WuMa."

"WuMa?" asked Yatou, with a puzzled look on her face. "But the aunties and uncles said under no circumstances would we ever be transferred from Shanghai Orphanage or Chongming Island."

"Zhu was evidently transferred by the hospital, not the orphanage. He's in an orphanage in WuMa. I've arranged for you to visit him there."

"Oh! Oh!" It seemed, for once, Yatou was stumped for words.

"Brother Tom, that's amazing!" I said. "How did you come up with all this in one day?"

"Connections," he said, smiling and shrugging his shoulders. "In China it's not what you know, it's *who* you know. This trip will be dangerous for both of you, but especially for Yatou. You will need to maintain your cover as Kwan Zhu, okay?"

"Okay."

"The train station will be filled with PSB officers. I've seen your orphanage picture being shown by some of them at the train station and the bus station."

Yatou put her hand over her mouth, fear mounting in her eyes. "I'm scared."

"Yatou, we will pray for safe passage," I said. "God is our Father. He will help us."

"Yes, but you'll have to be a tough little boy, not a pretty little girl. Think you can do that?"

"Sure!"

"Here," said Tom, taking something out of his bag. "These clothes are very American. It's a Baltimore Orioles baseball hat and a T-shirt and jeans."

Brother Tom took off his silver wire-rimmed glasses and handed them to Yatou. "I thought these glasses would be a good disguise, since the PSB is still looking for you. At the Shanghai train station, you'll need to be my nephew, and Mei Lin my niece. I'm your Chinese American uncle who's come back to Shanghai for a visit. And so, the American clothes."

I looked down at what Chang had given me to wear and wondered if it would work.

"Oh, and for you, Mei Lin, from America."

Tom pulled another pair of jeans and a T-shirt from his bag.

"It looks very American," I said. "What does the T-shirt say?"

"The Gap. It's an American clothing company. *The* American clothing company as far as most American girls are concerned. And here. These are Nike sneakers."

"Oh! Chang told me she's wanted a pair of these all of her life!" I exclaimed. I couldn't help but wonder what Chang would think when she saw me in them.

"Your train leaves tomorrow morning at ten. I'll be here at six o'clock to show you the way. It'll go better for you if I go as your self-confident Chinese American uncle. Have you ridden on a train before?"

"No."

"It is best to go early so that you can get in the front of the line. It's pretty peaceful until the train doors swing open. Then you'll do well to stay on your feet and make it inside."

"Tomorrow at six?" I asked.

"Right. I'll bring a bike for you to use. That way if I'm followed, they won't trace the bicycle back to Mother Su."

"I feel like I'm dreaming," I said slowly.

"It's important that you understand what to do. When you ride the train, you and Yatou will sit together in the same compartment. It'll take about eighteen hours, which should bring you to WuMa at about four in the morning. That's good, because the train won't leave again until ten the next morning, which means the train station should be less crowded. Pastor Wong will be at the WuMa station waiting for you. If you don't see him, that means he's probably being followed. In that case he will send someone in his place. We don't know who that would be as of yet. So look for someone with glasses just like these." He pointed to the ones he'd given to Yatou.

My head was spinning. Everything was happening so fast— so gloriously fast. To think that I might see my family within a week's time! "What's the plan once we're in WuMa?" I asked, supposing Brother Tom probably had one.

"Pastor Wong has already carried your Bibles on the train this morning, Mei Lin. He didn't want you and Yatou to endanger yourselves any more than you already are with a runaway orphan."

"Bibles too? This is just so incredible."

Tom smiled. "You have one day to rest up and say good-bye to Mother Su," he said. "I'll see you in the morning."

I couldn't even answer him. And then he was gone.

CHAPTER

Twenty-One

I miss you both already," cried Mother Su when we told her the story of Brother Tom's visit. "You have been such a joy to have in our home!"

"You've been so good to us," I replied. "You've treated us like family."

"You are my family, in a way," said Mother Su. "But you must be tired of being a *youzi*, a person away from home."

I turned to Chang. "Chang, I'm grateful for your friendship as well. You loaned us clothing and shared your food. Thank you."

"You're really going home?" she asked. "Tomorrow?"

"We're really going home," I said, smiling in a triumphant sort of way.

"But you didn't even get to see the university yet," Chang protested. "You've come all this way, and you haven't even seen the place you always dreamed of."

"It's amazing," I said. "But you know, I don't even think of the university anymore. All I can think about is going home!"

"I'm glad you get to go. Your father must be awfully worried."

"Yes, and we're going to look like real Americans tomorrow too," said Yatou. "Look at my baseball hat and funny wire glasses!"

Chang laughed. "Now all you need are heavier eyebrows."

"Eyebrows?" I asked.

"Sure, a little eye makeup to those eyebrows and Yatou will look more like a boy than ever. It'll help change her appearance, especially if the police are looking for her."

"That's a great idea!" said Yatou. "Let's practice right now!"

Chang and Yatou ran off to Chang's bedroom. I was glad for an opportunity to talk to Mother Su.

"Mother Su, have you thought about giving your husband's name to Brother Tom?"

"You're reading my thoughts, Mei Lin. My husband is not a great preacher like you and Pastor Wong. But he is a Christian."

"Then, you're planning to attend the house-church meetings?" I asked, ignoring her allusion to my being a preacher.

"Oh yes, every week!" exclaimed Mother Su. "Let's get you and Yatou to safety. Then I plan to approach Brother Tom. He seems to have a big heart for prisoners."

"He does. He also has a big heart for Christians without Bibles. That reminds me—I'm going to leave our two Bibles with you. It'll be too dangerous to take them on the train with us. But Pastor Wong carried Bibles on the train this morning to give to my house church in DuYan."

"Now, how is that?" asked Mother Su. "Your home is in Tanching Village, but you travel over the mountain to DuYan Village to attend a house church there?"

"That's right. We don't have a pastor in Tanching. Our pastor was taken to prison after one of our meetings was raided—oh! Why didn't I think of it before?"

"What's the matter?" asked Mother Su.

"Oh, Mother Su, perhaps Brother Tom has connections at the laogai camp where Pastor Chen was sent. I don't remember which one he's in, but Brother Tom seems to be able to find out anything. Maybe he'll be able to help Pastor Chen come home. Oh, Liko and his mother would be so happy! And Pastor Chen wouldn't have to suffer anymore."

"Be sure to talk with him before you leave tomorrow. Now, I'm going to market. I'm going to make you girls noodles, fish balls, and dumplings for your trip. Oh, and rice for you, Mei Lin. Just in case the spicy noodles are too much for you yet."

"Thank you. But how will you do all that in one night?"

"I'll do it if it takes me all night," said Mother Su, her jaw set as she walked out the front door with her market bag. "You girls are on your own for dinner. I'll bring you some pastries for dessert, okay?"

I found it amusing that while everyone else was in a flurry about preparing for our trip, I really had nothing to do. I opted for one last warm bath in that beautiful basin in the bathroom. After my bath I laid out my clothes and shoes for the next day, and then took out my New Testament. I sat on the couch and opened the precious book to Revelation 2:10, the verse I'd seen on the scroll above the high desk Saturday night. *"Be faithful even to the point of death, and I will give you the crown of life."*

I spent the next hour reading the chapter and praying. This little Bible was priceless. I'd never forget the day Brother Tom pulled it out and gave it to me. It was my souvenir from Shanghai.

I planned to wear my T-shirt outside of my jeans tomorrow so that I could conceal the little New Testament in my back pocket. I'd keep the money and tickets tucked safely in my front pockets.

Chang and Yatou walked into the living room.

"What do you think, Mei Lin?" asked Chang. "We did our best."

"She's—I mean *he's* hardly recognizable! I really can't tell you used makeup at all. Where is it?"

"Oh, a little up here and a little in the center," Chang answered.

"I guess I ought to play baseball, huh?" said Yatou, giggling at herself in the mirror.

"I'll give you this makeup stick," Chang said. "Then you can freshen her up a bit if you need to."

"Thanks, Chang," I said sincerely, realizing how much her makeup meant to her. "And I have something for you." I reached under my cot and pulled out the Nike sneakers. "I won't need them. My old shoes are working just fine."

"Oh, Mei Lin. You have Nike shoes? How did you—"

I could see Chang was caught off guard.

"Mei Lin, thank you. I'll never forget this kindness."

"They look a bit big."

"Just a little. I'll stuff paper in the toe. Who knows? Maybe I'm not done growing yet. My feet may get bigger!"

Chang was truly pleased, and I was glad to leave our friendship on such a pleasant note. I knew Brother Tom wouldn't mind.

———

Five in the morning came soon enough. Mother Su and Chang

got up with us in spite of the early hour. Mother Su had finished the food only three hours before.

"How will you work today, with so little sleep?" I asked her.

"I'll have the energy of the joy it brings me to know that you'll soon be reunited with your family."

"I'm truly happy for you too," said Chang, helping to straighten out Yatou's disguise again. "Your Christian God can certainly work miracles."

"Yes, He can." I sensed that Chang was leaving something out. "What miracles are you thinking of?" I asked.

"Oh, I guess I can tell you. When you first came here, you said God cares. So I actually prayed one night, like you pray, and asked God to get my father out of prison. Mother tells me that this man may be able to help us. Then, well, I guess it's a little selfish, but I've wanted a pair of Nike sneakers forever. When you gave those to me last night, I felt like they came from God. Like it was His way of saying He really was watching. Know what I mean?"

"I know what you mean," I answered.

"I think I'll go with Mother to the house-church meeting this week. I want to see it for myself."

I looked over at Mother Su. She was beaming. I thought of the verse in Romans, *"God's kindness leads . . . toward repentance."* Somehow I knew everything would turn out right for their whole family.

"Here's my address," I said. "Please write to me. Let me know about the house-church meetings and how things are progressing with your father."

We parted with hugs all around. Everyone was laughing, and Mother Su and Yatou were wiping tears.

"Careful, Zhu Yatou, your heavy eyebrows will droop!" Chang said. I checked my gear. I had the shoulder bag with our jackets and food, the money in the front left pocket, the tickets in the front right pocket, and the New Testament in the back left pocket.

"You both look very American," Chang said. "Here, try on these shoes, Mei Lin."

Chang handed me a comfortable pair of leather shoes that were very Western looking.

"Hey, they're a perfect fit," I said. "Thank you, Chang."

I looked at Mother Su and Chang, then I bowed formally to show them my deepest respect and gratitude. "You are wonderful friends. I'll never forget you."

"And you'll write to us as well?" asked Mother Su, wiping tears away with her apron.

"Of course." We hugged one another one more time, then Yatou and I headed down the dark stairwell at five minutes before six.

CHAPTER

Twenty-Two

The crowd was relatively calm and courteous until the Shanghai Express pulled into the dock. Yatou and I had been standing in the gate for two hours with only a dozen or so people in front of us. We felt the first wave of anxiety as the train pulled up.

A stout woman in a railway uniform barked at us to back up while she slammed the entry gate back and padlocked it. We held on to the sidebars for stability. Shanghai PSB officers walked up and down the aisle in front of the gate. Brother Tom had told us that if we felt we were being watched or about to be questioned, we should turn and nonchalantly wave to him. That way the officers would be distracted into questioning him instead of us.

"Zhu, hold tightly to my hand now," I said, nervously trying to stay balanced between my shoulder bag and my little cousin. People began pressing and squeezing to get to the front.

Then the doors opened! The woman slammed the bars back, and Yatou and I locked arms, barely able to shuffle toward the train door.

"Hey, you! Hey, kid! Let me see some I.D.!"

Needles of fear tingled down my legs. I kept going, turning once to wave at Brother Tom, a signal that we were in possible danger. I caught a quick glimpse of Tom waving back.

"Hey!" an officer yelled again.

"Wave to your uncle Tom, Zhu." I felt as if I had a rock in my stomach.

"I can't see him!"

"It doesn't matter—wave *now*!"

Yatou turned slightly and waved. It worked! The officers could not reach us now and turned instead to Brother Tom. We allowed ourselves to be carried forward by the crowd, panting and pushing to get onto the train.

Someone tried to push past us. I felt a jolt, and Yatou's arm slid out of mine.

"Zhu!" I shouted into the roar of the crowd. She had disappeared. I looked into the sea of black hair, trying to pick out a black-and-orange Orioles baseball cap. Nothing. Afraid she might be trampled, I watched the floor while shuffling forward. Panic pounded in my chest. "Zhu!" I shouted again. The sheer force of the forward motion of people pushed me onto the train. I stepped up and quickly turned one last time to scan the dock for Yatou.

Brother Tom caught my eye. He was smiling and waving a black-and-orange baseball cap! He pointed to the front of the train.

No longer allowing myself to be wedged into the flow of people, I broke rank and pushed my way to the front of the train. "Zhu!" I shouted. There she was, stuck halfway out the window, waving her hands wildly at Brother Tom. I didn't know if I wanted to hug her or shake her.

"Good-bye, Uncle Tom!" she yelled, then pulled her head and arm back inside. "Mei Lin, you made it!" she said.

"I made it?" I countered.

"Look," she said, pointing out the window. "My hat fell off while I was waving, and Uncle Tom found it for me."

"It's no wonder it fell off," I answered. "The whole front half of you is hanging out of the window!"

"You said to wave at Uncle Tom!"

I looked out the window and waved at Brother Tom myself. I saw the PSB officers questioning a man at the ticket counter.

Brother Tom threw the cap, and somehow I caught it.

"Good catch," said Yatou.

By the time we found our seat numbers, my adrenaline had settled down to a slow simmer.

"Look, Mei Lin, we get a window," said Yatou, totally oblivious to the terror we had just been through.

The ticket agent collected our ticket stubs and then left us alone. I breathed a sigh of relief as the train pulled out into the sunshine, and we settled back to watch Shanghai go by.

This part of the city wasn't very pretty. The gray concrete industrial suburbs of Shanghai went on for what must have been one hundred miles. I watched intently, while Yatou grew bored with the sight of it and dozed.

I was leaving Shanghai, the place of my dreams . . . and the place of my worst nightmare. Something stirred within me, something deep that had been inside me ever since I could remember. Maybe Shanghai was really God's dream all along. Maybe I had just added *university* to the dream and confused it for a while.

I kissed the top of Yatou's baseball cap. *My Shanghai dream is right here,* I thought. *All wrapped up in a little girl who looks*

*like an American boy . . . and in Mother Su and Chang and the
Shanghai house church . . . and in Sun Tao and other nameless
prisoners who now have the hope of the good heaven.*

The rhythm of the train was soothing after the eventful morning, and I too dozed off from time to time. After a short stop in Hangzhou, the train jerked and wheezed ahead, chugging by the paddy fields of Zhejiang Province.

"Look, Zhu," I said, nudging her awake and pointing to the treeless landscape. "This looks very much like Jiangxi. Only my village has a mountain beside it that's just thick with bamboo, poplar, and pine trees."

It was harvesttime, and I marveled at the speed with which a modern tractor harvested a sugarcane field. Later I saw the familiar sight of a long line of farmers up to their chests in a wheat field, rhythmically disappearing and reappearing as they stooped to swing their scythes.

The rice paddies were dense and golden, furrowed in by man-made walls terraced into the hillsides. Some of the paddies were filled with peasant laborers, harvesting long shoots of rice from the black mud. In front of a green-blue mountainous background, the fields were in perfect symmetrical form and strikingly fertile. Square fields of rice with narrow paths between them went on and on for miles, interrupted occasionally by a hillside of bushy bamboo.

"It looks kind of bumpy," said Yatou.

"Those are the rocks," I said, remembering the rock An and Liko and I had run to on a rainy night the year before. "See, that's a tea field, and over there's a canal."

"Look at the houses!" Yatou exclaimed. "They're so tiny, and just one floor!"

We passed tile-roofed huts, vegetable gardens, and peasant workers in light-colored shirts and pants under coolie hats. I suddenly felt very homesick.

"What's that?" Yatou asked, pointing.

"Those two boys are working a tread wheel. See?"

She looked back to catch a last glimpse. "What's it for?"

"The tread wheel operates a chain-driven water pump. Did you ever learn about it in school? It's been around for eighteen hundred years."

"I didn't have much school," said Yatou. "But I can read some!" She continued to watch as the slashes of black and green and white went by.

I began to contemplate what I'd do with her once we returned to Tanching. She would need a home, schooling, sufficient clothing, and food. Where would she go? Closing my eyes, I pretended to doze and made Yatou's future home a matter of serious prayer.

At lunchtime I nibbled on the rice, while Yatou ate Mother Su's fish balls and dumplings. We ordered one drink to share. Yatou had never tasted a carbonated drink.

"It's tickling my nose," she said, slurping more through her straw. Once she choked, causing the drink to go up her nose. We laughed until we had made a spectacle of ourselves.

I heard the woman across the aisle mutter to her old husband, "Hmmph. Children used to be more polite and respectful."

Later on Yatou tugged at my T-shirt. "Mei Lin, I gotta go."

I followed her to the toilet cubicle, pretending to be interested in helping her find the light switch.

"Oooh, what's that?" Yatou asked, pointing to a bucket beside the toilet.

"Eels," I answered, feeling a little nauseated. "A big bucket of dead eels."

"Ugh. What are they doing with a bucket of dead eels in here?"

We got our answer later, when I asked an attendant what was on the supper menu.

"Eels," the attendant said, and Yatou made a terrible face.

The woman across the aisle stuffed her mouth with the delicacy, clucking again about the ill-mannered youth of China. Yatou and I were happy to pull Mother Su's cooked rice and vegetables out of the shoulder bag. We entered Jiangxi Province right after supper. Pink, red, and purple splashed the skies over the rice paddies. We saw the purple deepen into a dark blue. Eventually stars appeared across the great expanse, dotting the skies with cheer. I was anxious for four in the morning to come!

Soon there was only pitch darkness outside the window, with one dim light in the aisle for those who needed to find the bathroom. Yatou had the window seat and was using the shoulder bag as a pillow. I settled down into my seat and was finally lulled to sleep by the monotonous motion and sad whistle of the steam engine.

★ ✶ ★

CHAPTER

Twenty-Three

I awakened to the howl of the train whistle. It sounded like a rooster, and rightly so. It was four-thirty in the morning. The old engine huffed and puffed, slowing to a stop. I woke Yatou and asked a passing attendant, "Miss, are we in WuMa?"

"Yes."

My heart raced, but I was relieved that I had awakened when the whistle blew. Yatou and I locked arms once again. Getting off the train was another crazy game of push and pull, but as soon as we set foot on the dock, I saw Pastor Wong. There weren't nearly as many people at this middle-of-the-night train stop.

I waved. "There he is, Zhu."

Pastor Wong greeted us warmly. I noticed he wasn't wearing his bandages. His fingers were various shades of purple, deeply bruised, and the ends were still somewhat scabbed over.

He saw me looking at his fingers and commented, "The bandages were too obvious. They'd have made the PSB suspicious. You want to throw this little boy up on my shoulders? I'll hang on to Zhu's legs. My hands feel better when I hold them up. Besides, it'll make us appear to be a happy family."

Pastor Wong bent down, and I gingerly hoisted Yatou onto his shoulders, where she enjoyed the attention and the view.

"Did you get to sleep at all on the train?" he asked.

"A little."

"Good. You'll need it today; things will happen quickly. I have an appointment for you both at the orphanage just outside WuMa."

"Thank you for doing this for us," I said. "I feel honored. You've been so kind."

"It's my pleasure. Of course, I couldn't do much without the rest of the body of Christ in China."

"You mean Brother Tom?" I asked.

"Yes, but not just him. There are the saints who storm heaven with their prayers. And the people themselves. God is doing a great work in China. He establishes our connections! We're just the hands and feet. He's doing all the work of the ministry."

I thought about that. "Pastor Wong, my pastor, Chen Biao, is being held at a labor camp. I can't remember which one. Is there any possible way to seek his release? Or at least send word to him?"

"I remembered his name from when you mentioned him while we were in prison together. I've already asked Tom to work on it."

"How does he get them to let the prisoners go free?" I asked.

"Money. It's all economics, Mei Lin. Everything comes down to connections and bribes in the prisons. There is much corruption. Our meals were kaoliang every day because those in charge of the prison were embezzling the money and foodstuffs that were supposed to be ours."

"Oh, I didn't know."

"It's true," said Pastor Wong. "Some of the torture that goes on is backed up by the bureaucrats. Some of it is just made up by the guards and warden when you get there."

"I wonder why the warden died so suddenly," I said.

"I checked into that story. The warden was promoted—probably so the Party wouldn't lose face. He'd been involved in black-marketing organs, and the Party found out about it."

"You mean body organs?" I asked.

"Yes. There is a lot of money to be made in selling organs. That's why they often execute criminals in the hospitals. They immediately take out their organs for selling."

Yatou made an awful face, and I patted her leg reassuringly.

"So he left, and I was released?" I asked. "Just that simple?"

"I'm not sure. You were probably a thorn in their side. Working hard, responding in forgiveness, convicting them of their sin with your life. You did say that some of the guards said they were afraid of your God."

"God is so faithful," I said. "The Bible says that the king's heart is in His hand. God turns it whatever way He wishes."

"A good verse in this circumstance," he replied.

We now stood outside the train station, and Pastor Wong hailed a taxi. It was five in the morning, and our appointment was at ten.

"Are you hungry, Zhu?" asked Pastor Wong.

"Yes. But please, no eels."

"Ah, you don't have the stomach for fine Chinese cuisine, eh?"

"At least not the cuisine that's sitting in the toilet cubicle," I said with a laugh, and explained our supper experience on the train.

"Well, then, driver, take us to a restaurant. One without eels, okay?"

"You got it, fellow."

We watched the sun come up while the driver zoomed in and out of back streets, practically vacant in the early-morning hours.

"Mei Lin," Yatou said in a whisper, looking up at me earnestly. "I can't wait to see Zhu!"

"I'm so happy for you, little one. He will be so surprised!"

Yatou's eyes widened. "Yes. And he will be surprised when he hears all I've learned—about how Adam and Eve sinned and then God said He wanted a family and then Jesus died on the cross to give God His family back and then Jesus didn't stay dead at all and—"

I couldn't stop myself from giggling.

"What's so funny?" asked Yatou, her mouth forming a little pout.

"Well, that's quite an ambitious speech you're planning to give. You are going to slow down a little when you deliver it, aren't you?"

"Oh—was I talking too fast?" asked Yatou. "Zhu used to tell me that all the time."

"Well, at least you're saying all the right things," I said, still smiling.

Pastor Wong paid the driver, leaving a tract on the back floor of his taxi.

After a leisurely breakfast, we returned to find the driver waiting for us on the quiet street.

"You want a ride now?" he asked us, his whole head sticking out of the car window.

Pastor Wong cautiously looked into the taxi. "No, I don't think so. We'll walk."

The driver shrugged and drove off.

"What's the matter?" I asked. "I thought we needed a taxi to get to the orphanage."

"We do. But the tract I put on the back floor was gone. The driver may be okay. Then again, he may have been assigned by the PSB to drive us around."

"Oh, I see," I said.

"You can't be too careful. Always try to go to different places, take different roads, different methods of transportation. It's the only way to remain anonymous. You both must remember that on the trip to Tanching."

"We will."

"Besides, traveling evangelists usually take the bus or walk to save money," said Pastor Wong.

"Are we going to walk to see Zhu?" Yatou asked.

"No, little nephew," answered Pastor Wong. "I'll hail another taxi."

But doing that took longer than we anticipated.

"WuMa is quiet and lifeless in the morning," Pastor Wong explained. "It's totally different from the congested traffic in Shanghai. Zhu, you can be Yatou while we're outside the city, but when we come back you will be Zhu again."

Yatou nodded with a big smile. "Okay."

We finally spotted a taxi and climbed inside. Soon we found ourselves on a two-lane paved road leading away from WuMa. The houses were crowded side by side, each with a gaping hole in the front for a doorway. I couldn't tell if some of the buildings were going up or coming down. There were no sidewalks, grassy yards, or parks. Dust covered everything.

Finally we arrived at the orphanage, a run-down building surrounded by iron fencing. The gates were tightly locked. Pastor Wong banged loudly on them, and soon a man in light baggy pants and shirt came around the side of the orphanage to let us in. His face was drawn and pale as he nervously opened the gate.

"Wong San Jun?"

"Yes. You are Tom's friend?"

"A friend of a friend. You may call me Si Yi. We must hurry. We'll go around the side of the building. I'll show you the orphanage there. My supervisor isn't here, but the others know you're coming. Remember, if you're asked, you are an uncle looking for a daughter or handicapped boy to adopt."

"I'll remember," said Pastor Wong. "We understand you are taking a great risk. Thank you."

Yatou was very quiet. Her lips were pursed, and her hand was locked tightly in mine as she paced her steps to keep up with me. It was hard to comprehend that this little lame boy named Zhu was the only family she had left.

Si Yi turned to us before entering the back door. "This room is where we keep the new arrivals. They're all newborns, mostly girls."

We walked through the back door to find ourselves in a shabby, dimly lit room that reeked of urine and feces. There were four rows of rusty cribs and cots, with four to five infant girls crammed in each one, lying in their own waste. Some slept on the filthy mattresses, while others could be seen looking around from under torn blankets. Most of the ones awake were crying. Under tiny tufts of black hair I could see ugly sores.

"Dear God," I murmured under my breath.

The babies' faces had open and scabbed-over scratches, where their little fingernails tried to scratch their dry, cracking, jaundiced skin. The only air came from a small open window, which allowed mosquitoes and flies to land on their faces.

I shut my eyes and tried not to faint. I was sure I'd open my eyes to find it was all a bad dream. Pastor Wong offered his arm to steady me.

I opened my eyes to see the caretakers busying themselves to feed the babies. Bottles were put beside each baby girl, but many of them couldn't find them or lift them to their mouths. A few older babies in the front row grabbed their bottles and ate lustily, but most of the babies appeared to be newborns, incapable of holding their own bottles. I immediately moved to assist them.

Si Yi stopped me. "We must go," he said.

I looked down at Yatou, stiff and nervous at my side. I realized that she too had been an abandoned baby, thrown in a trash can before the old woman she called Mother found her. I wondered if we had made a mistake in bringing her here.

Si Yi led us into another room, a toddler room. The little girls were tied to wicker chairs with holes in the middle. Their filthy trousers were split wide at the crotch, and their legs held wide with ropes. Some of the chairs had pots or wash bowls beneath them. Other children simply urinated and defecated on the concrete floor.

I'd seen many Chinese women toilet train their children in these types of chairs—only these children had been sitting there for hours. One little child had fallen asleep in that uncomfortable position. Several of the little ones rocked back and forth. I watched and found myself terrified that one of them would topple over and smash her head on the concrete floor.

Some of the little girls cried out to us, spreading their arms to be held. Their eyes begged for human affection. Others were withdrawn, fear shadowing their countenance. I felt glued to the floor, sickened by the neglect that I saw. But Si Yi led us quickly into the next room, which held the physically and mentally handicapped.

There were a few older children, including a few boys, but most appeared to be no older than three or four. Their plight seemed no better than the infants and toddlers. Several were tied to their beds with strips of cloth. Others rocked in their cribs, calling out for attention or crying.

The stench of human waste mixed with the cries of human hunger and loneliness gnawed at my stomach. I wanted to gather each one of them into my arms and offer them the basic things every child needs: human love and touch, food, and in their case, medical care.

Si Yi led us to another door, then turned to us. "Your friend Zhu is very sick," he said in a warning tone of voice. "He has contracted pneumonia, and I'm afraid he may not live long. He's been unconscious for several days."

"Oh no," cried Yatou. She threw her arms around my waist and cried. "This place is so awful," she whispered huskily. "He can't die. He just can't."

Pastor Wong looked pensive. He leaned down to look Yatou in the face and asked her gently, "Are you sure you want to do this?"

She gulped and nodded.

Si Yi opened the door, and we all gasped. Infants were scattered all over the concrete floor, like so many rugs. Most of them were stiff and quiet, breathing ever so faintly. Si Yi pointed to the far corner. "Over there. I think that is your friend."

Yatou released my hand for the first time since we had walked into the orphanage. She led the way now, carefully stepping over dying infants.

Si Yi left. Pastor Wong seemed frozen in grief. I followed Yatou, to offer her my support and comfort.

"Zhu, Zhu! It's me, Yatou." Yatou gently shook the shoulder of the little boy.

Zhu's complexion was ashen, his hair thin and sparse, his lips cracked and parched. His lame leg was smaller than the other, his bones protruding under his translucent, drawn skin. He was wrapped in a diaper-type cloth, and his shirt was lying open, exposing thin layers of skin over his ribs. The only comfort in the room was that some of the children and babies were either unconscious or sleeping. I tried not to imagine what this little boy had suffered.

"Please, he needs a glass of water," Yatou requested. Pastor Wong stepped out to get one.

Yatou shook her friend again. "Zhu, please, wake up!"

Zhu didn't respond. I placed my finger under his nose. "He's still breathing, Yatou. Try again."

"Zhu! You must wake up! I've come so far to find you. Please, wake up and look at me!" It pained me to watch little Yatou lay her head on his chest, heaving sobs of grief. I knelt beside her and put my arms around her shaking frame.

The time dragged on. We hovered over Zhu's frail body for such a long time that Si Yi kept returning to check on us. It seemed hopeless, but I didn't know how to tell Yatou that. She continued to call Zhu's name, dipping her finger into the glass of water and rubbing it over his parched lips.

Pastor Wong was on his knees, examining each child, mostly infants. I watched as he prayed in anguish over each one.

"Zhu, Zhu." Yatou shook him again and again. "Please, wake up and speak to me. I want to tell you of the One who made the earth and skies. You must know about the good heaven."

Suddenly Zhu's eyes fluttered. Slowly he blinked them open, looking past us, up at the ceiling. Pastor Wong saw he was awake and joined us.

"Zhu! You're awake! It's me, Zhu. Yatou. I'm here with you."

For a moment it looked as though he would lose consciousness again. Then he spoke, his face shining as he again focused intently around the upper corners of the room.

"Oh, look, Yatou. Aren't they beautiful!" His voice was raspy, and he took his breaths with difficulty. The three of us looked behind us and above us. What we saw around us was far from beautiful.

"What's beautiful?" asked Yatou, leaning her face closer to his.

"Oh, they're so tall and strong. I keep trying to go over there, but they told me you were coming to talk to me. They told me I had to wait."

Yatou glanced up at me, her face streaked in dirt and tears.

"He sees angels, little one," I told her gently, stroking her hair. "God has sent beautiful angels to take him to the good heaven. But they told him to wait until you came. Tell him about Jesus. He'll be so glad to know."

Yatou took Zhu's hand and told him the story of Adam and Eve. "You see, Zhu, Adam and Eve sinned, and then their children sinned, and then right down to us. We sinned too, although not as much as the aunties and uncles thought."

I had to smile at her childlike perspective.

She continued. "But our sin messed it up so God couldn't have His family anymore. You can't go to the good heaven with sin."

Zhu looked at Yatou now, his eyes bulging with fear. "You mean I can't go?" he gasped.

"Oh yes!" cried Yatou. "You can go! God sent His only son, Jesus, so that He could get His family back. Isn't it wonderful, Zhu? Even though nobody ever came to adopt us at the orphanage, God decided years ago that He would adopt us. You and I, we're just like God—we all want a family!"

Pastor Wong began to weep as though Zhu and Yatou were his own children. I bit my lower lip, trying to hold back my tears.

Yatou put her little hands around Zhu's drawn, skull-like face. "Just believe Jesus died for you. God wants to wash away all the things you've done wrong."

Zhu closed his eyes, struggling to find his breath. "Help me, God. I do believe in Yatou's Jesus. Please take me to that beautiful place—please take me now."

We were all quiet, taking in the miracle of a new birth into God's family. Then Yatou broke the silence, whispering excitedly, "Zhu, you're not an orphan anymore!"

Zhu smiled, his eyes still closed. He opened them and searched Yatou's face; his own countenance was full of peace and light. "Thank you, Yatou . . ." He stopped to wheeze and cough. "Thank you for coming. Look for me when you come to the good heaven."

"No, you're going to get better, Zhu, you wait. We'll talk tomorrow," said Yatou.

"I want to go now, don't you see?" The little boy put his hand over Yatou's and whispered, "They're waiting for me."

Yatou looked wildly from me to Pastor Wong and back to Zhu.

"But—"

I put my hand on her shoulder to stop her. "Yatou, Zhu wants to go to his family. It's better for him there."

Suddenly the room brightened. Zhu sat upright, lifted his hands to the ceiling, called out, "Jesus!" and slumped back into Yatou's arms. She held him, rocking him back and forth and weeping. I reached over and closed Zhu's eyelids, then stood back to let Yatou have a few last moments with her special brother.

Si Yi walked in the door. He looked at Pastor Wong, who shook his head, indicating that Zhu was dead. Si Yi left and returned again with a tattered blanket. "A shroud, to cover the body. We'll need to take the body to the morgue before it gets too hot."

"Thank you," I said lamely, hardly believing I had thanked him for such a poor shroud. I was happy for Zhu now. He was truly in the good, beautiful heaven. But what of all these suffering children? What kindness would they ever know? And after seeing room after room of languishing children, thankfulness was not an emotion I was feeling. These children were starved, thirsty, and caged, like unwanted trash. I dropped to my knees, hugging the blanket, and broke down. I couldn't pray. I could only call out "Jesus!" and weep some more.

After some time I felt Yatou's arms around me, and I turned to try to comfort her. Instead she took the blanket and wiped my face. "Don't cry, Mei Lin. Zhu is happy now."

"Oh, Yatou, you're so right. And you're such a good little sister!" I swallowed hard, trying to gain control of my emotions, not revealing to her that my tears were for the living.

Si Yi walked in the door again, motioning to Pastor Wong. "I'll take him to the morgue now."

I handed the tattered blanket to Yatou, and she took it to where Zhu's body lay. She touched his hair, holding his hand for a moment. Then she leaned over, sweetly kissed his cheek, and covered his face and body with the blanket.

"I'd like to carry him," said Pastor Wong. "Please."

"I'm not supposed to allow anyone in the morgue," said Si Yi. "I could be fired if we're seen there."

"Then, please, let's wait until the caretakers are at lunch," said Pastor Wong. "We'd like very much to pay our last respects to our friend."

Si Yi looked nervously toward the door and window. "All right. I'll be back in ten minutes."

"Why do you want to say a prayer over him?" asked teary-eyed Yatou. "He's already in heaven, isn't he?"

Pastor Wong picked her up and put her baseball hat on sideways. "Yes, he's already there. But I'd just like to take a look inside that morgue. I want to see if there are many children there. And I'd like to see the death certificate."

Si Yi returned with a short, robust woman in light baggy pants and shirt much like his. She felt Zhu's wrist and forehead, then moved his arms and legs. She jotted down a few things on her clipboard, then gave it to Si Yi and left.

Si Yi nervously watched the door. "We must go now," he said.

Pastor Wong again covered Zhu's lifeless body, picked him

up, and followed Si Yi outside to a little shack outside the main orphanage. I walked behind them, not at all sure that I really wanted to look inside the morgue. Yatou was very solemn during the little procession. She held my hand again, her eyes never leaving the covered body in Pastor Wong's arms.

After convincing Yatou to stay outside and wait for us, I stepped into the morgue. The stench was suffocating. There were five bodies lying on the concrete floor. I looked closer and saw that two of them hadn't even been properly shrouded and were no more than bags of skin and bone. I staggered, imagining the suffering they had endured before their deaths. Si Yi put a crematorium slip into a rack on the back of the door. While the men arranged Zhu's body beside the others, I took a quick peek at the medical form. The date of birth was blank. The psychiatric hospital listed his condition as physically fair, mentally competent when he was transferred to the orphanage. It was clear from reading through the record that Zhu had been purposely and systematically starved to death.

Could that woman Si Yi brought in possibly be a doctor? I wondered. She didn't even carry a medical bag. And what treatment did Zhu receive that he failed to respond to?

"What are these for?" I asked Si Yi, picking up several cartons of juice.

"It's our way of thanking the crematorium workers for disposing of the dead bodies. They sometimes refuse to take the bodies in summer."

"Oh," was all I could say. I remembered Mother Su's story about similar payoffs in Shanghai Orphanage.

"Thank you for your help today," Pastor Wong said quietly.

"I am sorry about your friend," replied Si Yi. He jingled his keys, then turned to Pastor Wong, his eyes searching. "It's as though he was waiting for your visit before he could—you know, leave us."

Pastor Wong smiled. "Yes, I think you're right. Here."

Pastor Wong shoved a tract and some money into the man's hand.

"Thank you," he replied sheepishly. "I'll let you out of the gate."

Si Yi took his large set of keys out of his pocket and led us to the exit. As he locked the gate behind us and left to go back inside, I couldn't help but remember Shanghai Prison Number Fourteen. Something inside of me burst with anger.

"Now which one of those children does he think may escape? The toddlers tied to potty chairs? The infants jammed into cribs? Or how about those in the dying room? They looked like they were going to break out of here any minute." I was fuming. "And I can't believe we thanked him for anything. Why? Are we more Chinese than Christian? Afraid to lose face to a small orphanage caretaker? What are we truly thankful for here?"

I looked at Pastor Wong with rage and then caught Yatou gawking at me, the way she did when she was scared. My heart sank. "I'm sorry, little one. I'm just so angry at the neglect here. It's so . . . so . . ."

"Sinful," finished Pastor Wong.

"Yes, sinful." I had been a Christian most of my life—perhaps too sheltered a life—for I had never seen how low men could stoop in sin. Such cruelty!

Pastor Wong and Yatou just stared at me. For a moment we shared the pain of this horror in silence. Finally Pastor Wong said, "Let's walk back to town. We could all use some fresh air and exercise."

CHAPTER

Twenty-Four

We are all capable of such terrible, cruel acts, Mei Lin," said Pastor Wong, breaking the silence as we walked. "Apart from knowing God, that could be you or me in the position of an uncaring orphanage worker."

"But why? Why starvation? They had plenty of juice for the crematorium workers, but Zhu's medical record showed he was dehydrated. Where's the justice in all of this? Why does our government have such orphanages?"

Yatou looked up at me. "That's simple. Don't you know there's a population problem?"

"Yatou!" I was astonished that she would side with these people.

"That's what we were told every day at Shanghai Orphanage. There are too many people in China. So some, the weaker ones, have to die so there's enough room for the rest."

"Do you believe that?" I asked, practically shouting now.

"It's what they told us. Our orphanage was bigger, but we had rooms like those. And only those of us who came there after we weren't babies anymore or those who were real strong babies made it the first few years. The aunties always told me I had good fortune because I made it to nine years old, even though I didn't go to the orphanage until I was five."

"Yatou, that's awful." I felt tired, confused, and grieved. "What do you say, Pastor Wong?"

"I repeat Psalm One Thirty-nine: 'You knit me together in my mother's womb. . . . I am fearfully and wonderfully made; your works are wonderful . . . O God!' God sees each of us as special and worth His time. I say, let's pray. Seek Him. We have collected a great deal of information today. Let's ask Him what He wants us to do with what we know."

"I will pray," I said with determination. "But I will also hate communism. I will pray for freedom and democracy to reign in China so that all people will have the right to live."

"Mei Lin, democracy would give Christians the right to live, but it would not necessarily stop the neglect of infants, born or unborn."

"What? You mean people would do this to little children without a government forcing them to? That is impossible!"

"It's not impossible. The United States is a free democratic country, but millions of American women abort their own babies. Not because their government said to, but just because they don't want them. And there are a few cases of abandoned babies, born to mothers who left them in garbage dumps or fields."

"In the United States?" I couldn't hide my astonishment. No one had ever told me this.

"Most women in the United States love their babies. But some of them are deceived into abortions. Many of them are teenagers.

They're led to believe it's their freedom to abort a baby if they don't want to be pregnant."

I was shocked, and I suddenly remembered what Fei had said to me that day in DuYan. "My friend Fei from DuYan said that Satan hates babies. He tried to get Moses and Jesus killed when they were babies. And he's still up to his wicked schemes today."

"It sounds as though your friend Fei has a lot of wisdom," said Pastor Wong. "Just remember that communism, socialism, democracy—none of them can change a person's heart. Only Jesus can do that. Whatever government we find ourselves under, living for Jesus is the only freedom."

"Are all of our country's orphanages this way?" I asked.

"Not at all," replied Pastor Wong. "I know of one wealthy Chinese man in Beijing who used his own money to start an orphanage. And he had the government's permission. However, the money ran out this year. He was planning to sell his lung to keep the orphanage going a while longer."

"What happened?"

"He could have received twenty to forty thousand dollars for his lung on the black market. But a Christian found out about his trouble and helped him collect money to keep the orphans fed and taken care of."

"How wonderful!" This story was heartwarming after the horrors I had just experienced in Zhu's orphanage.

Pastor Wong continued. "There are other government-run orphanages even in WuMa that have caring people running them. The children in those orphanages are well cared for. And I've never seen a roomful of dying children there."

I walked on quietly now, trying to digest what Pastor Wong was saying. The road that had been so deserted this morning was now a continual flood of traffic. Bicycles, trucks, cars, and several buses drove by. We were the only people walking. Pastor Wong leaned over and whispered to Yatou, "It's time for you to be Zhu again."

Yatou nodded in her wiser-than-her-age way.

"Are there orphanages like that one in America?" I asked.

"Oh no. And most American doctors would be appalled at what's going on in the orphanages here. Many people in America believe in human rights and ask their leaders to pay attention to countries like ours whose human rights are so violated. Still, America has its own set of problems. That's why I say, sin is sin. And Jesus is the answer, whether we're Asians, Americans, or Africans."

"I see." I knew that Pastor Wong spoke out of the knowledge he'd gained from his own American friends, and what he said must be true. Still, it was hard to believe.

"Is everybody in America a Christian?" asked Yatou.

"No. Everyone in the world has to make his or her own choice, Zhu," replied Pastor Wong.

Everyone was quiet for some time, each of us lost in our own thoughts about the events of the day. Yatou was the first one to speak.

"Where are we going?"

Pastor Wong smiled. "I wondered when that question would come up. We're heading back to WuMa to spend the night. We'll stay with a young Christian couple, friends of mine. I decided it would be safest for us to walk back from the orphanage. It's about a ten-mile hike."

"Are you hungry, Zhu?" I asked.

"A little. I don't think I can eat, though. Do you still have that water jug?"

We all took a drink, then picked up our pace. I wondered when we'd leave for DuYan, and when I'd be home again in my Tanching Village. The more we walked, the more my heart ached for home.

I laughed to myself, picturing Amah scurrying around the stove, fussing about how she was going to fatten me up. I longed for my father's strong arms around me. I thought about Liko. How would he feel when he saw me? I was barely more than a bag of bones, although my eyes were a little less sunken than they were two weeks ago. Once Liko had said he would wait for me. I wondered if he was still waiting.

"How far is it to Tanching?" I asked.

"About fifty miles," replied Pastor Wong. He leaned over and spoke closer to my ear. "Have you thought about what you're going to do about little cousin Zhu? Everyone there will know she is not really your cousin. You'll need to have another plan."

"I think it best if I tell the truth. Perhaps there are Christian cadres in DuYan Village, the one across the mountain from Tanching. The pastor there has some connections."

"Couldn't I stay with you?" asked Yatou. "Oh, please, can't we try?"

"We'll try, little one. Just remember, even Si Yi said he could see the perfect timing in your visit with Zhu. His comment gave Pastor Wong the chance to slip him a tract. God has a wonderful way of ordering things. But remember, there are no guarantees it will work out exactly as you want it to."

"I know. I just can't imagine not living with you. I'd miss you terribly."

I looked down at this little nine year old who had just held her dead childhood friend in her arms. She was strong for being so young. And so full of life and wonder. I put my arm around her slight shoulders as we walked. "I can't imagine living without you, either. God will make a way. Somehow."

"I'd like to accompany you to DuYan and Tanching," said Pastor Wong. "How much money do you have left?"

"I counted fifty yuan."

"That's more than enough for two bus tickets to DuYan," said Pastor Wong. "I'll pay my own way there."

"And we can walk to Tanching from there," I said excitedly. "Oh, I can't wait. What about the rest of the money?"

"The rest of the money may be used for your family or to get Zhu settled in," said Pastor Wong. "Dinner's taken care of. We'll eat at my friends' house in WuMa right after I look at the bus schedule."

I immediately picked up my pace.

We entered the bustling WuMa at four-thirty in the afternoon. Pastor Wong led us through the city, always careful for the watchful eye of the PSB. We were tired and hungry, but everyone agreed to go to the bus station first.

"The next bus to DuYan leaves tomorrow morning at eleven," Pastor Wong said, returning with the tickets in his hands. "And we'll be on it!"

"Oh, that's wonderful! How much were the tickets?"

"Ten yuan each," he replied.

"I can't wait!" Yatou exclaimed.

The young couple received us with great enthusiasm, obviously delighted to entertain Pastor Wong. Because we were with him, Yatou and I were treated like royalty. After dinner all three of us took turns sharing our testimonies with the couple and a roomful of their Christian friends. I was beginning to comprehend the vast network of Christians and house churches in my country.

When bedtime came I was thankful for a chance to sleep in before catching the morning bus. I wanted to look and feel refreshed when I saw my family. The next morning the gracious couple gave us an additional offering as well as food for our trip.

I noticed that Pastor Wong carried two large backpacks.

"Bibles?" I whispered.

"Enough for your whole church, I hope," he answered, smiling.

The taxi pulled up, and we turned to say good-bye to our new friends.

"Thank you for coming," said Gui Jian. "You are all welcome here again."

"Yes, please come soon," said his wife, Sheng. "God bless you."

As we climbed into the taxi I looked over at the couple on the sidewalk, studying them, memorizing them and the street they lived on. Somehow I felt I would return one day. Perhaps to help the orphans. Maybe I would bring Father or Liko and Pastor Chen.

"Kwan Mei Lin is my name," I called out the taxi window. "Don't forget!"

"We won't forget!" they called back, waving furiously.

CHAPTER

Twenty-Five

Pastor Wong boarded the bus separately from us. He didn't want Yatou and me to be seen with him in case he was caught with the Bibles.

The road to DuYan started out paved and fairly smooth, with two shoulders for bicycle riders. But after a time we were riding in a cloud of dust, bouncing over ruts and potholes. We were crammed three to a seat, but Yatou was having a good time, giggling over the bumps and doing her best to bounce higher than anyone else on the bus. When she tired of the game, she nestled in beside me to talk.

"Is your Amah a nice woman?" she whispered, her little face scrunched with worry.

"Very nice, even though she wishes I were a grandson instead of a granddaughter," I replied, smiling down at her baseball cap.

"And your father? He's a Christian?" Her mouth was so close to my ear that her breath tickled me.

"Yes."

"What if they don't want me? I'm a girl too."

"Oh, they'll want you, little one, don't worry," I answered, bumping shoulders with her in a playful way.

"But nobody wanted the real Zhu," she said soberly. "Just because he was lame."

"Jesus wanted him," I said gently in her ear, "and you wanted him. And if he had lived, I would have wanted him too."

"Really?"

"Really. But let's not talk about all this here, okay?"

She nodded.

I spent the rest of the trip nibbling on our food while I described the villages of DuYan and Tanching to Yatou. The talk seemed to calm her.

After three hours the bus finally bumped its way into DuYan. I felt my back pocket. The New Testament was still there. Yatou and I discreetly got off, and Pastor Wong followed us from a distance until we were well away from the station.

Taking back alleys that I barely knew myself, I led the little procession to Pastor Zhang's house. With more excitement than I could contain, I gave the coded knock. The same old woman opened the door.

"Mei Lin? Is that you?" she cried.

Suddenly I felt embarrassed. Had I changed that much? Was I so skinny now that I was unrecognizable?

"Yes, it's me."

The old woman clasped my hands and cried with delight, "Oh, come in, please, come in!"

The old woman was Pastor Zhang's mother. She called him, and he quickly came out, still dressed in his factory clothes. There was rejoicing all around us, so I tried to forget about my skinny frame and introduced the two men. Pastor Zhang reached out to grip the other pastor's hand. Pastor Wong hesitated. When Pastor Zhang saw the bluish fingertips, he bowed his head slightly to Pastor Wong in an outward sign of respect.

"It is an honor, Pastor Wong."

"The honor is mine, Pastor Zhang. Mei Lin speaks highly of your DuYan house church."

"Pastor Wong has a present for you," Yatou piped up.

Pastor Wong and I laughed, and he said, "This is our friend Zhu. And yes, I do have a present for you." He winked at her and reached for one of his backpacks, which he laid in front of her.

"Would you like to give him the present?" he asked her.

"Oooh, could I?" she asked, nearly dancing.

She took Pastor Wong's smile as a yes and quickly unlatched the bag, opening the top wide so that Pastor Zhang and his mother could see.

Pastor Zhang's mouth fell open. "Are they . . . are they really Bibles?"

"Enough for the DuYan and Tanching Christians, I hope," replied Pastor Wong.

"The other backpack's stuffed with them too," said Yatou, opening the second bag to reveal another mound of Bibles.

"Glory to God!" cried Pastor Zhang's mother. She clasped her hands and then raised them to heaven. "Our God is faithful."

Pastor Wong and I looked at each other and grinned. "That seems to be the testimony lately," I said. "Pastor Zhang, how is my father?"

"Delighted to receive your letter, Mei Lin. He only received it yesterday, and you're here already. He's in for a wonderful surprise."

"Oh, I just can't wait to see him," I said. "But tell me, how's Liu An? Her baby must be ten months old by now."

"I have a present for you, Mei Lin," said Pastor Zhang. "An!" he called.

I whirled around to find myself face-to-face with An and the most beautiful baby I'd ever seen.

"Oh, Mei Lin, I could hardly stand waiting in there," said An, the words rushing out of her as we embraced. "I was here to pick up Manchu. Mother Zhang has been keeping him for me while I work. She chased me to the back room to surprise you when she recognized you at the door!"

"Oh, An, how often I thought of you and prayed for you. And look at this beautiful boy! Do you remember a year ago when you looked like a brown Buddha?"

"And you looked like a mud monster!" It felt so good to laugh with her. Manchu held his chubby little arms out to me, and I snuggled close to his face, taking in the feel and milky smell of a healthy baby. After the orphanage experience, I needed to hold this little one. I managed to introduce An to Pastor Wong and Yatou while rocking Manchu and cooing to him.

"How was the birth?" I asked An.

"I gave birth to a healthy baby boy the day before Christmas," she said. Pastor Zhang motioned us to sit down for tea while An told her story. "My husband and mother kept little Sha for me while I hid at your friend Fei's home for a month. They were very good to me. They helped me with the birth. I missed little Sha terribly, but I waited for another month before going home, just to make sure they couldn't take the baby from me. When I finally returned home with a beautiful baby, the Women's Federation came to visit us. They handed my husband and me a bill for four hundred fifty yuan, saying it was a fine for all the trouble I had caused them."

An was beaming now. "The evening after the Women's Federation left, half of DuYan Village poured through our home for the full-month feast. We proudly showed off our rosy-cheeked son, and I told them of the miracle God performed in saving his little life. Of course, my mother handed a scarlet-colored egg to each guest so they could have a share in our good fortune. It was quite a celebration!"

"Oh, how wonderful!" I exclaimed. "Gongxi, Liu An! And God bless you! Were you able to pay the fine?"

"Oh, after a time. We sold our beds and furniture and totally depleted our savings." She looked down at Manchu, who was playing happily at our feet. "But it was worth it. A week after I returned home with Manchu, the militiamen came again in broad daylight. I thought they were coming for my son and gave him to my mother to escape with him out the back door. But they came for me. They grabbed me and put me in their car. I was so dumbfounded, I didn't resist!"

"Where did they take you?" I asked.

Liu An looked hesitantly at the men. Then she said, "On orders from the Women's Federation I was forced to have a tubal ligation at the hospital."

"Oh no! You won't be able to have any more children."

"It was a high price to pay," said An. "But I look at our little treasure, and I know it was worth it all. God kept little Manchu safe. Sha adores her new little brother, and now my husband is warming to the Gospel."

"What a testimony, An. Listen, I'll share my testimony with the DuYan house church very soon, okay? But now, please, we must leave for Tanching before dark."

"Mei Lin, I've been praying," said Pastor Wong. "I think I'll stay with Pastor Zhang for a few days, if that's all right with him."

"All right? It's wonderful," said Pastor Zhang. "We have so much to talk about. And we want to hear your testimonies."

"You will." Pastor Wong looked at me. "I'll meet your family here on Sunday at the house-church meeting, okay?"

"The house-church meeting for Tanching is now in Tanching," said Pastor Zhang.

"It is?" I asked. "Is Pastor Chen back home?"

"Mei Lin, I'm afraid I have distressing news for you. It may be better for you to hear it before you return home."

Pastor Zhang's tone made me uneasy. "What happened?"

"Your beloved Pastor Chen is with Jesus."

I sat down. I couldn't believe my ears. "How did it happen?"

"On January sixth he was interrogated and beaten for hours. They hung him by his wrists from the ceiling and used boards to beat him around his head."

"Oh no," I gasped as my eyes filled with tears. Pastor Wong put his twisted bruised fingers over my hand to comfort me.

Pastor Zhang continued. "We heard from another prisoner that his front teeth were knocked out. After he died the police removed all his organs and cremated his body—without his family's permission."

"Poor Liko!" I cried. "And Mrs. Chen." Thoughts of grief and confusion rushed over me. An stood behind me, putting her hands on my shoulders to comfort me.

My mind raced. Why was I so gloriously delivered, while poor Pastor Chen was beaten to death without ever seeing his family again? For the first time since my release I felt guilty for surviving the beatings in prison. I felt guilty for being alive. A deep wave of sorrow and hopelessness began to overwhelm me.

Pastor Wong seemed to know what I was thinking. Putting his scarred hand on my arm, he said, "Mei Lin, it wasn't our choice or even God's choice to beat you or me or Pastor Chen. It was our government's choice. Three years ago Premier Peng Liko signed two new anti-religion laws that have brought on massive suffering in China. But they are making their laws out of fear because they are losing control over the people, especially the Christians."

"I feel so awful," I said, my head in my hands.

"You must not feel guilty that you are here and he is in heaven. You must trust God and His plan." Pastor Wong's words were so comforting and heartfelt, I sensed he had experienced this guilt as well. I began to feel it and the terrible hopelessness lifting from my heart.

"Thank you, Pastor Wong." I tried to smile reassuringly, then turned to Pastor Zhang. "How are the Chens managing?"

"It was hard for them at first, Mei Lin. They had prayed day and night for his release. But it seems that God has taken what was meant for evil and turned it around for good."

"What good could come from such a tragedy?" I asked.

"It may be best if you see that for yourself when you return to Tanching. I will tell you that it seems Cadre Fang had a change of heart after your arrest and imprisonment. Although he's not a believer, he's been looking the other way, not reporting the house-church meetings."

"Oh my!" I could hardly believe my ears. "God is faithful, isn't He?" I said solemnly. But I couldn't stop thinking of Pastor Chen. A tear escaped my eye and trickled down my cheek. "Such senseless suffering at the hands of ruthless tormentors. Pastor

Wong, I know you said only Jesus can give us true freedom. But we must pray for democracy in China. We need the freedom to worship in China. I can't help it. I feel we must do something else too, but I don't know what."

"Perhaps you're right, Mei Lin," said Pastor Wong. "It is difficult to imagine such freedom. I try to imagine what it would be like to have both freedoms—free within through Jesus Christ and free without to express my beliefs openly."

"One day I believe we'll know," I said. "One day people will look at our red flag and think of freedom instead of torture and communism." I looked at the roomful of Christian friends. "For now I count myself blessed to be in the company of such saints of God." I hugged my dear brothers and sisters and said, "Yatou, we need to go to Tanching now."

"I'll come to your house church on Sunday, Mei Lin," said Pastor Wong.

"Good. I'll send someone here to show you the way."

"No need," said Pastor Zhang. "I'll accompany him."

"It's settled, then," said Pastor Wong. "Peace to you, sister. And to you, little sister Zhu."

"Sister?" Pastor Zhang asked.

"Ah, you see we do have you well disguised, Zhu," Pastor Wong said. "Pastor Zhang, let me reintroduce you to Yatou."

"Pleased to meet you," said Yatou. "Everybody in Shanghai thinks I'm Zhu, Mei Lin's boy cousin, but I'm really just a friend—a girl friend."

Pastor Zhang laughed. "I can see you've been a wonderful friend to Mei Lin."

"Let's go, little one," I said. "I want to get home before dark."

Yatou and I said our good-byes and headed down the familiar path to Tanching.

CHAPTER

Twenty-Six

Liko's wide pathway from the year before was narrowed now by overgrown shrubs and bamboo, but I quickly maneuvered my way through the brush.

"I've never seen so many trees at one time," said Yatou, struggling to keep up. I scolded myself for hurrying her and tried to slow down. It was around four o'clock, and I knew some of the villagers would be close to finishing their work in the fields. We finally came to the old barn, and I decided to take the road.

If Yatou had not been with me I would have run. Instead I hoisted her up on my shoulders, which were muscular from scrubbing cell floors. I touched my hair. It was still so brittle and thin. I looked down at my skinny legs and arms. Tears stung my eyes. I bit my lip and pressed forward. *Chen Liko,* I thought, *you're going to have to see me as I am. I can't be anyone else right now.*

"Mei Lin! Mei Lin, is that you?"

I looked at the rice paddy to my left, and running through the hedge was my dear friend Ping.

"Ping!" I ran toward her, Yatou flopping on my shoulders.

"Look at you, Mei Lin! You look like an American in those blue jeans!" she laughed. "And who is this with you?"

I squatted and let Yatou jump off of my shoulders. "This is my new adopted sister, Yatou. Yatou, this is Ping, my closest friend since childhood." They smiled and giggled and bowed to each other playfully. It was then that I noticed the change in Ping's body. "Ping, why are you in the fields? Why, Ping! Are you . . . are you . . ." I couldn't finish my sentence.

"Yes, Mei Lin. I have happiness."

I stared at the roundness of her belly and was at a total loss for words.

"It's all right, Mei Lin. I hope you don't mind. I've married Cadre Fang."

"You what?" My mouth was gaping, and I couldn't seem to close it.

"Are you angry?"

"Indeed not! Why? Why did you marry him? I'm sorry, that question was much too direct. We haven't even seen each other for nearly a year."

Ping smiled. "I married him because he asked me to. And we wanted to have our child right away. You know, he felt very bad about what happened to you. He blames himself and has been most kind to your family."

"Kind?" This was the second time I had heard that the cadre had willed himself to kindness. I could hardly believe my ears. "You're finished in the field?"

"Yes." She put her arm through mine. Yatou took my free hand and we started down the road together.

I didn't mention Ping's dream to attend the university or that she planned to marry a soldier or that she didn't want to remain in Tanching all of her life. It was obvious that both of our dreams had changed in the last year. But I did wonder if she had thought more about becoming a Christian.

"Did Cadre Fang, your new husband, tell you why I was arrested?" I asked.

Ping nodded. "Because you wouldn't stop being a Christian. Not even if it meant being beaten or not going to Shanghai. I couldn't believe it when he told me. I thought you weren't being sensible at first."

"At first?"

"Well, I never knew how strongly you felt. I was shocked that you would go so far to defend your faith. It made me think."

"And what do you think now?" I asked, probing to find out where my old friend stood in her own faith.

"I want to talk to you sometime. I want you to tell me again about the One who made the earth and skies. I want very badly to believe like you—if my husband will allow me."

We were close to my home now, and I could hardly contain my excitement. "Let's plan to talk. How about tomorrow after dinner? Will the cadre let you come to my house for tea?"

"Oh, could I? I thought you might be angry that I married the man who got you into so much trouble."

"I'm not angry. I have been praying for you both! You and your husband are both welcome. I'll answer any questions you have."

With that we parted ways. My heart was set to see Father and Amah.

I entered the courtyard still hand in hand with Yatou. "Father, Amah! Father, Amah! I'm home!" I cried.

Amah appeared at the door. Her hands flew in the air as she ran in her hobbling way to greet me. "Mei Lin, Mei Lin, my granddaughter!" Then, for the first time in my life, Amah hugged me. "This is the happiest day of my life. Oh, Mei Lin!" Suddenly she seemed to catch herself and pulled away from me. "Are you well? Let me look at you."

I bowed my head, ashamed of my appearance.

"Ah, still pretty as a lotus blossom, I see," said Amah, lifting my chin. "You'll need some fattening up, though."

"Mei Lin! Is that you!"

I turned around to see my father in the garden on the hill, his brown skin glistening with sweat. "Oh, Father!" My heart raced at the sight of him. He ran down the hill, and I gloried in watching his strong gait and outstretched arms.

"Oh, Father," I cried again. Within seconds he swept me into his arms and twirled me around.

"Oh, my little Mei Lin. How I've longed for you. Thank God you're safe. Oh, thank God." We hugged and laughed and hugged again. I could feel months of tension and uncertainty drain out of me under his secure embrace.

"Oh, Father. God has been so faithful," I said, my voice cracking with a dry sob. Then I felt a little tug on my shirt and remembered Yatou. "Father, this is my new little friend, Yatou. And we have quite a story to tell you!"

"Yatou? This is . . . Yatou?"

Yatou and I looked at each other and giggled. "Yes, Father! I will explain later, but this is really Yatou."

"Hello, little Yatou. Welcome to our home." Father bowed, and Yatou timidly bowed back.

We turned to walk into the house, and I saw neighbors standing at their doorways watching Father and me, gawking at the new little stranger and me dressed in Western clothing. Fresh boldness filled my soul, and I turned to speak to them. "The Lord God who made the heavens and the earth is faithful! He is faithful!"

The neighbors looked at one another, some of them whispering to each other.

Father took my hand. "Come, daughter. There will be time to talk to them later."

"Wait, Father."

The people continued to stare. They were listening, and I had a message.

"The One who made the earth and skies loves you. His son, Jesus, died for you, to take away your sins. Believe on Him, and you will have new life."

"Ah," said Mr. Lang. "Kwan So's daughter speaks of new life."

"Yes, new life in Jesus. He will send His Holy Spirit to help you. He has helped me. He loves you." I looked around at all their questioning glances. "Please, come for tea tomorrow evening, and I will tell you more."

"We will be there, daughter of Kwan So," said Mr. Lang.

"Welcome home, Mei Lin," said Mrs. Lang.

"Welcome back to Tanching," said another.

I smiled at them and waved. I never felt such love for them before. I motioned to Yatou to follow us into the house.

"You know, Mei Lin, you preach just like your mother used to years ago." Father took me by the shoulders. "Let me look at you. You look thin and pale."

I hung my head. "Yes, I know."

"But you have never looked more beautiful to me than you do right now."

"Oh, Father . . ." I fell into his strong chest. For the moment I didn't feel brave and strong. I didn't even feel like preaching. I was just relieved to be home and safe in my father's strong arms.

"Come! Supper is ready," said Amah, bustling around the little kitchen. "You two young people look like bamboo poles in American clothes. I won't have any of that around my house. Sit, sit!"

I smiled down at Yatou and winked.

"Mei Lin! Mei Lin!" someone called from the courtyard.

I jumped up and went to the door. It was Mrs. Chen. I embraced her warmly.

"Mrs. Chen, how did you know I was home?" I asked, blinking back fresh tears of grief over Pastor Chen's horrible death.

"Ping told me," she replied.

"My heart was truly saddened when I heard your good husband passed away," I said. But the words didn't seem comforting enough.

The widow searched my face, then spoke quietly. "Thank you, Mei Lin. You may be the only person I'll ever know who can truly tell me what prison was like. Will you come to see me one day soon, so that we can talk?"

"Oh yes! And there's another preacher friend of mine who was in the same prison I was in. He and Pastor Zhang are coming on Sunday."

Mrs. Chen beamed. "I'll be so glad to hear your testimonies. But we will talk privately, just you and I?"

"I'd love to," I replied. "Where are the meetings held now?"

"We're meeting at the barn again."

"Incredible. And Cadre Fang knows about it?"

"He knows, but he pretends he doesn't. Mei Lin, I have a note for you. It's from Liko."

I quickly opened the note. *Meet me in the cow shed tonight at seven.*

I trembled inside. "Please tell Liko I'll be there."

———————

It took me quite a while to convince Amah that I wasn't able to eat more than plain rice and vegetables. As we ate dinner I briefly told Father and Amah about my Shanghai prison experience, my release, and meeting Mother Su, Chang, and Yatou. I did not want to cast a shadow on this sweet homecoming and our first meal together by telling them everything. And my first concern was Yatou.

"Father, may Yatou stay with us for a while?" I asked. "She is an orphan. I won't say what orphanage or what city, because it doesn't matter. She's never going back there. She is a Christian now too, and I'm going to try to find her a permanent home. I'd like it to be with us."

"My little Mei Lin, you are full of surprises," Father said, shaking his head. "Yatou, our home is yours as long as the authorities let you stay."

"Please, Amah, would you entertain Yatou? I'd like to take a bath and put on some of my own clothes before going to see Liko."

"Yatou, eh?" said Amah. "Well, Yatou, how would you like to see a fishpond?"

"Mei Lin and I saw goldfish at Old Town! And you should

have seen the big Buddha there. Mei Lin called it a fat, voiceless, earless god!"

We all burst out laughing—even Amah didn't seem offended.

"Yatou, you're telling on me," I kidded her. "Amah will show you the chickens, ducks, and fish, okay?"

"Mei Lin, I want to hear more about your prison experience tomorrow," said Father.

"We will talk. Oh, Father," I said, getting up from the table to hug his neck. "God has been so faithful."

I carefully hid my precious New Testament under my mattress. Then I bathed in the wooden tub that Amah set up in our little bedroom. I was thrilled that Liko asked to see me at our old spot. I anxiously put on my plaid shirt and old school pants. My clothes looked as if they were hanging on a peg instead of a person. I combed my hair, arranging it the best I could, and lifted the tub to dump it.

"Now you look like our Mei Lin," said Amah, hurrying to help me carry the tub through the central room to the side of the house.

"Amah, do I look terrible?"

"You are very thin, Granddaughter. You know I will not lie to you. But don't worry. You will gain weight again. And your hair will fill out again. Besides, there is a light in your eyes and a glow on your face that makes you very beautiful."

"Oh, Amah, do you mean it?"

"One thing I do not do, Granddaughter, is tell lies." She reached over and patted me on the cheek. "Go to him now. He's waited all year for this day."

"He has? Are you sure?"

"I'm sure. Time has a way of working things out."

The sun was beginning to set. I squeezed Amah's hand and headed up the hill through the tilled gardens to the cow shed. Timidly I stepped into the little shack, thankful it was dimly lit.

"Mei Lin!"

I turned to look at Liko. He was taller than the year before, and definitely more muscular.

"Liko! Why, you're crying. I heard about your father—"

"No, it's you, Mei Lin. You're safe. I'm so glad. After Father's terrible death, I . . . I never stopped praying." Liko stood there limply, as though he didn't know what to do with himself.

Then he said, "I . . . please. May I hold you?"

Liko's tears touched something deep within me. "Yes, yes," I answered.

Liko wrapped his arms around me and held me close. I felt his chest heave with emotion. I'd forgotten how tenderhearted he was.

"I missed you, Liko. Pastor Zhang told me about your father. I'm so sorry."

"Oh, Mei Lin. Father suffered so. And I know you suffered too. I thought my heart would break when I learned how he was treated. I wondered if I'd ever see you again. After he died, I was tormented with thoughts of what they were doing to you. I need to hold you now, to feel you alive in my arms."

I clung to Liko, wanting with all of my heart to comfort him. And I wanted to be wanted. "I was afraid you wouldn't want me. I'm so skinny and—"

Liko moved me slightly away from him and put his finger to my lips. "Shhhh. Don't say it. You are *shiquan shimei*, perfect and beautiful. Your eyes are radiant, like lotus blossoms in a pond of clear water."

I lowered my head and tried to squeeze the tears back. My lower lip quivered. But Liko lifted my chin and brushed my hair out of my face. Suddenly I wanted him to kiss me. I wondered if he could tell. I closed my eyes and drew closer to his face. I felt his breath on my cheek. His lips grazed my hair. "May I?" he asked. "Or am I still a man in waiting?"

"There's no longer a need to wait," I whispered. His mouth found mine and he kissed me softly. I responded, ever so willingly, lingering in his gentle caress.

When he withdrew his lips from mine, his face was earnest. "Mei Lin, I want you to be my wife. I want to protect you. I want to love you for the rest of my life. I haven't much to offer—"

"You have everything to offer, Chen Liko. Your heart is worth more than the salary of ten doctors. And I love you for it."

"Do you mean that?"

"Oh yes, I do mean it," I said and flung my arms around him, longing to be held by him forever.

"Then you won't mind my new job?" he asked.

I drew back and looked intently into his eyes. "A new job?"

Liko grinned, and I saw that wonderful old twinkle again in his eyes. "How would you feel about being a pastor's wife?"

"You mean . . . you mean . . ."

"Pastor Chen. Pastor Chen Liko. I hope to do as well as my father."

"Liko, no one told me. Pastor Zhang told me God took what was meant for evil and turned it to good. You're really the new pastor?"

"Yes, a pastor. A pretty lonely pastor too." He grinned.

I laughed. "Be lonely no more, Pastor Chen Liko. The government won't let us get married until I'm twenty-one, but then

Kwan Mei Lin will be proud to be your missionary wife!"

"Let's go to the rock in the rice paddy, Mei Lin. We can watch the sunset, and you can tell me about your prison experience."

I slipped my thin hand into Liko's strong one, and we walked to the same rock we'd hidden on with An the year before. The sun stretched out into patchy streaks of pink and purple and deep red as we related both the tragic and glorious details of our lives in the last year. We talked until we saw the full yellow moon rise over the tall golden stalks of ripened rice.

I looked up into Liko's strong, handsome face. "You know, even though Cadre Fang is ignoring the meetings, the PSB will probably come to secretly check on me."

"Yes, that is their way," Liko answered thoughtfully.

"Liko, your father and my mother were tortured mercilessly and became martyrs for their faith."

Liko was quiet for a moment. "And you're afraid the same thing may happen to us?"

"Well, yes. But not just that. There's so much to overcome. We can't marry for two or three years, and then we can only have one child. Then there's the matter of what to do with Yatou. Did I tell you I want to go back to that orphanage outside of WuMa and somehow help those baby girls?"

Liko smiled. "Yes, you've told me about returning to that orphanage at least a dozen times now." He was teasing me, but then he grew serious. "There are problems, many problems. It all seems to be part of the struggle of being born Chinese."

"Yes, and the greater struggle of being born a Chinese daughter. You should have seen those beautiful orphaned girls paying such a high price just for being female."

Liko looked over the fields of rice and pointed. "Do you see these rice fields, terraced into steps far up that distant hill?"

"Yes."

"Our engagement is a first step, Mei Lin, just like the field we are in right now. There will be steps the Lord will lead us to take day by day, month by month, and year by year. And before we know it, we'll be at the top of that hill over there, looking back at the steps that brought us that far."

I smiled, remembering our childhood races up the hill behind my house.

Liko looked at me quizzically. "What?" he asked. "What are you smiling at?"

"We're racing up to the top of the hill again, are we?" I asked, searching his face to see if he remembered.

Liko grinned. "Maybe. Only we're a team this time, climbing together."

I scooted closer to him, nestling under his arm to keep warm. "A team," I repeated. "Still reaching forward to make the next step, however difficult it may be."

We sat quietly for a while. I thought about the enormity of what lay ahead.

I lifted my eyes to the dark expanse and spoke to the One who made the earth and the skies. "Help us, Lord. Walk with us to the top of that hill."

A CKNOWLEDGMENTS

I'd like to acknowledge those who have contributed to the facts in this book through:

- Writings

    The Coming Influence of China by Carl Lawrence with David Wang

    In the Lion's Den by Nina Shea

    Their Blood Cries Out by Paul Marshall with Lela Gilbert

    Death by Default: A Policy of Fatal Neglect in China's State Orphanages by Human Rights Watch Asia

    Broken Earth: The Rural Chinese by Steven W. Mosher

    A Mother's Ordeal: One Woman's Fight Against China's One-Child Policy by Steven W. Mosher

- Videos and Documentaries

    China Cry

    Bamboo in Winter

    China Cry

    Life Today television programs, "China's Orphans," 1995, 1996

    Return to the Dying Rooms, television documentary, True Visions Productions

- Organizations that provided facts about persecuted Christians
  Amnesty International
  The Center for Religious Freedom at Freedom House
  Christian Freedom International
  Christian Rescue Committee
  Christian Solidarity Worldwide
  International Christian Concern
  Open Doors with Brother Andrew
  Population Research Institute
  Voice of the Martyrs

I glanced at the television set as I cleaned—it was the horror of any mother. Life Outreach International showed toddlers strapped to potty chairs, reaching out their hands to be held. As many as four to five babies were crammed in each crib, with flies covering open sores on their little faces. In another room, children who were sick and dying were lying on the hard floor, scattered about like so many throw rugs. I felt as though each child were reaching out his arms to me, calling me into his world to taste, hear, see, touch, and smell. Then the camera zoomed in on the cardboard box on the floor—the newborn baby inside the box had just arrived on the orphanage doorstep.

"China's One-Child Policy," someone mentioned. I had to do something—this book is what I finally "did."

I called and interviewed Life Outreach's Director of Missions, Phil Caldwell. One phone tip led to another until I uncovered a world of people I didn't know existed—the persecuted Christians of China.

I owe a debt of gratitude to those who willingly offered their valuable time and insight during interviews with me while researching the facts for this book. Paul Marshall, Steven Mosher, Steve Snyder, Phil Caldwell, Jim Jacobson, Randy C., Wina, Jun, and little Hope are just a few who have been invaluable resources of insight, encouragement, criticism, and strength.

My deepest appreciation and esteem will always be to those who asked that their names not be mentioned. You are my heroes.

I am indebted to the editorial work of Elizabeth Sherman, Sherry Mitchell, and L. B. Norton, who have spent hours meticulously preparing this manuscript for publication.

Blessings to Dave Horton, Teresa Fogarty, Brett Benson, and the Bethany House Publishing team—you guys are the greatest!

I'd like to thank my writing mentor, Dandi Daley Mackall, and Marlene Bagnull, who was the first to tell me, "This book needs to be published."

A palm-slapping "high five" to Steve Laube and Pat Judd, who found me in the wrong line and decided to keep me anyway.

Thanks to Carol Johnson, who not only supports the daughters of China but shares a kindred heart for the nations.

To my friends who have walked with me in my heart for China—Diddie, Diney, Cin, Etta, Giovanna, Glenn, Grace, Janet, Jim, Kathy, Louise, Latinya, Marie, Mom and Dad F., Sally, Selena, Shirley—thank you all. I must admit there were a few times when I groveled at the feet of my two volunteer computer techs, Steve and Dennis, who repaired more shutdowns and computer changes than I care to remember. Steve, I'll never forget the time your parked car rolled down the dark parking lot while you were in the store buying my new motherboard. Thanks for the rescues!

Although LOI's television clip of China's orphans spurred me into action, the seeds of love for China were planted at my mother's feet, where she engaged my young heart with stories of Asia's missionary greats like Adoniram Judson, John and Betty Stam, and Hudson Taylor in large flash-card picture stories. My father nurtured those seeds when he gave me biographies to read as a teenager about the courageous missionaries to China and the challenging writings of Watchman and Witness Nee. I have a rich heritage—with God's grace I hope to pass this heritage on to my children and their children for many generations to come. Thanks, Mom and Dad.

An affectionate thank you to my husband, Scott, for listening to my countless versions of chapter one, for supporting my vision for this book, and for "holding down the fort" time and again so that I could have extra minutes to write.

I am forever indebted to and in the trust of "the One who made the earth and skies" for showing me what He is doing in China and letting me write about it from my heart.

If you, too, have the urge to "do something,"
visit the author's Web site at *www.seehope.com*
for more information about China.

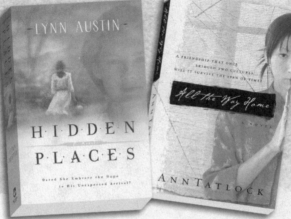

Thank you for selecting a book from
BETHANY HOUSE PUBLISHERS

Bethany House Publishers is a ministry of Bethany Fellowship International, an interdenominational, nonprofit organization committed to spreading the Good News of Jesus Christ around the world through evangelism, church planting, literature distribution, and care for those in need. Missionary training is offered through Bethany College of Missions.

Bethany Fellowship International is a member of the National Association of Evangelicals and subscribes to its statement of faith. If you would like further information, please contact:

Bethany Fellowship International
6820 Auto Club Road
Minneapolis, MN 55438 USA

www.bethfel.org